THE SOJOURNER

CLINT WESTGARD

ALSO BY CLINT WESTGARD

Unspeakable Rites: An Alkemya Novella

The Shadow Men:

> *Realm of Shadows*

> *Council of Shadows*

> *Dance of Shadows*

The Sojourners Cycle:

> *The Forgotten*

> *The Apostate*

> The Acolyte

> The Double

> The Sojourner

The Maleficio Chronicles

Trials of the Minotaur

The Farthest Reaches: A Collection

Published by Lost Quarter Books
www.lostquarterbooks.com

This edition 2019

ISBN: 978-1-928035-46-6

For Mary Shelley

.

CONTENTS

ONE   GOLDEN DREAMS   1

TWO   THE PACT   38

THREE   THE FUTURE IS MURDER   108

FOUR   THE AURELLANO   174

GOLDEN DREAMS

1

The sound of birds chirping outside my window awakens me. Sparrows or swallows, or some other tiny, dull species that covers the globe in endless numbers. I sit up carefully, having made the mistake earlier in my stay of forgetting how close the ceiling is to the loft bed. Several painful mistakes, actually. But then I am always forgetting where I am. It takes effort to remember, to fight through whatever happens to me when I sleep.

At least I am certain of who I am. That part of me remains stable. Aeida is gone. Suon assures me I have not taken to wandering and plotting in the night. I trust her, as far as that goes.

It seems she did not betray me when I was with her at Osahi's fortress, and she was not lying when she said she loved me. She does, though I cannot fathom why. I am a lost and broken soul in a foreign body. A pitiful thing who has done terrible deeds. The evidence of my failures is still with us: Ana and my self. It is Ana's presence that provides the window to allow me to finally see the truth of Suon's feelings for me. She is jealous of Ana and how much I care for her.

Envious that we share a bed, though that is at Ana's

insistence, not mine. It makes me uncomfortable, especially with the always-present threat that Aeida may return. There is no doubt of what he would do to her, given the chance. I have experienced it, and that is not something I can forget. Or forgive myself for. But there is so much that is unforgivable in my past that it is hard to know where to begin with an accounting, let alone trying to set it right.

I have decided I will begin with Ana, though I have no means to help her and no idea how to go about acquiring them. That is not entirely true. The Seeker would be able to help her and would perhaps even be willing. She was a Society agent, after all. At least for a time. More importantly, I am one now, ostensibly, though I have done nothing for them. That is another accounting I will have to face soon, and it amazes me I haven't yet.

Where is the Seeker? Why hasn't he come to see that I make good on what I promised him? For that matter, I don't understand why the Society didn't remain at the Church campus after their raid until they had driven me to ground. Surely, having destroyed the Church, they have no need for me to do the same. Molijc was the one who did the destroying, but it seems he was working for them too. I cannot believe that was always the case. My mind refuses to contemplate it. My life cannot be more of a lie than it already is.

The question of when the Seeker or the Society will descend to seize me is just another specter that clings to me, along with the threat of Aeida's return, haunting every hour of every day. I expect to spend however much time remains to me trapped in this false body on the run from those who wish to destroy me, or locked away and forgotten in some cell. If Aeida were to somehow manage to return and banish me to the void again, it would almost be a relief.

I swing my legs so that I am sitting on the edge of the bed, looking down on the rest of the house. Ana stirs but does not wake beside me. I decide I should get up before I disturb her further, and walk, back bent, to the ladder and descend from the loft as quietly as I can manage. The door to Suon's room is beside the ladder, and though it is closed, I suspect she is already awake. She has trouble sleeping. I have different problems.

We are staying in a ski lodge in the mountains several hours west of Calgary, near a place called Golden. Once it was a resort town, but now, like so much else in this world, it has fallen into disrepair. When Calgary—the world really—collapsed, there few people able to travel and pay for expensive ski holidays. As a result, the town here has been mostly forgotten, with a few dozen inhabitants left. One of them runs the lodges here, halfway up the mountain from the town. We are his only guests and have been since we arrived almost a month ago.

I start the coffee maker and sit at the kitchen table to watch it drip into the pot. As I expected, Suon is awake, and she emerges when the pot is almost full. We have our routines now.

"How was your sleep?" she says in a faux-cheerful voice.

I glare at her. "I dreamed again."

"Do you remember any of it?" Suon gets up to pour us both coffee.

I shake my head as I watch her spoon sugar into my cup. In my old body, I preferred coffee with milk and sugar, but in Aeida's, I drink my coffee black.

"Really?" she says. It is a challenge. She does not believe me.

"Really," I say, which is a lie. I remember the dreams clearly, even if I would rather forget them.

Suon takes the hint and decides to leave matters be. She pulls a box of cereal from the cupboard and pours herself a bowl. "We're out of milk," she says, when she goes to the fridge and returns to the kitchen table to eat her cereal dry.

4

I listen to the crunch of her chewing, staring out the window at the tree-covered mountainside, taking nothing in and trying not to think of anything at all. Suon is watching me as she eats—I can sense her gaze—working her way up to ask me another question. Already I know what it will be.

"We need to go into town for groceries," she says. "At least one of us does."

I make a noncommittal noise, not turning from my scrutiny of the mountain.

Suon waits and, when I don't reply, says, "I think you should go. You haven't really left the lodge since we got here."

I don't bother to say anything in response. We have variations of the same conversation every day. It always ends the same. This discussion will too.

"How long are we planning on staying here?" Suon says.

The question surprises me a little. She hasn't asked it in so long. "Depends," I say.

"We can't stay here forever."

"With the money I have, I can stay here for at least a year," I say.

"And what then?"

I sip my coffee, still not looking at her. She doesn't want to hear what I will say. I am just waiting for the Seeker, the Society, or the Church to find me. Someone will eventually, no matter where I go. There seems no point in running or trying to hide, when it will end the same regardless. In this body, I can be found anywhere in this universe.

"No one's asking you to stay here," I say.

Suon does not reply, and when I finally look over, I see she is weeping.

2

In my dream, I am Joseph Aurellano. Not the Joseph Aurellano who lived in the Vancouver of Aeida's universe under Meredith's supervision. Some other Aurellano. Though Aurellano never existed. He was a construct of the Acolytes, a simulacrum of a person, intended only to keep me imprisoned and hidden. I remember almost nothing of his thoughts, what he did during those months when I was imprisoned there. Only a few glimpses, shadows of things, came to me, usually when I was lost to myself, in battle with Aeida for command of this body and mind.

Those times I managed to return during my imprisonment, Aurellano was already gone. Aeida returned, though without his memories, which made him pliable. How many times did I come back and surreptitiously make contact with Morris, before being thwarted by Meredith? I never dared ask him that. Never asked him how long it had been since I was exiled. Though it hardly matters now; it is something I don't want to know.

In this dream—for they are all different, these dreams of Aurellano—I am in what appears to be a small colonial town. Spanish, if I had to guess, though it could be

Portuguese. I am near a square with a large Catholic church. Facing it is an official-looking stone building. None of the other buildings nearby has any of the impressive size or permanence of those two. They are all made of bamboo or other trees, with thatched roofs, some on stilts. There is salt on the air and the smell of fish pervades everything, but there is no sign of the sea anywhere.

The faces that pass by on the street are largely Asian, with a few Europeans and Africans thrown into the mix. The clothing, mine in particular, looks like something Osahi would wear. I stand under the shade of an awning, protecting me against the midday sun. Beside me, a functionary—a European, as am I—sits on a precarious-looking stool, an inkwell and some paper set upon a small table.

He is looking at me expectantly, pen poised to write, as are two women who stand facing me. Their dress is simple—a blouse and long, flowing skirt—though the colors are exquisite. Both have worn and thick fingers, of the sort that have done manual work, and their faces are lined from days spent in the sun. The notary clears his throat, as though to remind me that I am to speak.

"My apologies," I say, putting a finger to my temple. "I lost my train of thought."

"You were asking these women about their accusations regarding Doña Pía, Corregidor," the notary says, frowning a little.

"Yes, of course. Please continue."

Both women look at each other. "We've already told you everything there is to tell, sir."

"I want to hear it again," I say, making clear my irritation.

The women look from me to the notary, who shifts uncomfortably on his stool.

"Fine," I say. "Read it back to me."

"The women say that while they were at the docks this

morning working cleaning the day's catch, they saw Doña Pía, who was with them at the time, slip away and meet with a Chinese man. They think this man was Tingco."

I look at the two women. "And you are certain of this?"

They nod, and the older of the two says, "As certain as we can be, not having seen the man before. The men on the docks knew who he was, that's for certain. They were all watching him real careful, but none of them said a word to him."

"And did you ask them who he was?"

"After, yes. No one would say, which is why it must be him."

"I see," I say, not feeling the same confidence that she does. It is possible that the man they saw was just another pirate and not the Tingco. The docks of Manila are lousy with them, after all, and not every Chinese pirate is the notorious Tingco, despite what the easily impressionable might think. Though I sense this is a waste of my time, I continue with my questions. "Did he ask to speak to Doña Pía?"

The woman shakes her head. "No, he just went down by the warehouses, you know. She slipped away after she saw him. Left us to do the work."

"So you didn't see them together?"

"Oh, we did," the younger woman says eagerly. "We said that we weren't just going to let Pía run away to parlay with some ruffian while she was supposed to be working."

"I see," I say, letting them know by my tone that I am doubtful of their claims. Just because they do not like this other woman doesn't mean her consorting with a sea hoodlum is a crime. Now I will have to find this woman and see what she can tell me about this Chinese sailor.

The older woman glares at her younger companion, sensing that they are losing my interest. "We found them, all right. Back in one of the alleys. I don't expect I need to tell you what they were about." She sniffs as though such things are far beneath her. "But it's what they said that will interest you."

I resist a sigh. "And what was that?"

"It was Tingco, there can be no doubt. He said he was banding all the pirates together under his flag. He's recruiting locals, too, all through Manila. Even in the Intramuros. They're going to kill all Peninsulars. Every last one of you."

The notary and I share a glance. "Was there anything else?"

Both women look slightly insulted at my lack of reaction at their words. They shake their heads. I thank them for their report and leave the notary to get the details of where Doña Pía lives. I have stood long enough in the heat of the day, and I retreat to a nearby tavern, where I take a glass of brandy. I am just finishing my drink when the notary comes to find me.

"What do you think?" I say.

He wipes the sweat from his brow and stares longingly at the bottles behind the bar. "It's a pirate, no doubt. But is it Tingco?"

"Indeed. We'll have to find out? You have the woman's house?"

The notary nods, his gaze still lingering on the bottles. "Near the Alcaceria."

Though the Alcaceria is the Chinese district of Manila, I suspect it means little that this Doña Pía lives nearby. Far more likely she encountered the pirate through her work on the docks. The natives and the Chinese do not tend to mix, no matter how close the quarters they might keep. There is little love lost between them. After all, if it weren't for we Spanish, the Chinese might rule this place. That doesn't mean there isn't something to what the women told me. The Chinese are forever plotting to gain a stronger foothold on these islands.

"We had better go," I say. "I want this dealt with before nightfall.

"There's one other thing," the notary says, as we head toward the door. "About what the pirate was wearing. They both said he was wearing a black robe."

I glance sideways at the notary. "Like a priest?"

"Something like that, I gather. Though not precisely the same. There was an insignia on his shoulder."

"What sort of insignia?"

"They didn't recognize it. A symbol of some sort. Red."

A shiver of premonition passes through me, and it is then that I wake up.

3

I am sitting alone on the deck of our lodge, legs propped up on another chair, looking down the ridge at the river valley and the towering mountains on the other side, when a car pulls into the main yard by the office building. A man and a woman get out and linger by the door, which is locked. Neither of them speaks, though they share glances. They do not appear to notice me, and I go very still, blending into the background of the cedar planking on the deck.

Michael, the proprietor, appears on an ATV five minutes later, all smiles, no doubt having seen them arrive. He brings the couple inside the office, and I use the opportunity to slip inside our chalet, watching intently from behind the blinds of our kitchen window. My self materializes beside me, a blank look on my face.

"Go away," I say, not glancing at me. My self heads to the door to go out to the deck. "Not outside," I say before the door is opened. My self turns and goes back to the living room, no expression crossing its face.

When I am gone, I exhale in relief, feeling a tremor run through my body, which I let run its course rather than trying to hide it. There is no one here besides me to see it.

Ana and Suon have gone into town for supplies and a break from this stifling monotony. The monotony is what I crave more than anything now. Sometimes it feels as though it is the only thing keeping me together, while I wait for the inevitable in whatever shape it comes.

Michael emerges with the couple after ten minutes and leads them to the chalet on the far edge of the property. Trees block my view of it and also hide it from the road and the office. We chose this chalet because it offered a clear view of the office and anyone entering from the road, thinking that we wanted to see trouble as it arrived. The lodges are a short drive up an old logging road from the main highway. It is the only way in or out, unless one descends the mountain by foot. The logging road proceeds up the mountain, but is a dead end and starting to get overgrown by forest in places.

Michael and the couple return, and they take their car around the path out of view to where the chalet is, while Michael disappears into the office. I wait another five minutes to give them time to settle in before I return outside to the deck and resume my study of the mountains. Michael emerges at more or less the same time I do and spots me. He waves, a gregarious, excited gesture, and, unable to contain himself, wanders over.

"Hullo," he says, his accent one I cannot quite place, though he claims to have lived here most of his life. He has grey eyes that have a strange, dull sort of gleam to them. "Everything good for you folks? Enjoying your stay?"

"Very much," I say.

"Excellent. You don't need anything?"

I shake my head, careful to keep an empty smile on my face.

"Good. Good. Just let me know if you do."

"We will. Thanks." I wait, knowing that he will be unable to resist telling me what I want to know without me asking him any questions.

"You folks still planning on staying for another week or so?"

"We are," I say. "We'll decide in the next few days what we're going to do."

"That's great. You just let me know. Happy to have you stay as long as you want. And now you've got some company up here." Michael grins, counting the dollars he will be getting in his head.

"I saw that. Are they planning on staying long too?"

Michael nods. "A couple of nights, at least. Maybe longer. I told them about you folks, of course."

"Of course. Did they ask any questions?"

If he finds anything innocuous in my query, Michael does not show it. "Not a one. They were mostly concerned about being private. I expect they'll keep to themselves while they're here. Didn't say much about who they were, either. But then, I didn't ask. Don't want to be rude."

"Of course not," I say. "They're probably just looking for a little romantic seclusion."

"That's what I thought too," Michael says, happy that we agree. "That's what I thought too. Now, there's plenty of that here, as you folks know."

Michael seems convinced that we are some kind of polyamorous contingent, and we have done nothing to dissuade him of that assumption. As he has told me before, we are not the only ones to have used the lodges for that purpose. But I think he is wrong about the couple. I saw their expressions before they arrived, and those were not the shared glances of lovers on a sojourn. They are here on business, but what business that might be I cannot say.

"Did you recognize them?" Suon says, her face pinched with worry. She is afraid of the newcomers.

I shake my head. "Nobody we know. Maybe not involved at all. How would anyone know which way we went?"

"We didn't go very far."

This is Suon's usual complaint. In her mind, we should be running, staying nowhere long. She is probably right, though I wonder. There is nowhere in the universes we cannot be found.

"We haven't done anything to put us on anyone's radar. Besides, we don't know that anyone is looking for us."

Suon snorts in disgust. She knows the reason I remain here is because I believe any number of people are after me and that I cannot escape them, no matter what I do. Ana, who is sitting at the kitchen table with us, looks from Suon to me, a dim sort of concern on her face. I am tempted to ask her what she is thinking, but that seems cruel.

"I don't like it," Suon says. "I think we should go. Tonight."

"You're free to leave whenever you want," I say.

"Fuck you, Laila. You know I won't do that."

"Maybe you should. It would be better for you in the long run."

Suon slams her fist on the table, rattling the dishes. Ana studies her with the same faux-concern, not even blinking at her display of rage. "You think it'd be better for you if I wasn't here, you mean. Well, it wouldn't. You'd get to wallow in your despair, sure. Maybe throw yourself off the damn mountain."

She pauses to gather her emotions, aware that she is shouting and the windows are open. We both glance in the direction of the chalet where the couple are staying, wondering if they can hear us. Ana follows our gaze. She has become a mimic. It is hard to watch, but I cannot banish her as I do my self, when the absence at the center of her becomes too much to bear. She is the reminder of what I have done and what is left for me to do to make it right, as impossible as that is.

"Anyway, where the hell would I go? This isn't my

world, in case you've forgotten. The Society will be after me too eventually."

I don't answer, looking past her at the mountainside, where dusk is slowly taking hold. Suon shakes her head in disgust and storms out of the chalet to the deck. Ana and I watch her go, neither of us stirring from our seats. I turn my attention to the fire burning in the old stove that we light in the evening, for the mountain nights are cold, even in summer. Ana fixes her gaze on me, studying me with an intensity that makes me uncomfortable.

"Laila?" she says. It is not spoken in the voice of the half-thing she is now, but the way she used to say my name.

I go still, not even wanting to breathe, as I stare in her eyes. "Yes," I say at last.

She nods, as though that confirms something she suspected. It, too, is a familiar gesture. Tears begin to burn my eyes, and I fight to hold them at bay, while I watch Ana closely. She is watching me as well, and there is something like awareness in her eyes. I wait, unsure what to do, but she does not speak.

"Ana?" I say when it becomes clear she will not say anything further.

As I say the word, I can see the focus go from her eyes, the distant cloud returning as her awareness goes. For a moment, her eyes sharpen—a glimmer against the darkness that holds sway in her mind—and I think she will resurface. But just as it is there, it goes, her eyes dimming and her gaze empty again.

"Yes," she says, eager to please, as always.

"Why don't you go to bed," I say, struggling to hold my emotions at bay.

Ana nods and heads to the bathroom. I wait until she is inside before I go to find Suon.

4

Suon is sitting on the edge of the hot tub, her legs dangling inside. I go to sit opposite her. She refuses to look up at me, staring down at the rusted-out bottom of the tub. It is lined with dirt, pine needles, and other detritus, beyond repair, as so many things in this world are. While I wait for Suon to speak, I listen to see if I can hear anything from the other chalet, but the only sounds are the odd bird in the trees.

"I won't go," she says, finally looking up at me. "Don't fucking tell me to, because I won't do it."

"Okay," I say.

Suon looks away. She is embarrassed or overcome by emotion, perhaps both.

"You know we can't just stay here," she says. "We can't wait for something to happen. I know you won't tell me about those dreams, but you're not stable. We're barely holding you together with De Vroes' medicine. And the supply won't last forever, you know. What happens when you start to fall apart? Or Ana?"

"I don't know," I say.

"We need to get help. We need someone with access to Acolyte tech."

"There are the Acolytes, I guess." It is a poor joke, and

Suon glares at me to say I am not taking this seriously enough.

"There must be someone left from your allies. Or Osahi's people. If we could contact them."

"If any of my people are left after they took Morris, then I wouldn't trust them. Same thing with Osahi. Either the Society and the Seeker or the Acolytes will be grilling everyone to see what they can turn up."

Suon sighs, lets loose her hair, and ties it up again. It is an unconscious gesture, and for some reason I feel a stirring of desire, which I push aside. "I just don't understand what Molijc thought he was gaining by selling out to the Society. Does he think the Church is finished?"

"No. The Church is finished, but he would never believe that. He thinks he is the Church. So long as he remains, the faith does."

The crack of a branch somewhere on the ridge below makes us both go still. We listen, but no further sound comes. Motioning to Suon to say something, I creep from the tub and go to edge of the deck, which overlooks the ridge.

"He's a madman. No doubt about it," Suon says. "I can't believe...he was made Grand Regent."

I shoot an amused glance at her, knowing what she was about to say. To tell the truth, I can't really fathom now what attracted me to Molijc. He was a different person before we ascended the Hierarchy, or so I like to tell myself. Were we really so different, or did power simply remove the varnish we had put on our edges?

As I consider that question, I peer over the deck railing below. Our chalet is set upon the edge of a plateau where all the lodges are, with a steep incline beginning just beyond the deck, descending all the way down the mountain to the river and town below. The ridge leading to the plateau is covered with pine trees for the most part, and not thick, making it easy to see through them from our vantage point. Though it is getting dark, I have no trouble picking out a form scurrying through the trees toward the far chalet. It is hard to make out whom exactly, but I think it is the woman. I watch her go until she is far enough up the ridge that I cannot make her out through the trees.

"One of them," I say, turning back to Suon. "Maybe the woman."

"Was she listening?"

"Trying to, I would guess. I don't think there's anything else down the ridge that way. Maybe a bear. No other reason for her to be down there."

"Still think we shouldn't go?" Suon says, crossing her arms.

I shrug, heading inside. She follows me.

"Let's see what happens," I say.

Suon shakes her head and doesn't say anything, heading directly to her room. I stay in the kitchen, feeding another log into the fire and closing the blinds to the windows. Suon emerges from her bedroom and goes to the bathroom, coming out when she is finished for a glass of water. I remain where I am by the stove, my only movement to stir the blackened logs from time to time with a poker. She shakes her head, considering saying something, but deciding against it, returning to her room.

I stay where I am watching the light under her door. When it goes dark, some ten minutes later, I leave the lodge, as quietly as I can, and start toward the far chalet, clenching the poker in my hand. For the first time in weeks, I feel something other than despair and apathy and find myself grinning as I stalk through the trees.

5

I follow a different path to the far chalet than the woman who was spying on us. She came down the ridge, before presumably angling back up it to arrive underneath our deck. I stay near the path between the chalets, trusting that the growing darkness will hide me even if the few scattered trees won't.

As I come within sight of the lodge, I hear voices and pause to listen. I can't make out anything they are saying, only that it is a man and a woman speaking. Her voice is high with emotion, his calm and neutral. By the way their voices are muffled, I guess they are inside the house, not out on the deck, and decide to go closer.

Moving softly, and taking care not to make the same mistake the woman did, I come within sight of the lodge. The deck and most of the building are shrouded in darkness, but the kitchen lights are on. The blinds are drawn tight, but at least one window must be open, for I can still hear them talking. The woman speaks rapidly, excitably, while the man's replies are more languorous, almost mocking. I still can't make out anything they are saying.

Staying to the trees, I skirt around the chalet toward the

back, intending to crawl under the deck to get closer to the kitchen. As I pass by what must be one of the bedrooms, I can hear both their voices clearly, and I decide to stay where I am. The open window is obviously here, and I move to stand beneath it.

"They couldn't have seen me in the dark. The lights from the deck would have made that impossible," the woman says.

I grin and shake my head.

"Gloria, you can't know that for sure," the man says, his tone that of a teacher patiently explaining something to a pupil.

"Anyway, what does it matter?"

"Well, we don't want them suspicious, for one. The last thing we need is to draw attention to ourselves."

"They seem like the sort to keep to themselves."

"Yes. That's exactly why they'll be watching us carefully. They won't want us getting in their business. We might scare them off."

"Well, I'm sorry I made a mess of it, Hazim. If you'd wanted the thing done right, I guess you should have gone and done it yourself."

"I didn't say that, Gloria," Hazim says, realizing his misstep. "We each have our service to do, as you know."

"How is it that my service always requires me to put myself at risk and yours never does?" Gloria says.

"You know why. From each according to his or her abilities. Our duties in service are utterly clear."

"To you, anyway. I notice anytime I have a question, you think you have the answer."

I sense this argument has taken place before. It is immediately familiar to me, having been involved with persuading Regents to do the Church's bidding for so many years. Most do so without questioning, but there are some who do, usually because they are not favored in the way their fellows are, or something has happened that makes them question the entire enterprise of their faith.

Some people look past those moments, reconciling every betrayal of their belief, of their selves, until there is nothing left but the faith and what it requires. That was me, though it was easier for me than most to reconcile my faith to what I was doing, given I stood at the pinnacle of the Church for so long. But so many others I knew walked away, disappearing, and I never gave them another thought. What became of them?

While I am lost in my thoughts, the argument between the couple has continued, and they leave the kitchen, coming to stand beside the window I am under. I crouch down and press myself against the building, hoping neither of them happens to look outside. The poker in my hand suddenly feels ridiculous, and I set it on the ground next to the foundation, reasoning that my intentions will look better if I don't have it in my hands. Though that will hardly do me credit if I am discovered.

"Look, our service is clear here," Hazim says, "Now that we've found these people, assuming that we have, we're to observe them and report back. When we've confirmed they are who we believe they are, we'll be given our next steps."

"You make that sound so simple. How are we supposed to confirm who they are when we haven't really been told who they are?"

"It's simple enough. There's four of them. The two that you've seen match the descriptions we've been given. Once we get a look at the other two, we'll know. Tomorrow night you'll go back—and you'll be more careful—and listen to them again. If they say something about the Church or the Society, then we know, don't we?"

"I still don't see why it's me who has to do this."

"I won't have any complaints on the matter," Hazim says. "We have our service. From each according to her abilities."

He pauses, and I can sense him looking at Gloria,

daring her to contradict him. I urge her to as well, even as I know that will not happen.

When she doesn't speak, Hazim says, "Good. That's settled, then. We'll discuss it further in the morning, I think. Now, remember the other part of our service. To each according to their needs. Do you have a need?"

"I do," Gloria says, her voice flat. She is still angry, I can sense. "Do you have a need as well?"

"I do," Hazim says. "Let us satisfy those needs as prescribed by our being joined together."

Gloria doesn't reply, and I hear the unmistakable sound of kissing and fumbling at clothes to remove them. Now would be an ideal time to leave, while the two of them are distracted, but I stay, listening intently. Their sex, which seems pro forma at first, an obligation to be seen to, gradually builds in passion and urgency. My desire in response to what I am hearing is painful and confused, as always. How I wish it could be simple again.

I stay till they are finished and slip away as their breathing begins to still. The fact that these people are here looking for us should strike fear in me, or at least give me pause. Suon is right: we should be leaving tonight, trying to lose them before they can confirm our identities. But I have no intention of doing so. I want Gloria and Hazim to confirm who we are. I want whatever will happen once they do to take place.

My excitement builds as I make my way through the trees back to our lodge. Let them come, I think. I will be waiting. It is only as I return to the chalet that I realize I left the poker on the ground by their lodge. I turn around to retrieve it, but decide against it. Better that it stay there to serve as a warning to them, I tell myself. I will be expecting them.

6

Joseph Aurellano is a woman. She walks briskly down a gleaming, well-lit corridor. Only institutional hallways are made to gleam like that, to be so visible in their attempt at invisibility. I can discern nothing from the walls and intersecting corridors to tell me anything about where I am or where I am going. There are markers impressed in the wall where the hallways intersect, but I cannot interpret them. They are letters, but not from an alphabet I am familiar with.

I do not take another branch, and the corridor does not turn, yet as I go I have the distinct sensation that my path is curving. As I go further, I feel gravity shifting, lessening and then intensifying. For a time, I think I am walking upside down, gravity and my position in the corridor reversed. There is nothing to account for these sensations, except that I am in a dream. But none of the other Aurellano visions have had anything like the dislocations of time and space that are the regular habitat of dreams. They have been far too real.

As the shifts in gravity cease, several people appear in the corridor before me, materializing from the walls, if my eyes are to be trusted. I have passed no doors to this point, and part of me wonders if this is why. My main focus, though, is on the three people before me. They are wearing black robes with a red symbol upon their shoulders. Not the symbol of the Society, I notice, or not exactly. It is similar, as if they are part of the same category of things.

"Where are you going, Josefina?" one of them says. Their faces are shrouded behind hoods and masks, and the voice of the person speaking is somewhat distorted by it. I cannot tell if it is a man or a woman speaking. The robes obscure that as well.

"Where does it look like?" I say without hesitation, though I have no idea where I am going.

The three people move toward me, their stances threatening, though they carry no weapons. As they come closer, I can see beneath the shadow of their cowls that they do not wear masks at all. Rather, the armature is a part of their face, like the Seeker's eyes. The color and texture of it is the same, that blackness that is somehow absent of color and yet all colors at once, drawing in my gaze as if it possesses its own gravity. It appears both metallic and biological, and I wonder, with a shudder, if it has spread beyond their faces to cover their entire bodies.

What terrifies me most of all is that if were to put my hand up to Josefina's face, I am certain I would find the same armature. The thought is somehow as horrifying to me as my discovery that I was transplanted into David Aeida's body, and I have to fight the urge not to collapse and dry-heave on the floor.

Instead, I say, "You cannot stop me." I sound certain, though I have no idea what I am basing that certainty upon.

The one who is speaking to me laughs. "We'll see."

The three of them step aside, revealing an Acolyte's Eye floating in the corridor. I somehow failed to notice it before. It rasps and breathes like they all do, as if it is a living thing. It is a living thing. The insight comes to me, and though I want to reject it, to laugh at it as ridiculous, I cannot. Instead, I turn and flee.

I run back the way I came, not even looking to see if my pursuers are following me. They are; I know it. I can almost see them walking at a quick but unhurried pace, as if they have all the time in the world. Perhaps they do. For my part, I go down the first intersection I come to and take a different path whenever one presents itself, hoping I do not inadvertently lead myself to a dead end. The corridors all look much the same—officious, empty, and sterile.

I expect the walls to dissolve and more pursuers to emerge from within them at any moment, yet they do not. The longer I run without arriving anywhere, without any more people finding my trail, the more certain I become that this place is empty. No one is here but the four of us and the orb. I cannot fathom why that could be, for the place is vast, judging by the endless hallways. Though, for all I know, I am running through the same corridors endlessly. It is a dream, after all, I have to remind myself.

There is no sign of any pursuit, yet I dare not slow down. They are there somewhere, coming. There is no hiding either, not with the Eye present. Somehow I have to escape, to break free of these corridors and emerge from this building, whatever it is, to whatever strange world awaits me. It seems an impossible task.

When I do emerge, it feels as though I am climbing out of the ground, from deep within a cave, coming up to see the sun for the first time in ages. The gravity of the place drags at me, and, though I am still on my feet, walking the same as ever, it feels as though I am crawling, hand over hand, to reach the surface. Finally, the pull ceases, like chains unclasping from my ankles, and I step out from interlinked corridors to a new place.

It is a rotunda, vast as the corridors, with an arched ceiling curving high above. The ceiling is made of something transparent—glass, though it cannot be just that. It cannot be because of what is outside. Multitudes upon multitudes of stars, and nothing. Space. There is no world that I can see, no planets anywhere, and no sun. The universe that I know has vanished.

7

Suon is waiting for me when I climb down from the loft, standing by the stove, arms crossed and an accusing glare on her face.

"What?" I say, almost laughing. I go to the kitchen and pour myself some coffee. It feels as though I haven't slept at all. My mind is heavy and sluggish. When I close my eyes, I am still running down those strange corridors, or worse, staring up at the vast, empty space that surrounds that place. I am adrift there, trapped, without hope of escape. Despite all that, I feel strangely hopeful.

Suon comes over to stand beside the kitchen table once I sit, her arms still crossed. "You went over there last night. What did you do?"

"I did," I say, still smiling. "And I didn't do anything. Just took a look around."

"Where's the poker, then?"

"I forgot it by the chalet."

"What if they find it?"

"What if they do?" I say, shrugging.

Suon shakes her head. She starts to say something before stopping herself. "Did you find anything out?"

"They're definitely looking for us," I say.

"Fuck," she says, so loudly it startles my self. I poke my head around the corner from the living room and look about warily to see if anything is amiss. "Why are we still here?"

"They don't know who we are. They've got orders to confirm that and then report in. So they're not Travelers and they're not the Church."

"Free agents, then. They have to be working for one of them. Why else would they be looking for us?"

"I don't know," I say, smiling again. "I intend to find out, though."

"Jesus," Suon says, putting a hand on a table to steady herself. "Do you want to end up in black site? Is that the end game here?"

"Not mine, but that is where this is going to end. It has to. The Seekers want me to do something, and I haven't done it. They'll come for me eventually, and they'll make sure I pay for what I've done. I'm not going to run. I'm not going to hide. I'm going to enjoy the time left to me."

Before I can say anything further, Suon holds up a forestalling hand. "Don't even think about it. I'm not leaving you and the rest of this menagerie. Whether you want to hear it or not, you need me."

I simply nod in return. It seems we have come to the conclusion of that particular argument, or so it feels to me. She will stop asking me to go, and I will stop telling her to leave. We will both of us wait for what is to come. A strange elation comes over me. I have finally made my peace with my fate and decided what I want to do. I will not go back to the Church or Meredith. I will not do the Seekers' bidding, or anyone else's. Whatever consequences result from that, I am willing to live with. The rest, including Suon, doesn't matter.

"Why are you interested in these two?" Suon says.

I laugh, surprised at how perceptive she is. "They are interesting. They're members of a cult. Not ours. Somehow they've gotten mixed up in this. I'm just curious about their angle. And if we can use it."

"What sort of cult?"

"I don't know. They were repurposing communist slogans and talking about service."

Suon shakes her head and shrugs. She is not of this world, so she is not familiar with the religions that now exist here. Ours was not the only religion formed after the arrival of the Travelers in this world. Hundreds sprang up from the fertile soil left in the wake of a decade's worth of war and dislocation, while the old faiths withered. Most burned out within years of forming. A few, like the Church of Regents, became massive enterprises, growing at a rate that alarmed government authorities and the Society.

I knew little of the other faiths that came and went, none flourishing to quite the degree that the Church of Regents did in my part of this sorry world. Though that might be another lie of the faith, that we told and believed ourselves. How many Regents and Initiates are there now? How many had there ever been? I looked at the books we kept, but I have no idea if what Molijc and Lasinha showed me was anything resembling the truth. We had buildings and airships, all the visible signs of success, but they, too, might have been a sham. It all feels so pathetic now. It's a wonder I ever believed.

Our failure was that we pitched ourselves in a battle with the Society, which was not something we could ever win. We were fools, in short. Although if Molijc is a Society agent, as seems to be the case, and he worked with them since before our rise to the top of the Church, then it might have all been by design. So we are still fools, but of a different order. That is little comfort, given all the damage we did and are doing even now.

I have become lost in my thoughts, and Suon is staring at me with some concern. "Just thinking about the Church," I say, with a wave of my hand.

She doesn't look as though she believes me. "What did you dream last night?"

"Nothing."

"Don't lie to me," Suon says, pushing a strand of hair from her eyes. "I heard your screams. Was it about Aurellano again?"

I absorb myself in a study of the kitchen table, nodding. "Yes."

"This is not good, Laila."

"No."

"What if he takes over? What if you go back to where you were when the Acolytes worked on you?"

"That won't happen," I say.

"How can you be sure?"

"It's not like the other times with Aeida. Or even when I could feel Aurellano. Whatever it is they put in this body. Anyway. He's not trying to take over. He's not there in my head in the same way."

"Then why are you dreaming about him?"

I shrug. "Side effects. That's all it is. We can't keep pumping me full of Acolyte cocktails and expect there not to be some nasty consequences."

"I guess," Suon says, sounding doubtful. "But you need to tell me what's going on in your head. That way, I can do something before Aurellano or Aeida or whoever else you've got in there tries to take over."

"I will. I promise," I say, knowing that I should. "Aeida is the threat. Aurellano is not real. He's a simulacrum."

Then why are all my dreams of him? Him in the Philippines centuries ago. Her on some space station centuries from now. They are the same person somehow, even though that person is not real. Joseph and Josefina are real, but the Aurellano put inside me was just a mask put over Aeida to hide this body's true contents. I think of the armature that Josefina and her jailors had on their faces. Though it is impossible—Aurellano is not real; he is a creation—I am becoming that person, both of them. My hand strays to my cheek and rubs the unfamiliar stubble there

8

I stay inside the lodge most of the morning. My self and Ana I banish to their rooms, wanting them to remain out of sight, to force Hazim and Gloria to do something foolish to try to confirm who we are. Suon spends the morning pacing the deck outside, vigilant for any sign of them, which will only serve to put the couple further on alert.

She comes inside as I am eating a salmon sandwich, just like Aeida's mother used to make for him. "There's smoke," she says, casting a glance back outside.

I go out to the deck to find the sky has clouded over with a thick haze that seems to brush against the tops of the trees. The air feels thick and filled with noxious particulate, lining the inside of my nostrils and throat. Suon looks at me, frightened and clearly ready to load the car and go immediately.

"Better close the windows," I say. "Don't want the smell everywhere if we can avoid it."

I go inside to do that, while Suon follows behind me, exasperated. "If the mountain's on fire, we should get the hell out of here."

"We don't know where the fire is," I say. "We just

know the wind is blowing the smoke here. We could end up driving right into it."

"I don't know that I want to stay here to find out how close it is."

"Don't worry. I'll talk to Michael," I say, and head over to the office.

He is not there, but he gave us a key to use in the event of emergency. There is a phone line in there, the first landline I have encountered in a long time. I dial the number he gave us, and he answers on the first ring.

"Michael. It's David." I almost find myself saying Joseph instead, and experience a wave of vertigo. "There's a lot of smoke up here. We're not in any danger, are we?"

"Awful, isn't it?" comes his chipper reply. "No danger yet. The fire's up north near Prince George, apparently. Take quite a lot of burning to make its way down here."

"That's good," I say.

"Been a dry year, though. Wouldn't be surprised if there are more fires started. Supposed to get a few storms tomorrow, so that should help knock some of the smoke out of the air. Hopefully the wind changes."

"That's fine," I say. "We'll deal with it. So long as we know we don't have to get out of Dodge."

"Nope. No need to do that," Michael says with a nervous laugh that makes me wonder if the fire is closer than he is letting on. I decide that is unlikely. Michael may be desperate for our business, but he is far too kind a soul to put our lives at risk, at least in my judgment.

The door to the office opens behind me as I end the call, and I turn to find myself face to face with Gloria. She is surprised to see me, but recovers quickly to smile. It is a tired grin, and she has tired eyes to match. Her long dark hair appears uncombed, hanging over her eyes. I wonder if she resumed her argument with Hazim after I left.

"Oh, you must be the other guests. I'm Gloria," she says, holding out her hand. "We just arrived yesterday."

"I know," I say, not bothering to offer my hand in

turn. She has long fingers, I note. Everything about her is long and lean, spindly like some desert plant fighting for every ounce of water and nourishment it can.

She blushes and withdraws her hand. "What's your name?"

"Joseph," I say before I can stop myself.

"Oh," Gloria says, as though she hadn't expected to hear that. "Isn't it just wonderful up here?"

"If snorting campfire is your idea of a good time."

She laughs, putting a hand to her mouth. "There is that, I suppose. Is the fire close, do you know?"

"I just talked to Michael," I say. "He's says there's nothing to worry about. Just have to wait for the wind to shift."

"Oh, that's such a relief," she says, not looking as though she thinks it is. "I was worried we were going to have to go after just getting here."

"How long are you planning on staying?" I lean against the counter in what I hope is a relaxed, inviting pose.

Gloria will not meet my gaze and is suddenly evasive rather than effusive. "We haven't really talked about it. At least for the weekend, I guess. And we'll take it from there."

"No lives to get back to, I guess. Must be nice."

"Not right away, anyway," Gloria says, realizing she needs to be careful. "What about you folks? There's four of you, right?"

"Oh, we're on the run," I say, declining to answer her second question.

Gloria laughs as though I have said something hysterical, though nothing in my demeanor suggests I am joking. She cuts off her laughter quickly, seeing I am not smiling, and looks over my shoulder, shifting on her feet uncomfortably. It is clear she is torn between doing what she was sent here for and getting away from an awkward and difficult conversation as fast as she can.

I suspect that Hazim is not using her according to her

abilities but according to his wants and needs. He wants her to take the risk in this venture, as she herself guessed. Likely he is a coward, and also he thinks that her looks will overcome her lack of tradecraft, and he may be right. She is beautiful in a desperate sort of way that some people find irresistible. Hazim is likely the cause of much of that desperation, if what I overheard is any indication.

"We're planning to stay as long as we can," I say, allowing myself a small grin. "Assuming the mountain doesn't go up in flames in the next few days."

Worry sparks in her eyes. "Oh. Is there really a chance of that?"

"Let's hope not," I say, my smile growing deeper. "We're only just getting to know each other."

Gloria flinches imperceptibly at my words, but recovers quickly and smiles in return. She is now on familiar ground and feels more comfortable. "Yes, that would be a pity. What would your wife think about that?"

"She's not my wife. We're companions, of a sort," I say, hoping that the always talkative Michael has shared his theories on the nature of our companionship with the newcomers. By the way Gloria shifts on her feet again, considering and rejecting a response, I see that he has.

"What about you and your…" I trail off to let her complete the sentence.

Gloria swallows, considering her reply. "I guess we're companions of a sort too." She attempts a bold grin that only makes her seem more desperate.

"In service to one another, eh?" I say, as if making a joke.

Gloria stiffens, no longer sure of herself or where this conversation is going. "I don't understand, I'm afraid."

"We all have needs and they all need to be serviced, according to our abilities. What are your abilities, Gloria?"

She backs away, unable to hide the panic she is feeling. "I…I have to go. I forgot…I need to let Hazim know about the fire."

"Hazim," I say, as though she has told me something I was hoping to learn.

"Yes," Gloria says, pausing in the doorway, conflict visible on her face. Now she is wondering if she should stay to try to find out what I know about them, or if she should go report immediately that they've been made. The latter wins out. "I'm sorry, I do have to be going."

"Of course," I say. "Be seeing you."

She looks over her shoulder as she goes out the door, unable to disguise her fear. Aeida's general creepiness is useful for something, I decide, though I know I shouldn't be taking such pleasure in torturing that poor woman. She has problems enough already, I sense. As do I.

After waiting five minutes or so—time enough for Gloria to return and report our conversation to Hazim—I head back to our lodge. Suon is in my face as soon as I open the door. The stench of smoke has made it into the house; hardly surprising, given how much of it is in the air, but it will make for an unpleasant day if it continues.

"Well?" she says, once I have closed the door.

"Nothing to worry about. The fire is near Prince George."

"But there's no one to stop it, right? It could burn down to here."

"In theory," I say. "But Prince George is, like, eight hours' drive. It'll take a lot of burning to get down here. We'll have plenty of time to get out if it somehow manages to. Don't worry."

"Okay," Suon says, though she doesn't appear to accept what I have said. I suspect she will go call Michael herself later this afternoon.

"I also had a little chat with Gloria," I say, unable to stifle a mischievous smile.

"You've got a thing for her, don't you?" Suon says. She is unable to disguise her own hurt and need.

I laugh, which I immediately regret when I see the pained expression on Suon's face. "Beautiful, but not my type. Believe me. I prefer people playing at my level."

"You prefer people who're dangerous to you," Suon says, unable to hold back her bitterness. "Since you found out I'm not a threat, you've lost all interest."

I look at her with some curiosity. Is that how I seem to her, or is she just giving voice to her wounded pride? It does have the sting of truth, and my first impulse is to deny it. "Is that what you think? Maybe you're right. Even if that's true, she's still nothing to worry about. She's a pawn in someone else's game."

"Fine. I believe you," Suon says, glaring out the window. "What did you find out?"

"Nothing, really. She was fishing for information, and I put a bit of a scare into her. Then I implied we were in some polyamorous tetrad and that we'd like to play with her."

"Jesus fuck," Suon says, shaking her head and throwing up her hands.

I grin. "She's telling Hazim that right now. I imagine he'll send her back to us to play along and fish for more info."

"You're enjoying this far too much," Suon says.

"Why not?" I say. Better than listening to the thoughts in my own head.

Suon walks away, shaking her head and muttering to herself. I watch her go, smiling and thinking, How could I not be enjoying this? There is a knock at the door, and Suon sticks her head around the corner from the living room.

"Even sooner than I expected," I say, feeling triumphant. "Make sure that my self and Ana stay out of sight."

I give her a moment to organize the two of them, which Suon does by banishing them into her own bedroom. They go compliantly, as always. There is another knock at the door, and I step back and call out, "Be right there."

When Suon nods that all is arranged, I go to the door and open it, a ready greeting and explanation on my lips. It dies as I see who stands upon the threshold, shrouded in smoke, his grey cloak covering his head, obscuring his expression but not his terrible eyes. My fun is at an end, and the future I have been dreading and waiting for has arrived. The Seeker has found me at last.

TWO:

THE PACT

9

Despite knowing there is nowhere to run, no way to escape him, I back frantically away from the doorway, heading straight into Suon's arms. She is staring dumbfounded at the Seeker, stunned into immobility. This is the first time she has seen one, a distant part of me realizes, even as I try frantically to get past her to the room where Ana and my self are.

There is no point in doing so. I cannot protect them from the Seeker, or the Black Robes no doubt accompanying him. Even if I manage to open the window, remove the screen, and squeeze out through that narrow opening, there is nowhere for me to go. The Seeker will be able to track me down. It will only be a matter of time. That was always the case, only now the time is at hand.

"Laila Aeida," the Seeker says, with the same ironic detachment. "Or is it Laila Aurellano now? You are barely holding yourself together."

Suon is hyperventilating beside me, her worst nightmares being realized. She is expecting to go to black site, to disappear and never be heard from again. Her fear is paralyzing her. I put a comforting arm around her, to bring her back to herself. We will need both of us to have our wits if we're to get out of this whole.

"Close the damn door," I say. "You're letting the smoke in. Unless the rest of the Society is coming in after you."

The Seeker's expression doesn't change, but he steps through the door, closing it behind him. He looks around the interior of the lodge, nodding a little to himself, as if his suspicions were confirmed, before pushing back the cowl from his head. Long, dark hair spills out and again I am struck by the feeling that the person before me is a woman, though I know hair is no way to judge. His voice has a masculine timbre and his face…all I can see of his face are those terrible eyes.

I am back in my dream again: Josefina Aurellano, standing and facing some further evolution of the Seeker. The thought makes me shudder violently, and I begin to cough. That is enough to awaken Suon from her paralysis, and she puts her arm around me, rubbing my back. Our eyes meet and she gives me a pleading gaze to say: Don't go. I attempt a smile to reassure her, but my lips spasm and contort.

"What do you want?" Suon says, turning from me to glare at the Seeker.

He looks at her, and I can feel her stiffen under the power of that gaze. It is the sensation of someone cracking open your skull to peer at all that is within. I straighten and move to stand between her and the Seeker.

"Don't look in his eyes," I say, putting my hands on her cheeks to force her to look at me. "If you can help it."

I turn back to the Seeker, who still has not moved from in front of the door, as if he is reluctant to further intrude.

"Well," I say. "Are you going to answer her question?"

"Suon Som," he says. "You are not of this universe."

"Neither are you," I say.

"That is not true. It is also immaterial to the current discussion."

"So is Suon," I say. "This is between you and me. I've

been expecting you. Honestly, I wondered what took you so long."

The Seeker is looking past both Suon and me toward of the back of the lodge where Ana and my self are. "Who else is here with you?"

"Please, as if you don't know," I say. He doesn't reply, and I stifle a laugh at the absurdity of this conversation. "Don't you?"

Still he doesn't answer and turns to look at Suon. Before I have time to warn her or step between her and the Seeker, she says, "It's Ana and Laila's body."

"Show me," the Seeker says.

I watch helplessly as Suon goes to retrieve Ana and my self. When she returns from the bedroom, leading the two, she is weeping. "I'm sorry, Laila. I'm so sorry."

"He was going to find out anyway," I say. "There's no stopping him while he's here. Anyway, this isn't your fight."

"Isn't it?" the Seeker says. "She is of the Church. She is with you now in a universe that is not hers."

"We've left the Church. We're done with all that."

The Seeker regards me with his implacable gaze. "Is that so? What about our agreement?"

"The Church is already destroyed," I say, waving my hand at him and going to sit at the kitchen table. I want his attention on me and not the other three. His intentions are still unclear, but I assume he is here for me. If so, I may be able to protect everyone else, though it is foolish to think I can do anything to stop a Seeker.

"You didn't need me to do that. Molijc did it himself. But then, you would have known that too. So I'm at a loss to figure out why you needed me in the first place. Morris. Molijc. Who else did you have in the Church?"

"Ana Arajuano. After a fashion," the Seeker says. He has not moved from the doorway, his gaze now intent upon Ana, who looks at him with her usual blankness. There is something in his expression resembling human emotion, which I have never really seen before. Is he mourning what she has become?

At last he breaks his gaze from Ana and comes over to sit across from me at the kitchen table. He looks at me, but the power of his gaze is absent for the moment. A sign of respect, I think. Or he is lulling me into a false sense of security. Suon risks moving up near the fireplace to look at us. The Seeker has his back to her, and I give her a look of warning to come no further. Ana and my self stay where they are. They are obedient, if nothing else, and will not stray.

"So it was Molijc, was it?" the Seeker says, musing to himself. "I did not think that possible."

"What the hell are you talking about?" I say, looking at him in disbelief. "Of course it was. He pushed Osahi and me away once he allied with the Acolytes. And then he pushed Lasinha away. Who knows what's happened to him. When Osahi made his play, he called on the Black Robes to clean up his mess."

The Seeker is looking up at the ceiling, still lost in thought. He continues as if I haven't spoken. "Never thought it possible. Lasinha. You. Even Osahi I thought might be, however unlikely. But Molijc, Molijc I was certain believed."

"He does. That didn't stop him from going to the Society to save his ass when it suited him. How long was he one of yours?"

The Seeker doesn't answer, though he looks at me again.

"You didn't know," I say, shaking my head. "You didn't know."

"Why else do you think we wanted you to go back? Or Ana, for that matter."

My hands are shaking. I don't bother to hide the fact. "You said you wanted me to restart my rebellion against Molijc."

"We both know you had no intention of doing so. You

42

wanted your body back and you wanted revenge. Morris had already told us you did not have the assets to do that. No, what we wanted to find out was who was the conduit between the Society and the Acolytes."

"Why would they need a conduit? The Acolytes left the Society to join De Gofroy."

The Seeker shakes his head. "The Acolytes never left. They have always been a part of the Society. Just as we have. An opposing part, no doubt, but a part nonetheless."

"I don't understand," I say.

He looks at me, considering what to say next. His eyes are still empty of their usual power. He opens his mouth to speak, before pausing, cocking his head as if to listen to something.

"We must go," he says, making no move to stand.

"No," I say, though I know any resistance I offer will prove futile. "I want to know what the hell the Society was doing to the Church."

The Seeker's lips move slightly, as if he is speaking in an undertone, though I hear nothing. He waits and receives a response, before turning his attention back to me. I expect him to order us from the chalet, but instead he provides an answer to my question.

"The Society is at war with itself and has been for some time. The Church of the Regents was a useful proxy for that war. You and the rest of the faithful were subsumed within it."

As soon as he says it, I can see the logic in it. Why else did the Society allow us to continue to flout their laws so blatantly and for so long? They needed no proof; they could have raided the Church and its Protocol Centers at any time. Who would have stopped them? The governments of whatever countries we were in would have gone along with it. They viewed us as a nuisance at best, a threat to their rule at worst.

Yet only twice that I am aware did the Society move openly against us. Once when Molijc, Lasinha, and I were taken. And only a few short days ago, when Molijc called upon them to save his hide from Osahi. There were disappearances, of course, Black Robes and Seekers dispatched against Protectors, and, once we started crossing over, sub-Regents of the faith. Just as when Meredith thwarted my attempt to cross over and brought the Seeker to Aeida's world. But all of that could just as easily be a part of the proxy war, the Acolytes and Molijc working with their allies in the Society to disappear Protectors and sub-Regents they didn't trust.

But once the Watchers' Order was created and the Acolytes perfected their techniques, that would no longer be necessary. The other side in the battle—the Seekers and their allies—would want to know what was going on, though. So arrests and renditions would continue and people like me would fail to notice any difference. The threat of the Society changed, but it remained the same.

The Seeker is still watching me, judging how I am taking this revelation. There is a simple way for him to discover that, yet he does not use his eyes. Why? And why tell me this now? What does he hope to gain from me in telling the truth of the Church? He wants me to go with him willingly for some reason. Yet his revelation ensures I won't. I cannot stand any more of the betrayals, subterfuge, and hidden alliances, and my faith is utterly gone. There is nothing left for me in what was apparently his war.

"Now, we must go," he says, rising to his feet.

I make no move to follow. There are questions I want answered. "Did De Gofroy know?" I have to know. Was it all a sham, right from the beginning, right to the very core?

The Seeker shifts from foot to foot, unable to hide his impatience. I expect him to demand that we go immediately, or to summon whoever he is communicating with. They will come bursting through the door to drag me out. Perhaps Suon and the others as well. Instead, he answers.

"Not to my knowledge. The Acolytes, and their followers within the Society, only approached the Church once the power of his following became clear. They saw an opportunity. From the beginning, they placed people in the faith, hoping that they would gain positions of influence so that it could be guided. We did the same, hoping to thwart what they were planning."

I look at Suon. She appears crestfallen, and I can understand why. It is one thing to go into a faith, see it lose its way, and abandon it as a result. But to know that the faith, our faith, was perverted to the ends of those we thought we were opposing is too much. We stood against the Society. Our battle against them for the true souls of all those in all the universes was the one thing that allowed me to keep the faith all these years. Yet I was doing the Travelers' bidding the whole time, one side of the Society or the other. What difference did it make?

"Now, I have answered your questions, and there will be time for more later. But we must go."

"Absolutely not," I say, allowing myself a thin smile. "Why should I go with you?"

"There is much you can do for us. You have a part to play, to set the universes right again, and I am here to see that you do." The last is uttered mildly, but I know a threat when I hear it.

"You'll have to make us," Suon says.

The Seeker gives her a mocking look to say that he is more than willing to do so. Another message comes to him, and he says, "There is no more time for discussion here."

"I have plenty of time," I say. "Don't you, Suon?"

"I'm in no rush," she says, crossing her arms.

The Seeker looks from one of us to the other, clenching his fists. Suon shrinks when she sees but stands her ground.

"I'll help you," I say. "But there is a price."

The Seeker sighs, no longer able to conceal his

frustration. "That is not your body."

I stare at him blankly.

"That Laila," he says, "is not of this universe. It is not your body. Assuming your price is the restoration of yourself to your body, we cannot do it without the body in question."

A multitude of questions and emotions crowd my mind at this new revelation, but I push them all aside. "That's not my price."

Suon makes a small sound of protest, and I glare at her. There is a sharp rap at the door, which makes everyone go still. Only the Seeker does not turn in that direction. His lips move with no sound emerging again. His eyes, still absent their power, are intent upon me.

"Your price?" he says.

"My price is Ana. She's restored and set free. The Society, the Church, none of you fuckers has any claim to her. You return her to Aeida's world, or whatever world she chooses, and let her live her life with Sebastien. And you make sure that nobody else goes after either of them. Don't give me any bullshit about polluting universes or whatever. You owe her that much at least."

To my surprise, the Seeker looks uncomfortable, shifting almost imperceptibly. "That is in contravention to our—"

"I don't give a fuck," I say. "That's my price. You might as well restore this other Laila too while you're at it. Send her back where she belongs."

"And this Laila too," Suon says, pointing at me. "Assuming we find her true body."

I look at Suon and shrug. "When we're done, we get to walk too. You send us to some other universe where we can do whatever we want."

The Seeker looks at both of us for a long time, his eyes somehow seeming to meet both of ours, though his head doesn't move. "Very well," he says. "I agree to your terms. Now you must agree to mine. We need to leave here immediately."

Before I can agree, Suon interjects. "We need a moment to discuss this before we agree. Alone."

The Seeker looks as though he wants to argue, but he nods curtly instead and goes to the door. When he opens it, I catch a glimpse of someone standing on the deck looking through the thickening haze at the road. After the door is closed, neither Suon nor I move for several seconds, both of us in a daze at what has just transpired. She emerges from her stupor first and comes over to sit across from me, taking care to avoid the Seeker's chair.

"Do you trust him?"

I snort and roll my eyes.

"Do you think he can hear us?"

"I assume so," I say, and shrug to say that it doesn't much matter either way.

"I don't think we should do this," she says.

"You say that as if we have a choice," I say. "We go willingly or they take us. Something's coming, and it's got them worried. Whatever it is, we have to assume it's coming for us too."

"How do we know that what's coming will be any worse than the Seeker?"

"We don't. All I know is I've never seen a Seeker scared before. And I've definitely never heard of one willing to negotiate favorable terms. Whatever he thinks we know or can do, it must be valuable to them, and they must not want it to fall into someone else's hands. So I'd say we're in a good position, all things considered."

It does not feel like a good position to be in, a thought I can see reflected on Suon's face. There are no good choices now. I am as trapped as I've ever been. The only way forward is deeper into the morass, but there is no guarantee I will find a way out. I don't expect to. If I can keep people like Suon and Ana from joining my fate, I will count it as a victory.

Suon considers what I've said and nods. "I guess I

agree. I'd rather the Seekers than the Acolytes anyway. At least we know they won't tamp your brain."

"I wouldn't be so sure of that," I say, thinking of my dream of Josefina and her altered body, and stand up.

Before I can move to the door, it opens and the Seeker enters, followed by a Black Robe.

"We have no more time," he says. "Your answer?"

Suon and I look at one another. "We accept your terms," I say.

"Good. We must be quick now."

Before he can say anything, an explosion reverberates down the mountainside, nearly spilling us to our feet.

10

The aftershocks of the explosion continue to rumble through the mountain, vibrating everything in the chalet. My jaw itches with it, and I have to clamp my teeth together to stop them from chattering. Someone is screaming in terror and agony, and I realize it is my self. I am lying on the floor, clutching my head, while Ana stands over me, a distant and confused look on her face. The Seeker motions to the Black Robe, who goes to my self and pries open my eyelids, which are pressed tightly shut. He looks at the Seeker and shakes his head.

"Do you have any of your dampeners or suppressants left?" the Seeker says.

"Some," Suon says with a caginess that surprises me. How much is left? Her expression seems to indicate not a lot, which would explain her growing desperation these last weeks to leave here and find help.

"Give her something. We need her stable."

Suon goes to retrieve the supplies, which she keeps in a duffel bag in her room, ready to flee at a moment's notice. While she does that, I unsteadily climb the ladder to the loft and pull the hard drive with De Gofroy's files from its hiding spot under a loose floorboard, sliding it into the pocket of my jeans. I look around to see if there is anything else to bring with me, but all that is here are clothes and other detritus of a life that feels best left behind.

When I return to the main room, Suon has subdued the half-thing and is supporting her with the Black Robe. Ana is looking around confused, some panic in her eyes. I go to her and take her hand, squeezing it with my damp one. The reverberations are continuing, and it now seems clear that there was no explosion and the vibrations are the result of some weapon.

"What the hell is going on?" I say.

The Seeker ignores my question and leads us out the door. Outside, the smoke has grown thicker—I can barely see the road, and the trees and mountainside beyond it are obscured completely. There are no new vehicles parked by the office, only the car we came in and Gloria and Hazim's vehicle. The Seeker leads us off the deck and takes us around to the back of the chalet, where the mountain begins to slope down toward Golden.

There is something like a trail there through the trees, and the Seeker starts down it, moving quickly. I go next, leading Ana by the hand, and Suon, the Black Robe, and my self bring up the rear. Our descent is precarious, given the continued vibrations that seem to extend down the whole mountainside. What can be causing them? It has to be Society tech—no one else in any of the universes possesses anything like this—but it is beyond anything I am familiar with.

No one speaks through our descent, and we encounter no one as we go. I try to listen for sounds of pursuit, but there are none, though it would be difficult to hear anything over the vibrating rocks of the mountain. The sound is grating, not unlike a drill boring into concrete. As we descend, the noise lessens and the vibrations lose some of their intensity, the rhythm of each tremor longer.

The Seeker picks his way among the trees, locating a

trail I cannot, as if he has been down this way many times before. When I glance back, the chalets are no longer visible, obscured by the smoke and forest. The road up the mountain is somewhere to our left, and we are angling away from it, so we must be well hidden from it. Unless someone was able to track us as we left the chalet, they should not be able to follow us. Of course, the people who are after us do not need to have eyes on us to find us.

We descend for half an hour, the way growing steeper and steeper as we go. When I look up at the smoke-shrouded tree line, it seems that we have covered no distance at all. The vibration is now a dull tremor that I only notice when the slope grows precarious. Even its sound recedes until it cannot be heard over our own breathing and footfalls and the chatter of the birds and wind around us.

Just as the slope becomes so steep that we have to scramble down on our backs, we come to a narrow ridge where the ground levels. There is no way forward, only a sheer drop onto the tops of pine trees stretching up from the next ridge to almost reach the one we are on. Beyond that is a plunge to the river valley, the water gleaming in the sun. Looking down is simultaneously terrifying and entrancing. I have a vision of myself floating down amid the treetops, carried by currents of air.

The Seeker grabs me by the shoulder and pulls me back from the edge. The others have moved down the ridge as it spirals along the mountain, but they are looking back at me. It seems I have been standing here for some time. Suon looks as though she is about to cry again, whether from relief or despair, I don't know. Perhaps both. I know I feel both in this moment, as the Seeker leads me to them.

We haven't gone far along the ridge when we come upon the transfer engine. It is like nothing I have seen before, yet immediately recognizable. A small box, a vibrant black, made of a material that looks to me like a distant cousin to the Seeker's eyes. It is strange to me that they have left it here, even in so isolated a spot. Its exterior is smooth but for the small bulge where I assume the channels will show. There are no obvious buttons to enter them in, but the object blinks to life as we come near, lights of green and blue cycling toward synchronicity. I watch it, as hypnotized by it as I was by the treetops.

"Do we have to?" Suon whispers behind me. "She doesn't handle crossings well."

I do not, and the thought of attempting one again is terrifying. My stomach twists uncomfortably, and I worry I will have to throw up or defecate off the side of the mountain.

"We will stabilize her on the other side," the Seeker says. "Any trouble, Rahim?"

This question is directed at the Black Robe, who crouches over the transfer engine, frowning at the lights. "We're still too close to the pulse. It's upsetting the calibration."

"Can you compensate for it?"

The Black Robe shrugs and turns back to the engine. He doesn't touch anything, but I can see the rhythm of the lights changing, trying to match the distant reverberation that I can feel only if I close my eyes and concentrate. No one else speaks, and the forest around us is quiet but for the wind stirring through the branches. I look around, sensing a foreign presence, expecting to see someone descending through the air toward us. A squirrel dances across the limb of a nearby tree.

I can feel the channel begin to open, and I turn back to look at the engine. The other side is not visible, but the tug of the other universe is already present. The Black Robe frowns as the lights continue their pattern and the channel refuses to solidify. Beside me, the Seeker shifts slightly, an unconscious gesture. A nervous one. Again the thought occurs to me that I have never seen a Seeker so exposed before. I didn't think it possible.

The channel begins to coalesce, and the air by the

engine changes, like a hazy window has been placed between us and the rest of the forest. I cannot make out anything on the other side. The drag of the other universe makes my hands shake and the bottom drop out of my stomach. I fight the urge to flee.

My mind seems to be running to thoughts of its own accord. I see Aeida as a child playing with a rocking horse. Except the horse is mine, but the house we are in is unfamiliar. Joseph Aurellano steps around a corner, looking down upon me with a soft smile, a dishtowel thrown over his shoulder. His hands are damp, I know. I can feel the water on them.

These visions are interrupted by a murderous scream. All of us, except the Black Robe, turn to look back up the ridge in time to see Hazim emerge, his lips twisted into an enraged grimace. He has a sword in his hands, held above his head as he charges toward us. It is long and narrow, with a slight curve at the end. A saber—the word comes to me. The metal of the sword is an odd color—a light, almost sky blue—and it glimmers strangely when the light catches it. I have the sense of sparks emerging from it when the sunlight does touch it, but that is only in my head.

Hazim heads straight for the Seeker—a sensible move, I suppose, given he and the Black Robe are the only real threats here. The Seeker stands his ground, watching Hazim approach, his expression betraying nothing. He doesn't move, even as Hazim lowers the sword with a vicious swing, intending to cleave him in two.

To my surprise—and Hazim's—the sword bites earth, cutting deep into it. Hazim frantically tries to jerk it free, while looking around for the Seeker, who stepped aside from his blow and now stands behind him. He moved so quickly that I did not see it happen. Neither did Hazim, but he seems to know where the Seeker is, for when he frees the sword, he whirls around to face him.

"End the Seeker interference. Leave the universes to

their true ends and means," Hazim says, raising his sword again.

He is gripping it with a single hand now, and, before he can attack, the Seeker grasps him by the wrist, twisting and bending his arm. I hear bones breaking or separating, an awful sound, as Hazim's arm is now held out perpendicular from his body and behind his back. He screams and drops the sword, falling to his knees and weeping. The Seeker releases him and retrieves the sword, turning from Hazim to look at the Black Robe.

Rahim nods. "The channel is ready."

"Excellent," the Seeker says, motioning for us to go forward.

I look from him to Hazim and back to the channel, filled with trepidation. The treetops below the ridge fill my mind. I want to float among them. Before I can, Ana takes my hand and moves toward the open channel, eager to comply with the Seeker's order. It breaks the spell I am under, and I follow her, though my fear does not quiet. Suon watches me go, her own fears on her face, before following with the other Laila. The Black Robe moves to help her, and we all step through the channel, the Seeker coming last.

11

Sweat sticks my shirt to my back and runs down my face. My only movements are to brush the droplets away before they reach my eyes. The Manila night offers no succor from the heat. The air is still and murky, heavy with the stench of people and animals. It chokes out even the salt of the sea.

How I wish I were back in Granada, where the climate is more salubrious. But I will never return there. My life is here, my career here. No matter how high my station rises in the Philippines, I will never gain the wealth that will allow me to return to Spain. It is a mournful thought and a foolish one. I knew the consequence of my coming here, and the reward as well. That it has not arrived, that I am condemned to a miserable existence in this squalid place, is no one's fault but my own.

A form enters the shack I have hidden myself in, a shadow deeper than the shadows around it. There is a shout from somewhere down the street—a child waking from a nightmare—that leads the form to pause and glance back outside. Though I can barely make out the figure in the doorway, I am certain it is not a woman, as I expected. It is not Pía, which means it must be Tingco.

"Aurellano," the figure says, turning back. "Well met."

I am uncertain whether I betrayed my position. The greater concern is how this ruffian is aware of me, a minor functionary. Does he know who is tasked with investigating him? Evidently.

"Tingco, I presume," I say, stepping from the corner where I secreted myself.

Tingco nods, a gesture I barely make out through the murkiness of the night. He crosses the small room, near enough for us to touch, to the kitchen table, where he strikes a match with his thumb and lights a small candle. The wax on it is already burned low, with leavings added back to stick to make it last a little longer. When the candle is burning, he sits at the table and gestures to the only other chair for me to join him.

Reluctantly I do, though I know it is dangerous to sit across from this man. His reputation precedes him. I keep my hand close to the dagger at my belt while I search for the words to begin this conversation. Tingco is too quick, though, and he will not allow me the upper hand.

"You've found me, then. Now what do you propose to do with me?"

I study him in the dim light of the candle, shadows moving across his face as the flame dances. It is a Chinese face, and his clothes are typical fashion for the Chinese here in the Alcaceria—and Chinese everywhere, I suppose. Except for the fact that they are entirely black, but for the red insignia on his shoulder. It is too dark for me to make out the symbol, but I do not think it a Chinese character.

"It seems you wanted to be found," I say, stalling for time. "I can only assume you have something you wish to tell me."

"I do, in fact." He smiles. "You think this is about the here and now, but it is not. There are greater matters at stake."

"I'm sure there are," I say. "There always are. But my concern remains my responsibilities to the Crown and the safekeeping of the Spaniards of this city."

"Not the Filipinos?"

"It is my understanding your lot intends no harm to them. If I am mistaken, I will extend my concern there as well. They too are my responsibility."

Tingco lets out a ha of air. "You are a responsible man, Aurellano. You always are. A credit to your kind. My responsibilities are different, though. And greater. They concern all the universes and all those who inhabit them. But then, yours do too, you are just unaware."

"Surely there is only one universe under Our Lord. Even you worshippers of the earth must not be so misguided as to believe there is more than one sun and one world upon which it shines. No one is so depraved."

Tingco smiles. "On the contrary; you will find me quite heretical, I'm afraid. There are universes as endless as the stars in the skies. I should know. I've seen more than I can count."

I stiffen at his words, wanting to dispute what he is saying. It feels unchristian to say nothing, but I do. Something in him compels me to hold my tongue and see what he wishes to tell me. It is important, I feel. This meeting, here and now, is no accident. It is happening because he desired it to.

He nods as if I have passed some test he set for me. "As I said, my responsibility is to the multitudes in universes you cannot begin to imagine. It is their futures that are at stake. If I must murder a few in this universe to do so, I sadly will. The price of doing nothing is far too great to bear. Though the weight of this is heavy enough. I find I can bear it, after a fashion."

I frown. It seems he is talking in code that he expects me to interpret. I want to argue with him, to dispute his points. Means and ends are for philosophers to debate— here in the world where life is lived, matters are different. It is one thing to say that you will kill one to save the many, but something else to actually do so. Especially for so obscure a cause. But that is what gives me pause, for it is fanatics who have no difficulty finding reason to justify their madness.

"Of course you don't understand," Tingco says, seemingly disappointed. "Some of you do, though, and that is why this must be done."

He nods as he says the last, and I open my mouth, ready to both argue and question him. Before I can speak a word, I sense a presence behind me and whirl around to see Pía approaching me, a dagger in her hand. Where did she come from? There was no one here when I entered—her shack is so small that we cannot both have secreted ourselves without the other one becoming aware—and she cannot have slipped inside without my noticing her. Can she?

My mouth hangs open stupidly, as does my hand, not moving to take my own dagger from my belt. Too late, I move to stand and draw the blade. Tingco is already at my side, pinning my arms with his hands. "See it done," he says, in a soft, almost seductive whisper.

Pía does not look at me. Her eyes are locked upon Tingco's. There is doubt there that gives me a moment's hope, but it vanishes, replaced by resolve. I don't feel the blade cut my throat, only the terrible warmth of the blood as it flows from my neck down my chest. Tingco holds me tight, keeping my arms pinned, as though I might somehow still escape. He makes soothing noises as though putting a babe to sleep, while easing me to the dirt of Pía's shack.

"Until next time, old friend," he says, then blows out the candle and takes Pía by the hand, leading her out into the night and leaving me with the darkness.

I stare at it—at nothing—for a good long while as blood and life seeps from me by degrees. It takes an impossibly long time to die, it would seem. I make my peace and pray to Our Lord for forgiveness for my multitude of sins, asking for release from this slow agony.

It does not come.

My concentration is broken by the whirring wings of a large dragonfly as it flits around my face. Already flies to the carrion, I think. Who knows what vultures will follow? The dragonfly does not alight upon me; it stays hovering near my face. Somehow, even through the darkness, I can see its eyes as it gazes upon me. They are a deep black, almost an absence of color itself, yet still visible through the night. Some light sparks within them.

12

Scattered images flow past me, carried by some invisible current. Some are caught in an eddy and stay for a time before moving on, but most are present for only an instant. I remember little of what I see. Suon is there sometimes; the Seeker as well. Various Black Robes come and go. We are in a blank room with walls that dissolve and reappear. Outside is the vastness of space, the sea, or a city street with people passing here and there. They are not people as I know them.

There are other things that happen, but I don't remember them. They do not happen to me, but to Aurellano. One of the Aurellanos. It is hard to keep track of them all, though they all reside somewhere within me.

Time passes, but I do not feel its passage. Everything is now.

Things come back into focus gradually. The images slow. Time slows. I can feel my breathing again, hear my heart beat in my ear. It is steady, as nothing else is, and I cling to it for stability in this turbulent sea.

I am lying on a bed in the middle of a large room. There is no other furniture but the bed, nothing else at all in the room. Three of the walls, the ceiling, and the floor are a dark, metallic grey that shimmers at intervals. Three seconds, three seconds, and then five. That is the pattern. One wall, to the left of the bed, is a window. We are in a tower, looking down upon other towers, in a vast city.

Suon is beside me. Has she been there all along? She follows my gaze. "They say it's Jakarta."

I cough and clear my throat. "Where's Ana?"

Suon winces, clearly wounded that my first question is about the woman she sees as her rival. "I don't know. As soon as we crossed over, you collapsed. They took you away and then separated the rest of us. I was put in a room just like this by myself. I don't know what they did. I don't know what they did to the others."

I reach out and take her hand to calm her. "It's fine. We knew what we were getting into agreeing to go with them. There was nothing you could do. How long have we been here?"

Suon shrugs and withdraws her hand, turning to look out the window. "A day at the most, I guess. They've fed me twice. They brought me here about an hour ago. No one's said anything, and I haven't seen the Seeker since we arrived."

I attempt to sit up in bed, a wave of nausea assailing me. Suon begins to rush over, but I wave her away. "He'll come when he's ready. They need us, let's not forget."

Suon makes a face, but doesn't argue. She watches with concern as I push myself off the bed and walk over to the window. I move slowly, my whole body tingling and unsteady, as if it has been days and not hours since I got up. As I come to the window, my stomach lurches with vertigo, the height of the tower we are in now evident. The streets below are barely visible amongst the conglomerations of towers, even the shortest of which seem to be fifty stories or more.

"Jakarta, you say."

"They say," Suon says. "It doesn't look like Jakarta."

"I've never been," I say.

"Neither have I, but I've seen pictures. There aren't this many towers. And there's nothing like this." She waves her hand at the room. "There are no doors anywhere here. They just walk through the walls and dissolve and re-form. Except when I try to do it. Which I guess makes us prisoners. I've never seen tech like that. Never even heard of it."

"I have," I say, still gazing down at the city, wondering if this is a window or a screen projecting something. "In my dreams."

Suon looks at me as if she is mourning something that died. "It's changing you, isn't it? Taking over."

"I don't know," I say. "The dreams aren't dreams, if that makes sense. These Aurellanos exist somehow. In another universe, maybe, and I'm connected to them. I don't know how that's possible. In the last one, the Aurellano was killed by some proto-Society person. It was in the past. Sixteen hundreds, maybe. I died. I felt myself die."

I shake my head, trying to chase the final images that were impressed upon the brain of the dying Aurellano. The Seeker dragonfly—did the Philippines even have dragonflies?—fluttering near my eyes, looking into them. To what purpose?

"Maybe these dreams are part of what they want from you. Whatever this is."

"Maybe," I say, though I can't imagine what use having dreams about a hundred Joseph Aurellanos might be.

"We need to figure out what they want. To put us in a better negotiating position."

"We've already gotten more than I ever imagined we would," I say. "The trick will be keeping them to their word."

"We always keep our word," the Seeker says. There was no warning of his presence. One moment, Suon and I were alone in the room, and the next, he was there with us.

He must have stepped through the wall, but I did not hear or feel anything to indicate that he had.

"You'll forgive me, but I'll need more than platitudes to go on," I say, going back to sit on the bed. I need stability if I am going to make it through another conversation with the Seeker in this place, and the bed is the only thing providing it here.

"What did you do to her?" Suon says, moving to stand guard over me. I resist the urge to shoo her away.

"We have stabilized you," the Seeker says.

"How?"

"By removing Aeida," the Seeker says, as though it were something insignificant, like removing a wart.

I shudder despite myself, putting a hand to my head. "This is his body," I say, simultaneously horrified and exultant. I am finally free of him and can be assured that Ana will be safe in my presence. Yet this is still so much less than what I wanted. I am stable, but trapped in Aeida, and the Seekers will have less incentive to remove me now. Presumably I can do whatever they need in any body, and from their perspective, this one is as good as any.

"It was the only way to ensure your stability. So long as there were two of you present in one mind, it was inherently unstable."

I open my mouth to say that there may be more than just me in my mind right now, but close it and look away. Better that he not know for now. Suon glances at me, a strange look on her face. The Seeker is watching us carefully, but his eyes have none of their power. Not that much escapes his attention anyway.

"I want to see Ana," I say to distract him. "Before we do anything further."

"That is impossible," the Seeker says.

"It goddamn well better not be."

"As well as unwise," the Seeker says, finishing his thought. "She is safe, I assure you. As I said, the guild always honors its agreements. Ours will not be any different. But she is not safe here. Nor is the other Laila, for that matter. Both of them have been removed."

"If it's not safe, then why are we being kept here?" Suon says.

"Laila's presence is the reason it is not safe. The Acolytes are looking for Laila; they are not looking for the other two. Removing them and keeping them away was the wisest course of action. We judged that you would not wish to abandon Laila, otherwise you would have been removed as well. If you wish to go—and it would be wise if you did—we can arrange that."

"I'm not going anywhere," Suon says.

I roll my eyes, while the Seeker nods. "As we expected. Now we must prepare you for what comes next. We cannot remain here long."

"Where is here?" I say.

"Jakarta. In another universe."

I look at the Seeker, prepared to argue the matter, before deciding against it. "Fine. Jakarta it is. What now?"

"We return you to your universe."

"Won't that be more dangerous for me, with all these people looking for me?"

"Undoubtedly," the Seeker says. "But we want them to find you."

I sigh and look out the window at the city. "I was afraid you were going to say that."

13

The transfer equipment begins to blink, synchronicity approaching. Blue, green, blue. I watch it intently, trying to have my breathing match it. The Seeker has assured me the transfers will give me no more trouble, that Aeida is gone for good, but I cannot trust him. Even now, after all we have discussed these past hours. My head still reels with what he has told me. Is any of it true?

Suon moves up to stand beside me, reaching out with tentative hand to touch mine. "Are you ready?"

I laugh and shake my head.

"We can always refuse to go."

"You can. I can't."

She sighs. "You can. They can't force you to do anything."

They can, I am fairly certain, though they don't seem to want to. But that is only because they have something I want from them, which will assure my cooperation. If it were otherwise, things might be very different.

"I have to," I say, glancing at her. "For Ana. I have to set that right. If nothing else."

Suon doesn't reply, though I can see her thoughts clear on her face. And what about me? she is thinking. She will not like any answer I can give her. So be it. She knows that, and she knows as much as me about what we are going into, and she is still here. Everything that happens to her from here on out is on her.

Even as I say it to myself, I don't believe it.

The lights reach synchronicity and the channel forms. I can feel the other universe, can see it forming. For a moment, I close my eyes and let it pull at me. I feel nothing, no reactions, no falling apart of body and self. Suon is watching me expectantly. I look at her and attempt a grin.

"Let's go."

"I want to know everything. I deserve that much, if you're going to be using me as your weapon against the Acolytes."

I made the announcement defiantly, but my voice trembled as I spoke, giving the lie to my confidence. As always, the Seeker's face betrayed no emotion, though there was a flicker of expression on his lips. It was the eyes, I realized. They didn't convey emotion the way human eyes did, and I was always watching them, not the rest of his cues, so he remained hidden to me, while I was forever exposed.

"Very well. What do you wish to know?"

"Gabriel Arajuano. He was one of yours? The whole play with Frederik and the Church funds, that was your game?"

The Seeker nodded. "Correct."

"Why?"

"Before Frederik, his role was to identify which Initiates might be allied with the Acolytes. He identified three critical possibilities: Molijc, Lasinha, and you."

"Jesus fuck," Suon said, drawing a glance from both of us. We were in the same room I had woken in. The bed was gone, disappeared into the floor, replaced by three chairs and a table where there was a version of gado gado we were all eating, unlike any I had ever tasted before. The window still showed the city of Jakarta, now at night, the buildings illuminated by thousands of points of light.

"Only three?" I said, raising a skeptical eyebrow.

"Three who gained De Gofroy's trust, anyway. You were positioned to run the Church, which meant that part of the Society was as well."

I thought back to the night of Arajuano's exile. That had been Osahi's show, and De Gofroy's. Lasinha and I were brought there as a test of loyalty, neither of us knowing a thing about Arajuano and his betrayal. Lasinha even told me he thought there was nothing to it, that it was all Church politics. How wrong he was.

The Seeker continued. "We judged we could not allow you three to gain control of the faith, because doing so would allow the Acolytes free rein to do as they wished."

"The Order."

"Yes. They have been developing the technology associated with the tamps for some time. Really, it was just an extension of what they had begun with the Eye. With Arajuano gone and your ascension, they were free to act as they pleased."

It was difficult to listen to this, to know that I was the author of the faith's destruction all those years ago when I thought we were saving it. "And Ana, was she always with you?"

The Seeker shook his head. "We recruited her when you sent her to the Society. Her father told her the truth of things."

I wanted to cry with relief, though I didn't know why it mattered so much that Ana had once been as true to the faith as I had. But it did. At least one part of my past was not entirely tainted by the Society. "So you arranged our rendition so she could make contact with me then. Was it always the plan to have her come back, to try to infiltrate us?"

"No. The Society's conduit arranged for the rendition.

We still aren't sure why. There must have been some information he needed or wanted to pass on. We simply took the opportunity to reach out to you. Ana felt we could trust you, that you weren't the plant. Her intuition proved correct. We knew it was a trap when you brought her back to the Church, but we decided we couldn't pass up the opportunity. We hoped we could get her out before it was too late."

"You were wrong," I said. My hands were shaking again, but this time it was from emotion, not the side effects of what the Acolytes had done to me.

"We were. And the cost has been immeasurable."

We all fell silent, each mulling our own thoughts. For my part, I was thinking of the woman with Ana when Aeida and Lasinha arrested her. She must have had evidence that Molijc was a Society agent, just as somewhere in the De Gofroy's files there must be proof as well. Why else would he have been so desperate to recover what I had taken? I had read them all, but I didn't see anything in them that showed the truth. But I was never very good at seeing the truth of things within the faith. I had allowed myself to be led astray so many times.

I looked up from my still hands at the Seeker. "Why did you send me back the last time?"

"To discover the conduit."

"You've got your answer."

"Perhaps," the Seeker said.

"You can believe what you want," I said with a shrug, though I wondered why he wasn't convinced it was Molijc. The evidence seemed clear—to me, anyway. Lasinha was gone to the winds, maybe out of the faith entirely, though I doubted that. Like Osahi, he could hide forever, and like Osahi, he would never leave if he thought there was a chance he could regain his influence.

Another question occurred to me. Even as I posed it, I knew the answer. It filled me with a sickening dread. "How could you expect me to find out who the Society agent was if you didn't tell me that's what I was there for? Hell, I was Aeida for most of the time I was with Molijc."

"Yes, we made of certain of that. Crossing over made you unstable."

I did not let him finish what he was saying. My whole body was shaking, this time with rage. "You put that asshole in control of this body. Do you realize what you did? He raped Ana."

The Seeker's expression didn't change. "Unfortunately, we couldn't foresee all the consequences. All we could do was ensure that you were able to resurface. We judged the risk worth it to discover the conduit."

"Of course you did," I said, still shouting. "You used her before. Had her use me. Nearly broke us both. And what was the result? She ended up a half-thing for Aeida and whoever else to play with."

The Seeker regarded me dispassionately. "I can assure you, we did not intend that. Ana was someone we cared for very deeply. She believed in what we are doing as strongly as we do. That is why she agreed to return to the faith. And because she trusted you. But she knew the risks and accepted them."

I was disconsolate, wanting to throw myself at the window, to plunge out into the Jakarta night. Only the suspicion that I was facing a screen projecting a city and not a window stopped me. "Fuck you. How could she know that this… Fuck you. Don't you try to put this on me. You did this. You made him come back."

Suon reached out to put a hand on me, but I pushed her aside and stood up. I had to do something. The thought of being in this thing's presence for a moment longer filled me with loathing. Not as much as I despised myself, though.

"Ana didn't deserve this," I said, beginning to weep and hating myself for it.

"No, she did not," the Seeker said. "Neither did you. None of your Regents did. Not even Aeida. If nothing else, we must try to set that right. But we will need your help to do it."

"I won't do it. I won't. Not for you bastards." I shook my head and wiped away my tears, refusing to look at him or Suon.

"You can't make her," Suon said, protective again. She stood and put an arm around me, trying to offer me something.

I had to choke back my anger. It was not her fault. She was just the easy target, the one who would never fight back against me. Gradually I forced myself to breathe, and my fury began to dissipate. I sat down, still refusing to look at either of them. Suon stood behind me, a hand on my shoulder, ready to defend me as necessary. I felt my rage at her building again.

The Seeker considered both of us. "Do you remember the first time we spoke, Laila?"

"Are you going to talk about fate again?"

The Seeker nodded. "I told you our fates were intertwined, that we would be together in the end of this. And we will, I can assure you."

"I won't help you bastards," I said, but there was no force remaining in my voice. I knew it was far too late for that. We had made our pact and now I had to see it through.

I open my eyes as the channel closes behind us. Beside me, Suon lets out her breath, which she has been holding tight. We are back on the mountainside we left only a short time ago. Days, though I am not certain how many. Time was difficult to ascertain in the Seeker's stronghold.

When the channel is closed behind us, Suon picks up the transfer box and, as instructed, slips it into the backpack the Seeker has given us. It is our emergency exit, programmed to take us to the place we just left. They have shown us how to start it, but not how change the channels to alter where we are going. Given time, I could probably figure that out, but for now I will play by their rules. I will honor my side of the agreement in the hopes they will honor theirs.

The backpack also contains the hard drive of De Gofroy's files, which the Seeker insisted we bring with us. He would not explain why, and nor would he say whether he had looked through their contents. There are secrets a Seeker might be able to discover, but he doesn't seem to care to. It is bait, just as I am. The threat of what it might contain, whatever the truth of the matter, will draw our enemies out in the event that I am not enough of a prize.

We start back up the mountain toward the chalet, where the Seeker has assured us our car will still be waiting for us. I wonder how he can be so certain of that, just as I questioned how he could be sure that Hazim and Gloria, and whoever was with them, didn't take the transfer box. I receive the answer to that question as we follow the curve of the mountain and discover Hazim lying unconscious on the ground. He doesn't stir as we approach. His arm is bent at an impossible angle and his breathing is ragged.

Suon kneels over him, checking his vitals. "He's stable, more or less. What do you think happened?"

"Probably passed out trying to climb back up because he couldn't use his arm. Check his pockets."

Suon goes through them while I scan the ridge to see if anyone else is there. It seems incredible to me that Hazim was alone when he attacked us, but evidently he was. Given how much time has passed since our escape, it is also unbelievable that no one has come to his aid. Would Gloria leave him on the mountain and abandon her faith? I hope so, but I doubt it very much.

"Just a pulse pistol and some money," Suon says, standing.

"Let's take them both," I say. "We may need them."

"Why would they leave him here?" she says, looking down at his still form.

"I don't know. Even with a broken arm, he should

have been able to get up the mountain. It's not that steep. If he's been here for two days, I'm amazed a bear hasn't gotten to him."

Suon nods and then tilts her head as if she is trying to hear something. "Do you feel that?"

I go still as well, and then I do. The vibration, though faint, is still there.

"Did they just leave it on all this time? He can't be the only one they sent after a Seeker, can they?"

"No," I say, thinking of Gloria. "She would still be here. She would come and find out what happened to him."

Suon looks down at Hazim and back up the mountain, struggling to find some explanation for what is going on.

"There's one possibility we're not considering," I say. "Maybe this isn't a couple of days later here. Maybe it's only a few minutes."

"Is that possible?" Suon says in a whisper, as if she is afraid someone might overhear.

"Not for us," I say. "We'd better get the hell out of here anyway."

"What about him?" Suon says, pointing at Hazim.

I shrug and start climbing back the way we came without a reply. We encounter no one on our way back to the chalets, the vibration getting stronger as we go. The higher we get, the more smoke there is in the air, yet more proof that not much time has transpired since left. It seems to coat my skin and the inside of my throat and nostrils, and when we reach the plateau with the chalets, the first thing I do is go into ours to wash my face and get a drink of water.

Suon does the same, and we spend a few seconds looking around to see if there is anything we should take with us. We stuff a few clothes and our toiletries into the backpack, but otherwise leave everything behind. Even the bag with the Acolyte medicine, which I no longer need, given how easily I passed through the channels.

"We better go," Suon says, as we both linger, looking around the chalet, wanting to find some reason to stay longer.

I nod, and we go out the door to find Gloria waiting for us, a pulse pistol in her hand.

14

Gloria moves the gun from one of us to the other, unsure of who she should be targeting. Her hand shakes a little with each movement. "Where's Hazim?" she says, trying to sound threatening, but sounding scared.

"Down the mountain a ways," I say. "His means met an end."

"You killed him," Gloria says, her face flushing.

"He's worse for wear but still alive. He'll probably need some help getting back up here."

"You just left him there?"

I nod, and Gloria wets her lips, unsure what to do now.

"You're coming with me," she says, thrusting her gun at us.

"I don't think so," I say. "We've got places to be."

"No," she says, growing in confidence now that she has made a decision. "You're coming with me. We're going to get Hazim, and then we're going to go see some people."

Suon and I look at each other. "And who might those people be?" Suon says.

"That's none of your concern, is it?" Gloria says, twisting to point the gun at Suon.

"They're using you," I say. "Your faith. The Society. They're both using you."

"You don't know a thing about my beliefs. We don't work for the Society."

"Yes you do. I know enough about faiths like yours work to know the truth of them. We were once part of one ourselves. You should get out while you can. Walk away and forget about all this shit."

Gloria sneers at me. "That would be good for you, wouldn't it? I don't think so. I don't know what nonsense the Seekers have been filling your ears with, but I know the truth about the universes. You should know they can't be trusted."

"Oh, I know far better than you."

"Is that right? You're nothing but a Seeker's pet, and I'm not going to listen to what you have to say. Now, let's go."

I can see the futility of arguing with her further, though it disappoints me to give in. She is young and vibrant, charged at the possibilities she sees before her. I see myself in her, the possibility of what I could be, before all my failures. Now I want to save her from those same mistakes, but that is a fool's errand, and I have promises I need to keep. Because she is right: I am now a Seeker's pet.

Gloria motions with her gun, and we go past her, down the steps of the deck. As we turn to go behind the chalet, Michael emerges from the office and waves. I freeze, uncertain how Gloria will react, and not wanting to put Michael in any danger. He starts toward us, smiling but concerned. Gloria swears under her breath and ducks behind Suon, who is nearest her, trying to hide her gun, but also wanting to keep it trained on us.

"Get rid of him," she hisses, glaring at me.

"Don't worry," I say under my breath. "Just let me handle it."

"Hey, folks," Michael calls out as he comes closer. "Glad you guys got a chance to meet. Hope the smoke isn't bothering you too much. Wind should shift tonight, I hope."

"Great," I say, mustering a grin.

"Say, do you know anything about this earthquake thing or whatever that's going on? It's a hell of a vibration."

I shrug. "It is. For sure."

As Michael comes closer, his smile disappears and he abruptly halts, spotting Gloria with her gun. "What's going on, folks?" he says in a quiet voice.

Before I can say anything, Gloria fires the pulse weapon. Everything after that happens in slow motion, where I can see what is about to happen before it does. Michael emits a sigh and crumples to the ground, his eyes rolling back in his head. I whirl to face Gloria, who is staring at his fallen body, the full weight of what she has done settling upon her.

"I told you to let me handle it," I say to her.

She looks at me, her eyes flashing with anger, raising the gun to point it at me. "Not another word—"

Suon doesn't give her a chance to finish. She moves to seize the arm that holds the gun, twisting it and Gloria's wrist, so that she drops the weapon. Before she does, the pulse goes off again, this time harmlessly into the air. They grapple together, Gloria trying to reach the gun, while Suon works to thwart her. Suon manages to keep Gloria's arm pinned under her own, her back to the other woman so that she cannot gain any advantage.

Just as I begin to wonder if I should intercede, Suon hits Gloria with an elbow to the nose, knocking her sprawling and stunned to the ground. I move over to pick up the pulse weapon and tuck it into my belt, while Suon readjusts her pack and gains her breath. Gloria sits up, blood trickling from her nose.

"You fucking broke it," she says, touching it and wincing.

"Lucky for you that's all that's broken," Suon says.

I go to Michael and look him over. He is unresponsive. While the other two watch, I attempt to resuscitate him, but it is too late. The shot was too close and the setting too high. I straighten up, look at Suon, and shake my head. Gloria begins to cry, head in hands. Suon looks as though she is about to say something biting, and I glare at her to be silent.

"Where's the machine that's doing this?" I say, getting to my feet.

It takes Gloria some time to realize that I am talking to her. "I don't know. Hazim connected with whoever set it up. He wouldn't let me know anything. He never tells me anything."

"We have to go," Suon says. She is looking at Michael's body. "Someone will be up to investigate eventually, and we don't want to be here when they find his body. What do you want to do with her?"

Both of us turn to look at Gloria, who refuses to meet our gaze, staring miserably at the ground.

"Bring her," I say.

"Seriously?" Suon says, hands on her hips. Gloria looks at me with undisguised hatred.

"Yeah," I say. "You're right. Someone will come up to investigate, or whoever is working the tech will come looking for Hazim. Either way, we don't want her here to explain what went on. Because we'll be the ones taking the blame. So she comes with us."

"What do we do with her?"

The disdain with which she pronounces those words makes me smile. "I don't know. We'll figure it out once we're out of here."

Suon shakes her head and stalks away toward our car. "Fine," she says, not even glancing over her shoulder. "She's your responsibility."

I smile, and Gloria winces at the sight of it. I pull out the pulse weapon and motion for her to get up, which she does, scrambling to her feet. We start toward the car, where Suon stands, the driver door already open, watching our approach. Gloria goes first, head down and defeated, and I follow, taking care to adjust the pulse weapon so that the stun is mild.

We get in the back seat one after the other, while I keep the weapon trained steadily on Gloria. She refuses to acknowledge it or me, staring straight ahead. Suon watches us and shakes her head, muttering something under her breath, before getting in the car and driving us down the mountain, back to where it all began.

15

It is at least a five-hour drive back to Calgary, assuming we can still get through, along a highway, fallen into disrepair, that winds through the mountains. In places, rocks have fallen or the pavement has become so degraded that the road allows only one lane of traffic through, making our progress torturous. It is one of the reasons we felt we could stop in Golden without fear of pursuit. Few people attempt the drive across the mountains anymore.

For the first hour, no one says anything. Even the radio is reduced to static once we are out of the Golden valley. I sit facing Gloria, gun in hand, though not pointed at her. She refuses to acknowledge me in any way, facing ahead, various emotions flickering across her face. At times her lips move silently, as she carries on an argument with someone. Me or Hazim, I am guessing.

Her silence doesn't bother me. Nor does Suon's, who has decided that she is done with me for the time being as well. It gives me time to think. Mostly I consider why I have brought this woman with us. Bad enough I am putting Suon's life in danger—she is here by choice, though she may be regretting that decision now. It amuses me greatly how easy it is to make her jealous, and perhaps that is the only reason Gloria is here. Because I want to annoy Suon, and I don't particularly care what becomes of this stranger.

But that is not true, or at least not entirely so. Gloria is here because she reminds me of myself when I first joined the faith. Driven and uncertain, absolute and wavering. I want to steer her away from the path she is on, for I know where it ends. Instead I am taking her into the belly of the beast, so to speak, from which escape is unlikely, especially for someone as unschooled as her in these matters.

There is also the fact she is beautiful. Suon is correct to be jealous. Gloria's caramel skin and sparkling dark eyes leave me yearning. She wears her hair in a sort of pixie cut that I find entrancing. I want to run my hands through its raven-black strands. Every moment she is near me, she is a danger and a distraction, I realize, yet I know I won't send her away. Just as I could never quite rid myself of Meredith, except for the one time it mattered the most. I am still paying for that mistake.

"Are you just going to sit there and stare at me the whole drive?" Gloria says, interrupting my thoughts.

"I am," I say, trying to smile suavely, though I am disconcerted. Could she tell what I was thinking about?

"Fucking creep."

Suon snorts and finds my eyes in the rearview mirror to say: I knew it. I am nothing if not predictable, it would seem.

"Where do you want us to drop you off?"

"What? You're not just going to push me off the side of the mountain whenever you feel like it?"

I narrow my eyes. "I hadn't been planning on it, but the more you talk, the more tempting it gets."

Gloria goes still, unsure of how serious I am, and returns to looking straight ahead. I catch Suon's eye in the mirror again, and she shakes her head in disgust.

"Tell me about this faith of yours," I say.

For a time, it seems like Gloria will stay silent. Finally,

she says, "It is the true faith."

"They all are," I say.

Gloria turns to sneer at me. "Just because you were led astray by false prophets who sold you a line about the true nature of the universes doesn't mean there aren't those who understand—"

"Forget I asked," I say. "Did we sound like that?"

"You definitely did," Suon says.

"Who was running that tech?" I say, deciding to try a different tactic with Gloria.

"I told you. I don't know. Hazim wouldn't let me know about any of that stuff."

"Means and ends, huh?"

"Something like that. Anyway, it's just anti-Seeker technology. They must be stopped, you know. They're a threat to all of us."

"I don't disagree," I say. "But you know the only people who have anti-Seeker tech like that are in the Society. Who else would need to worry about managing Seekers?"

"The Society is a plague upon all human civilization. They must be stopped at all costs."

"Then why are you working with them?"

Gloria laughs. "You people are fools. You really don't understand what's going on here, do you? There are more players in this game than just the Society and Seekers. They're not the only powers in the universes. They just presume they are. But those of the true faith are rising against their hegemony. We shall be triumphant."

I look at Suon, who ignores me while she negotiates a precarious turn, before sighing. This will clearly get me nowhere. "Still don't want to tell me where to drop you off?"

"You don't understand," Gloria says. "It doesn't matter what you do to me. Your kindness will count for nothing. You will pay for your sins in the end."

"Believe me, I know," I say. Mercifully, she does not

reply, and we drive on in silence.

After four hours of interminable driving, along roads that test the vehicle's suspension and our patience, with many more awaiting us, we come to a roadblock. It is visible only after we crest and come around a bend in the road. Suon swears under her breath as she sees it. We are too close now to stop and turn around without looking suspicious, even if we could. The highway is narrow, with no shoulder on either side, the traffic steady in both directions, except at the roadblock, where it is constricted to a single lane with barricades funneling the traffic. People in uniforms are checking each vehicle before waving it through, while others stand watch over the proceedings with what appear to be pulse rifles in their hands.

"Can you see who it is?" I say, squinting and trying to do so myself.

"Locals, I think," Suon says. "What should we do?"

I make a face. Local enforcement is no real assurance. They are likely to be in the Travelers' pockets. Even the Church could afford to buy them off when we were ascendant. Perhaps whoever is working with Gloria—though it is ultimately the Society, I have no doubt—has arranged this.

"Go through it," I say. "Can't exactly turn around."

"Do you think they're looking for us?"

I consider the question. "No. Doesn't make sense. Who would know we're coming back this way now?"

Suon doesn't reply, except to meet my eyes in the mirror and look in Gloria's direction. I shrug. It is certainly possible that Gloria and Hazim told the Society where we were, but the plan was clearly to capture us in Golden. Unless Hazim somehow made it back up the ridge, there is no one who saw where we went. More likely the authorities in Golden went up to investigate the vibrations, found Michael dead and all of his guests gone, and ordered up some roadblocks.

Which means we are dealing with a different sort of problem here. If the authorities have talked to anyone in Golden, they will have some of our descriptions. Suon's for sure, because she regularly went into town for supplies. Mine is less likely, as I rarely left the chalet. Ana and myself often went with Suon, and their absence now may help to confuse matters, as will Gloria's presence. It is unlikely anyone in Golden, except Michael, got a good look at Gloria and Hazim. That there are three of us, not four or two, will help to confuse any identification they may attempt to make as well. I hope. Unless they've pulled CCTV images of Suon, or any of us, in which case we are fucked.

There is also the matter of the pulse pistol and what Gloria will do once we go through the checkpoint. The weapon I can hide, but Gloria is a wild card. She may decide she's better off being arrested, even though both Suon and I were witnesses to her murder of Michael. I think not, though. If her faith is anything at all like the Church, they will be paranoid and suspicious of outsiders, doubly so for anyone in authority.

"Just smile, look pretty, and act nice," I say to Suon. "You can do the talking, too."

"Great," she says, and grits her teeth.

"And you," I say to Gloria, "do the same. But keep your fucking mouth shut."

Gloria stares daggers at me but doesn't reply. I smile in return and place the gun in the center console.

"Really?" Suon says.

"Are they searching the vehicles?"

"No," she says begrudgingly.

Gloria's eyes flick from the console to me, judging the distance and taking the measure of me. How fast will I be able to move, and Suon as well? Will she able to retrieve the pulse weapon while holding both of us at bay? Unlikely, her face seems to say. She looks out the window, careful not to telegraph anything, and I know she will try as soon as we are through the checkpoint. I catch Suon's eye in the mirror, and she nods, her gaze shifting over to Gloria.

As we get closer to the barricade, we slow to a crawl, inching forward and then idling as cars are stopped and allowed through one by one. While we wait, I watch the authorities carefully. They are local police, to judge by their uniforms—the same dark blue pants and light grey shirts police in these parts always wear, a holdover from the days of the RCMP. They have to be from Banff, I guess, though they may be from as far as Calgary. Two officers approach each vehicle on either side and look inside each window of the car, peering at every passenger's face for an uncomfortably long time. When that is done, they wave them through, no secondary searches conducted.

The silence in the car grows tenser and tenser as we creep nearer to the barricade. Four cars, now three, now two. Gloria shifts in her seat, coiled with intensity, still looking out the side of her window as if the checkpoint doesn't lie ahead. I can hear Suon's breathing, long and deep inhales and exhales to calm herself. It is strange to see them both nervous, while I feel nothing. I am but a piece the Seeker put on the table, to be moved around as he so desires. He wants me captured. This may be a little earlier than scheduled, but I have no doubt the end result will be much the same.

The car ahead of us is waved on, and then a car in the opposite direction comes through. One of the officers points and beckons us forward. Suon pulls up and stops when he holds up his hand. She rolls down her window, and the officer calls out, "Lower all your windows, please." Suon complies, and we wait.

The officers approach, one on each side, from behind the car. All of us stare straight ahead, trying to look normal. One officer peers in my window, and I meet his gaze with my own unblinking one, trying to look demure and forgettable. The officer on Gloria's side of the car does the same with her. They move up to the front of the car, each of them peering in to look at Suon, who sits rigid, not breathing. The officer on the passenger side moves on quickly, but the officer nearest Suon keeps staring. Something about her has intrigued him.

Not good. The other officer moves to the front of the car and the barricade, saying something to the officers behind and atop it. Not good at all. Now all the officers on duty are staring at our vehicle, while the one inspecting the car stares at Suon.

"Where are you folks coming from?"

His question seems to take the air from the car, all of us going even stiller than we already were.

"Kelowna," Suon says in a surprisingly even voice. "We're going to Calgary."

"What for?"

"To visit some friends and maybe look for work."

It is a mistake, though she doesn't realize it. She is not of this universe. No one would come from Kelowna to Calgary looking for work. Not with the tar sands abandoned. Not with Vancouver and the island and their ports to beckon them.

"What sort of work would that be?"

"I… One of our friends just said he might have something for us."

A smirk crosses the officer's lips and vanishes. "Is that right?"

Suon, realizing she has gone wrong somewhere, doesn't reply. At least he hasn't asked her for a license and registration. Not that he would need her failure to provide that to justify taking us in.

"How long you folks staying in Calgary for?"

"Just a few days."

"Unless you get that job you're looking for."

"That's right." Suon looks at him defiantly, daring him to challenge what she is saying. It is another mistake.

The officer straightens up and steps back from the car,

lifting his radio to his mouth and saying something in code. He receives an affirmative response and looks over at his partner, who nods. Leaning down to peer into the car again, he says, "Follow this man's directions here. Proceed straight ahead and then pull off to the right."

Suon looks in the mirror at me helplessly. I just shrug, hoping not to draw the attention of the officer. He has already stepped back from the car and is waving us forward. His partner is beckoning as well, and Suon shifts into gear and goes ahead, turning right and pulling off the road into a small rest area along the side of the highway. We pull to a stop as directed and Suon shuts off the car, none of us speaking, waiting for what happens next.

16

The officer looks up from her paperwork and squints at me. "We have no record of a Joseph Aurellano ever residing in Calgary."

I shrug. "Records aren't what they used to be."

She frowns and looks down again at the papers. I cannot imagine what information she might have there and am desperately curious to find out. "You have no ID. Nothing. You'll forgive me for wondering if you are who you say you are."

"It doesn't matter who I tell you I am," I say. "I can't prove it, and you won't believe it, so I decided to go with the truth. Why not, right?"

Her frown deepens, and she leaves the interrogation room they have placed me in, taking her papers with her. I suspect it was once a utility closet, given our close quarters, repurposed, as so many of the rooms in this small school have been. I don't know where exactly we are—somewhere south of Calgary is all I have gleaned from our journey here—or who has brought us here. It is not the local police, despite their uniforms, that much is certain. No local police in this part of the world can deploy the kind of tech I've seen here. I saw advanced pulse weapons and armor lying in the reception office, where they held us for a few minutes before sending us to our separate cells.

After directing us off the road, the officers made us get out of the car, not even bothering to search it. For all I know, the vehicle is still sitting abandoned on the side of the highway, a pulse pistol hidden in the center console. We were placed in the back of an SUV with bulletproof glass shielding the driver and another officer. There were no handles for the door or windows. No one searched our belongings to ensure we had no weapons, which either meant they considered us no threat or were particularly sloppy at their jobs.

They drove away, siren blaring, dodging the other vehicles and going at insane speeds, given the heavy traffic from their blockade. At some point after Canmore, they went off the main highway, heading south for a time and then east again, ending up in a small town with empty streets and buildings that looked dilapidated. Black Diamond or Turner Valley were my guesses, based on the direction and distance we had traveled. Which meant we definitely weren't dealing with local police. They would never bring us to this place.

The woman returns, papers in hand, and sits across from me, doing her best to look impatient. I wonder if Suon and Gloria are receiving the same treatment. Does Suon still have the backpack with our way out of here and the hard drive with the files that we are to barter with? If she does, I hope she has the sense to transfer out of here. There is something very wrong about this whole situation, though I can't quite say what it is that bothers me. It is a put-on, but I just can't glean the purpose yet.

"Are you going to start taking my questions seriously now?" the woman says, straightening the edges on her paper.

"That depends. Are you going to start taking me seriously?"

"Is being arrested a joke to you?"

"I haven't been arrested," I say. "You've just brought me here. You're playing some game and getting mad at me because I'm not playing along."

The woman looks at me, contemplating how best to proceed. "You need to tell me the truth. You're not Joseph Aurellano. We know that for a fact."

"I am Joseph Aurellano. Whether you choose to believe it is up to you. I won't change my facts to suit you. I'm more than willing to take a lie detector test or sit in front of an Acolyte's Eye if that will make you happy."

I am probing her for a reaction, but I don't receive one. Her face doesn't change at the mention of the Eye, which is interesting. It doesn't feel like I am dealing with the Society. They wouldn't bother keeping this charade going once they had us at their black site. There would be no point. Better to apply the leverage they can bring to bear than to pretend this is someone else.

Who could possess the tech I saw on my brief march through the school hallways to this interrogation room and want to keep their origins obscure? The Acolytes? Perhaps. Or someone I'm not familiar with. Gloria suggested as much, but she is a fool blinded by belief.

The woman leans forward, her jaw set, trying to appear threatening. "This will go badly for you if you don't answer my questions. We need your cooperation in this matter. We expect it, and we will get it one way or another. I've been patient with you to this point, but my patience is wearing thin."

"So is mine," I say.

"Tell me who you are."

"Only when you do the same."

The woman gestures at her uniform. "Calgary Police Service. My name is Constable Agathon. As I told you."

"Which one of us is lying now?" I say, grinning. "You haven't arrested me. Haven't charged me with anything. Haven't even mentioned a reason for bringing me here. Or bothered making up something. So let's just cut the bullshit here."

The woman sits back in her chair, crossing her arms, looking at me as though she is disappointed things have come to this point. "I will give you one last chance to tell me who you are."

"I already have," I say, mimicking her posture.

"You will regret this."

She stands and turns to go, almost forgetting the papers on the table. After retrieving them, she favors me with another glare and leaves the room. I smile to myself and shake my head. I have a feeling it will be a long time before anyone returns.

Two hours pass—maybe more; it is hard to keep track after a while. I fill the time by getting up and pacing the room and stretching, trying to stop this body from getting stiff. While I wait, I try to think about who these false officers might be, but I get nowhere. I am left frustrated and cranky, hungry, and needing to go to the bathroom. This is all part of the plan, of course, and I know that, but it doesn't make it any easier to endure.

There is a knock at the door, and someone enters. A man this time, not in uniform, wearing a bad, mustardy suit of the sort I've seen detectives on the police force wear. I sigh, putting a hand to my temple, as though the sight of him pains me.

"Hello," he says, with an awkward smile. He gestures for me to sit and does the same. "What are you calling yourself?"

"Let's skip past all that and get down to brass tacks," I say. "I'm not changing my answer. You can ask Constable Agathon, or whatever else she calls herself. Maybe you should try changing your questions."

The man frowns, looking down at the table, or off to the side, never directly at me. "There's a lot of things we need to discuss, but until we get the basic facts correct, we can't proceed."

"Where are the people I came with? I won't answer any questions until I see them and can confirm they're okay."

"They are being asked the same questions you are. They are far more cooperative."

I snort and don't bother with a reply. He waits, his eyes flicking to meet mine for the first time, before darting away. A minute passes before he speaks.

"Very well. You've made—"

"I demand to see a lawyer and to know the charges on which you are holding me," I say. "If there are no charges against me, I'll be going. If you won't let me leave, then I insist on seeing a lawyer. These are my rights under Canadian Common Law."

"You are no position to make any demands."

I repeat what I said before. If they are going to play pretend, then I will as well, and we can see how far they intend to let the charade go.

"This is a mistake, I can assure you."

"You level with me, I'll level with you. Once I see the others. Otherwise: get me a fucking lawyer."

The man stands up so abruptly that he tips his chair over and scrambles comically to catch it before it falls, dropping his papers in the process. They scatter across the floor, one landing near my feet. Before he can leave or deliver his parting words, he has to pick them up. I watch as he does that, trying not to laugh. He is flushed with anger and embarrassment, trying not show his wounded pride.

One piece of paper lands near my feet, but I make no move to pick it up. The man sees it and looks at me, clearly hoping I will give in to my curiosity and pick it up for him, if only to get a look at its contents. I don't, and he is forced to come around the table and bend down beside me to pick it up. I let him, but tense my body as soon as he bends down. He freezes, sensing I am going to attack him, but I don't move. As he straightens up, I get a glance at the paper. It appears to be blank.

The man stares at me, bristling with anger, trying and failing to think of something clever or cutting to say. When nothing comes, I allow a little smirk to bend my lips. He turns and walks out without another word, slamming the door behind him.

Another hour passes, and my bladder will hold out no longer. There is no bucket or receptacle of any kind that I can make use of, so I simply stand near the door and piss all over it, creating a nice puddle that someone will have to step in when they enter. When I am done, I sit in my chair and wait. Twenty seconds later, I hear someone running down the hallway, and the door opens. Constable Agathon looks down at the puddle in horror.

"You little shit," she says. "I should make you lick it up."

I give her a look that says try me, though I certainly hope she doesn't. She slams the door, apparently content to let me remain in the room deal with the smell. I have no problem with it either, for my little rebellion has confirmed two things. First, as I assumed, there are cameras in the room, and I am being observed. Second, judging by the fact that it took them close to a minute to respond to my protest, there is no one guarding the door and no one particularly close by. Which means they don't have enough people to do so.

If I can move quickly, I might be able to break out of this room and escape. As if they have just concluded the same thing, Constable Agathon and the mustard suit man return, stepping gingerly through the door, wincing as they do so. They come at me from either side of the table, grabbing me by the arms as I stand up, and start to drag me from the room. I go limp, making them work, though it means getting dragged through my own piss.

As they pull me down the hallway, I shout as loud as I can, "I demand to see a lawyer. I demand to know the charges against me. If there are no charges, I demand to be set free. If you will not do so, get me a lawyer."

I repeat these sentences, or something like them, as they turn a corner and drag me down another long corridor. Neither of them react to my shouting, but they are not the audience I am playing for. Suon is here somewhere, and I hope that my voice carries to her, so that she knows I am okay. If she can hear me, and is able, maybe she will respond in kind. But all I hear in response is my own voice echoing down the hallways.

Mustard Suit and Constable Agathon reach the end of the corridor, and we come to a halt in front of the final door. Agathon unlocks it while Mustard Suit tightens his grip on my arm and glares at me. Though I am sorely tempted to do something, just to further annoy them, I know that is dangerous. They are clearly under orders not to do me any harm—yet. I don't want to do anything that makes them reconsider.

They shove me inside the room, slam the door shut, and lock it. There are no lights on within, so I stand by the door, fumbling at the wall for a switch. I find one, but it does nothing.

"It doesn't work, I'm afraid," someone says, far away from me, across the impenetrable black of the room.

I don't need any light to know who it is. "Hello, Lasinha," I say.

"It's been too long, Laila," he says. I can almost see his grin through the darkness.

17

"What a happy coincidence," I say, my voice suggesting strongly that it is neither.

"Quite," Lasinha says. His voice is closer now, and I can hear him moving toward me, following the wall around to the door. "It's empty," he says, when he comes near. "Best I can tell, anyway. Windows, but they've been boarded up. Door seems like it's the only way in or out."

I don't reply, looking in the direction of his voice. What is he doing here? Is he a prisoner or just the next interrogator in line? This is exactly his sort of approach. He never came at me, or anyone, directly, always sidling up alongside with a smile. But he knows I will never trust him, so why try this again?

"How did you end up here?" I say, taking an involuntary step back, though I have no way of knowing how close he is to me in the darkness.

"They picked me up at a check stop when I was trying to sneak back into Calgary. Didn't think much of it at the time. Just thought it was the cops. Maybe somebody Molijc paid off. So I didn't worry. Big mistake."

"Yeah." The echoes of my own predicament in his story don't offer me any comfort. That coincidence, along with the fact that he knew who I was immediately, put me further on guard. Of course, he would recognize Aeida's voice, but he would have no way of knowing who was actually in command of this body. "Do you know who they are?"

"Not really. They were looking for me. And you. Getting the old band back together, I guess."

I grit my teeth, trying to hold my anger at bay. We are not friends now, if we ever were, and this pretense at camaraderie is almost more than I can stand. There is blood on his hands. The High Regents, Ana, myself and Aeida, and countless others. All sacrificed for nothing. The delusions of grandeur of a man who betrayed him. I feel some satisfaction at that.

"So they knew who you were?" I say.

"Of course," he says. "And they knew who you were, too. They told me they were bringing an old friend to visit right before you arrived."

It is an explanation of sorts, but not a satisfactory one. "Then why all the questions about who I am?"

"Did you tell them the truth?"

"Of course not," I say. I'm not even sure what the truth is anymore, or how to explain it.

Lasinha laughs. "I don't know what answer they were looking for, but you couldn't very well give them a satisfactory one, could you?"

You're the reason for that. I want to shout the words in his face, but instead I clench my fists and force myself to breathe. "Why were you coming back to Calgary?" I say when I can manage.

"I'd heard the Church had fallen and thought I would come back to see... I don't know what I thought I would do once I was there. But I had to see what was left. You were there, weren't you? Is there anything left?"

How does he know that I was there? It should make me even more suspicious, but I'm not surprised. He would still have people there loyal to him. That is one thing he would make sure of.

"It's done," I say, surprised at how emotional I feel at saying those words to Lasinha. We worked so hard to build the faith, to protect it from the Society. If we were not friends, we were allies in that at least. We gave everything we were to it. Certainly I did, all that and more. And now it is nothing, because of all we did. It is a hard thing to face, even now that I know that the faith is better gone and forgotten.

"What about Molijc?"

I sense this is the question that Lasinha has been building to all along. That we undoubtedly have an audience to this conversation is not lost on me.

"To the wind," I say. "With Meredith."

"Ah," Lasinha says with a little breath of air, whether of disappointment or relief, I am unsure.

"He sold the Church out, you know, just to get rid of Osahi. Called in the Society. Had the Travelers take all of Toma's people. He'd rather be Grand Regent of nothing than have the faith survive."

There is raw bitterness in my voice that I don't bother to disguise. I want him to know what the master he served has done, how he has betrayed everything that we stood for, all to elevate himself over the faith. None of this matters anymore, and yet it does. If Lasinha had stood with me, we could have stopped this madness and so much more. Instead I am compelled to be a soldier in a war I don't believe in, working for my enemies, to save those Lasinha has destroyed.

Lasinha is quiet for a long time before responding. What is he thinking? I am grateful for the darkness, because it stops me from trying to read his expression, which I know is a fool's errand. When he does speak, it is in a quiet voice.

"I'm not surprised. I wish I had been there to stop him, but… He was getting more and more unstable the worse things got. The constant incursions by the Society. Osahi's betrayal and taking so many of the faithful with him. And so many others just left. There was no one remaining really. And your betrayal, I'm afraid it cut the deepest. He was never really the same after that."

"Yes, I am always the one to blame, it seems."

Lasinha starts to say something and then stops himself. "It doesn't matter anymore, does it? The faith is gone. Nothing we can do will bring it back."

"What happened between you and Molijc?"

He lets out a soft, ironic laugh. "The Watchers happened. Once we unleashed them, it could not be controlled. We kept finding more and more people who we had suspicions about, for one reason or another. The Grand Regent started to wonder why we kept finding more. If all the faithful were found wanting, someone had to be to blame. It was him or me. We started the whole inquisition. And obviously he couldn't find fault in himself."

I don't respond, and he laughs again, that same knowing chuckle. "I suppose you think I deserve that."

That and so much more. "How long have you been here?" I say, changing tack. The past is a dangerous place for me still, and I have the future to think about, specifically my promises to the Seekers.

"A day, maybe. No more than two. They've fed me twice. I can't tell you much more than that. Like I said, I don't know who they are exactly. They're claiming to be local police, but that's obviously bullshit. They were expecting me, though, and they were probably expecting you, which means they've had time to plan."

"Maybe," I say. They couldn't have known I would be coming this way, unless Gloria is working with them and somehow managed to let them know what direction we were headed. It's possible, though it seems unlikely. "There's not many of them."

"No," Lasinha says. "But that may change now that they have both of us."

"Maybe," I say again.

"Was there anyone with you when you were taken?"

"Yes," I say. "Two people. I imagine they're being interrogated right now." The thought of Constable Agathon dealing with Gloria, assuming they are not somehow in league with each other, makes me smile.

"Anyone important?" Lasinha says. Again I sense this is not an idle question, that he has been waiting to insert it into our conversation.

"Acquaintances. Was anyone with you?" I already know the answer.

"No."

He begins to say something else, before we are interrupted by the sound of the door being unlocked. I step back, tensing myself, ready for anything. The door is thrown open, light flooding within, and I have to turn my head from the glare. Before I do, I see Gloria held by Constable Agathon, who roughly shoves her through the door. Gloria says something incoherent in protest, an inarticulate syllable uttered entirely in frustration.

The door is slammed shut, returning us to the darkness. Gloria stamps her foot in frustration. "Fucking Society," she says.

"I don't think they're involved in this," Lasinha says in his genial way. "Who is this?"

"Who the hell are you?" Gloria says.

I can feel both of them looking at me in the darkness, awaiting my answer. But I don't bother to reply, for I saw the brief look they exchanged before the door closed, that moment when they thought I was turned away from the light. They have met before, I am certain. Lasinha is right: whoever is behind this has certainly had time enough to plan.

18

"I'm not going to just sit here and wait for them to do something. I'm getting out of here. You two can join me or not. Up to you."

Gloria's voice is loud, surely audible down the hallway, but she doesn't care. After impatiently dealing with her false introduction to Lasinha, she has grown insistent upon action. Lasinha, too, was building in that direction before Gloria's arrival. His talk about the number of people watching us increasing now that we both were captured was clearly intended to lend urgency to our situation, to make it seem unstable and make the breakout he is planning seem inevitable.

"I don't disagree with your noisy friend," Lasinha says to me in a whisper. "There aren't many of them out there now, as you pointed out. That isn't going to last forever. We should take advantage while we can."

I make a noncommittal noise that might be agreement or disapproval. Nothing has changed as far as I can tell, and there is no reason to believe either that we are the only ones our captors are interested in imprisoning or that more people are on the way. The people who hold us are amateurs, or at least pretending to be. Putting all their captives in one cell where we can easily plot an escape is gross incompetence. The fact that the one person they know is my ally has yet to join us tells me they want the three of us together. They want us to try to escape.

"I should have known you would just collapse at the first sign of trouble," Gloria sneers.

"The first sign of trouble was you appearing on my doorstep. One of us panicked then, but it wasn't me. But then, I don't really understand how to bring means to an end."

"Insult me all you want. It won't get us out of here."

I elect to ignore her and turn in the direction of Lasinha's voice. "What's your plan, then? I assume you have one."

He comes near me, so close I can feel his warm breath on my cheek. It repulses me, and I flinch, glad he cannot see my reaction. "The only way out is through the front door, as I said. We just need something to pick the lock. The hinges are inside; we could take them off too."

"With what?" I say, matching his hushed whisper.

"We'll have to find something in here. It can be done."

I'm sure it can. "What then? Getting out of this room just puts us in the hallway. There may not be many of them, but we're still outgunned and outmanned."

"How much attention did you pay to the building when they brought you in? They've got their tactical room set up in the main office by the entrance. I'm sure you saw the same tech I did."

"Yes," I say begrudgingly. "That's my concern."

Gloria has come over to stand beside us so she can hear what Lasinha is saying. She is, I note, being conveniently quiet as Lasinha lays out his plan.

"Mine as well. There were two hallways going from the main entrance. They interrogated me in one of the rooms down the hallway to the left of it. I assume they did the same to you. When they brought me here, they didn't go back by the main office. They went the other way and turned down another hallway. We're at the end of that hall, which means we should be in the corner opposite their office."

"Granted," I say, not bothering to note how convenient it is that our captors have placed us so far from their manpower. His description of where we are matches my own sense of things. "They're a long ways away right now, but they have to be able to observe us somehow. They've probably got cameras or microphones. They'll figure out what we're up to pretty quickly."

"We'll have to be quick, no doubt," Lasinha says, as though this is easily achievable. "But it can be done. And my point is that once we're out, we don't have to go back via the main entrance. This is an old school. There have to be fire doors and other exits nearby. Once we're out, we can figure out what happens next. They don't have the manpower to do a search, and we should be able to avoid them. Getting transport out of here could be tricky, but we're resourceful enough. We'll manage something."

I roll my eyes. There is probably a vehicle waiting to be hotwired somewhere nearby, prepared especially for our escape. "I'm not leaving without my friend," I say.

"What friend?" Lasinha says.

"I told you there were three of us. I'm not leaving without her. If we break out, I'm going to find her. Or we can wait to see if they bring her here like the rest of us."

I can hear Gloria swallow, which I interpret to mean Suon is not being brought here. What has happened to her, I wonder, feeling a shiver of premonition run up my spine. Nothing good can come of this.

"Fine, we'll find your friend," Lasinha says.

"Fuck that," Gloria says in a loud voice.

"You are not a party to this discussion," Lasinha says coldly. "You can go your own way if you want to once we get out."

Gloria doesn't respond, and Lasinha continues. "They can't assume we'll go looking for her, and they can't assume we won't. It could force them to divide their people. And there'll be another exit somewhere nearby."

"Then we're agreed," I say, trying not to laugh. It was all so easy to get Lasinha to put his life at risk for me, which means he doesn't think it is any risk at all.

The three of us scour the room, going by feel to see if there is anything we can use to open the door. The room is empty, as Lasinha said, so we focus on the walls. They too are bare, but for the windows, where boards have been nailed over them. None of the nails are loose, though, and it would take hours of effort to try to work them free with no guarantee of success.

"What about the ceiling?" I say as we cluster again near the door.

"Worth a shot," Lasinha says, sighing with frustration.

He crouches down, and I clamber up on his shoulders to investigate. It is a drop ceiling, and I am able to lift one of the tiles away and feel my way around. There is conduit and cables running through the ceiling out into the hall just to the right of the door, which means there may be enough space for someone to slip through. I decide to try.

"I'm going up," I say, standing on Lasinha's shoulders. He grunts his assent, lifting me up as I pull myself into the ceiling. It is tight and hot up there, the air stifling. The ceiling groans and bends under my weight, and I try to shift so that the conduit bears some of it. The conduit feels weak, bowing under the pressure of my arm. I will be lucky if I don't come crashing down on top of Lasinha and Gloria.

I forge ahead, ignoring how precarious my position is, clinging to the conduit and using it as my guide. There are thin aluminum bars attaching the ceiling to the roof, and I have to snake by them in order to get out of the room and into the hallway. The path is constricted, but I am just able to squeeze my shoulders through, and the rest of my body follows.

Once I know I am past the wall and into the hallway, I pull up one of the ceiling tiles. I peer down into the corridor to assure myself it is empty, having visions of descending into the arms of Mustard Suit or Agathon. It is, and I wait a moment to see if there is any sound of footsteps approaching before twisting myself so that I drop down feet-first to the floor. I knock softly on the door once I'm down to let them know I've made it. Lasinha says something in a muffled voice that I can't make out.

I don't bother to wait for them—they are on their own if they want to get out—and head back down the corridor the way I came. The doors ahead of me are all closed, and the handles I try are locked. I peer under a few doors, but it doesn't look as though there are lights on in any of them. Behind me I hear someone drop down to the floor and turn to see Gloria steadying herself. A look of rage and triumph flashes across her face.

I ignore her, continuing my perusal of the corridor. When I check over my shoulder next, Gloria has disappeared and Lasinha is approaching. It is disturbing to see his empty grin in the flesh again. The last time I saw it, I was not in this body, though I was being brought to the Acolytes' implements for the transition.

"Any luck?" he whispers. I shake my head, and he shrugs. "Where's your friend?"

She's not my friend, she's yours, I want to say. Just once I would like to see Lasinha admit to what he is doing, to someone. Today will not be that day, I know.

"Gone," I say instead, casting my eyes down the corridor to where Suon is imprisoned.

Lasinha nods. "Further up, I think. Around the corner here. How do you propose we get inside once we find her?"

"Same way we got out," I say. "You get me in and stand watch."

Lasinha looks as though he wants to argue this plan,

but instead he shrugs again. We start forward, heading to the end of the hallway. I try each door as we go, though I agree with Lasinha's judgment that Suon is likely in one the rooms in the next corridor. As we come to the corner where the two hallways meet, Lasinha notes a door with an exit sign above it with a nod.

I start toward it, intending to see if it is open. As I do, I hear a shout from the next corridor and step out into the next hallway, exposing myself. Constable Agathon and Mustard Suit are there, leading Suon by the arms. Her head hangs down, almost limp, long strands of hair around her face. I cannot see her expression to know her state of mind, or if she is even conscious.

At the sight of me, both of them release Suon, who falls forward, sprawling onto the floor with a sickening thud. What the hell have they done to her? Agathon and Mustard Suit raise their pistols, letting off shots in my direction. One of the expanding pulse waves catches my right arm, rendering it numb and useless, before I manage to dive around the corner, out of their range of fire.

Lasinha is pressed against the near wall, where no pulse can reach him, sweat beading on his forehead. He pulls me beside him, and I have to fight the urge to shove him away. In the other corridor we can hear Mustard Suit and Agathon whispering something to each other, though I can't make out the words.

"Prisoners have escaped. We require immediate backup. Repeat, prisoners have escaped. We need immediate backup," Agathon says. Her voice is calm and loud, full of steel. She wants us to hear her announcing this to her nonexistent compatriots. The backup that will not arrive.

"Any ideas?" Lasinha says.

My answer is to start running back down the hallway we came. Lasinha hesitates, but only for a second, before following me. In the far hallway I can hear someone swear and footsteps retreating as well. It is a race to see who will make it to their control center. We both have roughly the same distance to cover, but I am betting that Aeida's body is quicker than both of them. He was always agile. Behind me, I can hear Lasinha cursing under his breath.

I turn right at the end of the hallway and race toward the entrance and the control room, where I saw all kinds of tech as I was brought through to the interrogation room. If I am right, it is sitting there unguarded. If am I wrong...

But I am not. Someone would have emerged from the main office to shoot me by now.

The office door is half-open, lights still on within. I dive through it as Mustard Suits lets off a few blasts of his weapon. Lasinha skids to a halt, out of the line of fire but stranded in the hallway. He backs away, expecting Mustard Suit to approach. After a pause—to adjust the settings on the weapon, or to get instructions?—Mustard Suit resumes firing in my direction. I kick the door closed, still lying on the ground, and listen to the glass reverberate with the pulses.

Not knowing whether the door is locked, I scramble to grab the first weapon I can find among those scattered conveniently on a table in the corner. It is an assault pulse rifle, far more advanced that anything I've ever seen. It is hard for me to know what the settings are, whether I will be shooting to kill, maim, or stun. I tell myself it doesn't matter.

Rifle in hand, I crawl back to the door. The glass is reverberating from Mustard Suit's continued shots, but he does not seem to be approaching, evidently worried about where Lasinha is and whether we have set some kind of trap. That gives me confidence, and I reach up, turn the door handle, and slightly open the door, just enough to make sure it will swing open with a push. I lie on the floor beside the door, rifle at my shoulder and finger on the trigger.

The shooting stops. Perhaps Mustard Suit has noticed

the door. When it resumes, I act, pulling the door open with my left hand and rolling over so that I am lying in the doorway, rifle ready to fire. Mustard Suit has a second to respond to my presence before I shoot, but he is not able to react in time. I squeeze the trigger three times in quick succession, and he collapses with a gasp.

I emerge from within the office slowly, rifle still at my shoulder, ready to fire. Lasinha is crouched down against a wall, his expression unreadable. For an instant—a second, no more—I consider shooting him. He has it coming, for all that he has done. Something of my thought must come across my face, because he flinches at my expression. As he does, my murderous intent dissolves. I cannot kill someone in cold blood, not like him. If Mustard Suit is really dead—and I fear he is—then I will be haunted by his visage, just as I can still hear the terrible silence that followed after I enacted the defense systems in the Order compound, murdering half of Osahi's extraction team.

I tell myself that, both then and now, my actions were necessary. Self-defense. And maybe that is true. It feels like the easy path, though, and it never takes me from the trouble I find myself in. More is always right behind.

Constable Agathon is that trouble coming, arriving as the thought passes through my mind. She approaches, pistol pointed at me, steel on her face. Her other hand clutches Suon, who stumbles behind her, still strangely limp, head hanging down as if she is asleep while standing. Or as if she is still dealing with the aftereffects of a tamp being applied to her mind. The thought makes me shiver, but I keep my weapon steady upon Agathon.

She pauses beside Mustard Suit, nudging him with her foot. "You've murdered him."

I don't respond, flicking my eyes from Agathon to Suon, judging how to handle this situation. Suon is my priority. If I have to kill Agathon in order to spare Suon, I will do so. For the moment, I hold my fire, waiting to see if there is a way out of this impasse. There is a very real chance any shot I take at Agathon will also hit Suon. And there is also something about Suon, beyond just the limpness of her frame, that seems wrong. Her movements are not natural, not hers, and her face is still largely obscured by her hair. Something is off. I don't think there are any Acolytes here, but she is acting as if they performed a procedure on her.

Agathon catches me staring at Suon and jerks her savagely to the floor, pushing her in the back with a knee so that she sprawls beside Mustard Suit's still form. I have a clear shot now, no chance of hitting Suon, but still I hesitate. Before I can reach a decision, Agathon does, lowering her pistol so that it is aimed at Suon's head.

We fire simultaneously. I can see Suon's body shudder and twitch from the blow and go still. Agathon tries to say something as the pulse wave hits her. Incoherent syllables sputter from her lips as she falls to the floor and doesn't move.

I lower the rifle and stare at the three bodies, not quite believing what has happened. Lasinha is beside me, shaking me, saying something. He goes over to check the three forms, and I start forward and stop. I don't want to look. I know what the results will be. And there is the backpack, which Suon carried, with my way out of this madness. My passage back to the Seekers. It is somewhere here, and I have to find it.

That seems a distant concern, though. I have failed Suon, just like I failed Ana. Like I failed everyone who stood beside me in the Church.

Lasinha is back beside me, speaking again. He has taken the rifle from my hands. "Laila, I'm sorry. I am. But we have to go now. We don't know how far away their backup may be."

He says more, but I don't listen, staring at the bodies feeling utterly lost and numb. Finally, Lasinha is forced to take my hand and lead me. He drags me out the front door and into the night.

THREE

THE FUTURE IS MURDER

19

The Acolyte's Eye floats above me, its rasping breath filling my ears. I stare at it with undisguised hatred.

"They would send your kind to deal with me," I say.

It does not respond, but they never do. That is not their way. I can feel its presence probing at the edges of my mind, searching for some means of entry. That is a sensation only, I know, and not the truth of the matter, though it still makes me uncomfortable.

"That is not all who has been sent here." A familiar voice and a familiar face appear before me, materializing from the wall of my cell, which shifts to allow their entry before re-forming behind them. It will not allow me to pass, unless I can fool it somehow. No easy task.

Tingco seems to follow my thoughts, or perhaps I have not been guarded enough and the Eye has penetrated them. "Don't bother. The walls have been armed against you."

I give him a thin smile. "It hasn't stopped me before."

"No, Josefina, it has not." He smiles as well. "My fellows in our order were lax. They didn't understand who they were dealing with. What you are. But I do. Perhaps more than even you do."

I frown at his words. Tingco is no one of particular note, at least to the best of my knowledge. He is of our shared order, wearing the sigil upon his shoulder, his face marked by the same transmutations as my own. Some distant part of me is repulsed by the armature that covers both our faces and more, though it is as much a part of my flesh as any other. I push those strange thoughts aside, though not soon enough.

The Eye's breathing changes. It has noticed. Tingco turns to look at it, a question asked and answered.

"Interesting," he says. "It is always the Aurellanos. I often wonder why. I could just as soon ask why it is always me. What it tells me is that my cause is just."

I stare at him, wondering what he is talking about, and decide to reply with defiance. "Your kind will never win. You can take me, take any of us; there will always be more. All your kind desire is power and domination. We fight for the liberation of the universes."

"It is a question worth asking, is it not, whether there are a finite number of universes?" Tingco says.

No smile is visible upon his masked face, but I feel it nonetheless, along with a shudder from that foreign place within me. The rasping of the Eye changes as it passes through me. How is it that I find myself so unguarded before it?

Tingco glances at the Eye again before continuing. "Or is it infinite, as everyone seems to believe? Each tiny change begetting another change, and another, ad nauseum. Each birthing a unique universe that must be protected at all cost from the depredations of people like me."

"You know what the truth is," I say.

"I do," Tingco says, assured. "Do you?"

His reply leaves me feeling uncomfortable, though I cannot locate the source of my unease. With each rasp the Eye makes, I fear I have revealed myself completely. But what have I revealed? There are no secrets left to me. That is why I am here, because my enemies have managed to expose them all. It is a risk to all of us who wear the sigil. For it is worn by both our enemies and our friends, and how is one to tell the difference. Here, now, I have no doubt as to what is facing me.

I have the sense that Tingco is looking above and past me, his focus on something else. A message. The rasping of the Eye seems to hush, as if it too is hearing what is being said. When it is over, Tingco glances at the Eye.

"Deal with it," he says, and the Eye vanishes through the wall. Was that fear in his voice? Do I still have friends left in this sorry universe? I know I do. Whatever happens to me here, I know there are others who will carry the fight. And we will be victorious, even if I fall, for just the reason I said to him. We know our cause is just and our enemies fight for nothing.

As if to tell me that my hopes are in vain, a chair forms from the floor and Tingco sits in it. He rests his arms on his knees and leans forward to peer at me where I sit in the corner of my cell. For a long while he stares at me, and I return his stare with what I hope is courage, though I feel none. His voice, when he finally speaks, is very low.

"I will tell you what I think, Aurellano. What I know. The universes are finite in their infinity. We are contained in a cell, all of us, just as you are now. You say your kind will liberate us, but all you seek is to rearrange the furniture in a closed room. I am here to tell you that I intend to liberate us all from this cell we find ourselves in, to take us beyond everything we know."

"What could possibly lie beyond the universes?" I say.

"What indeed," Tingco says in a joyous voice. "I intend to find out."

I suppress the urge to laugh. It never occurred to me that Tingco was a madman. I wonder if any of the rest of his lot are as well. They seem interested only in securing their dominion over the universes and the crossings, however they might justify it.

"You think I'm mad," he says, sitting up in his chair.

"No," I say. "I'm just wondering how you intend to break us free of our cells."

Tingco studies me, pondering how much he dares reveal. Why does he care, I wonder, what I know of his mad dreams? Even if he could do what he speaks of, which is impossible so far as I know, there is little I could do to stop him. Not in my current straits, anyway.

"How, how? Yes, that is the question indeed," he says softly. "There is only one thing I know of that stands in my way. Do you know what it is?"

I don't bother to answer. If he wants to entertain his delusions, I will gladly let him. If I am fortunate, an opportunity to escape will present itself.

Tingco stands up, the chair dissolving back into the floor. When he speaks, there is menace in his voice. "You, Aurellano. It is you."

The fierceness with which he speaks frightens me, even as I think what he is saying is absurd. I am no one special, and there is nothing I can do to thwart his mad designs. Their very impossibility will ensure that.

"It is so much easier when you don't believe," he says. There is disdain in his voice.

He shakes his head and strides from the room, the walls closing in behind him. I stare at them, wondering just what he was speaking about and feeling a despair I have never felt before. Everything feels lost, and I have never felt so alone.

20

The sound of tires on pavement, hypnotic and steady, penetrates my consciousness, so that I know where I am before I open my eyes. A vast prairie dawn greets me when I do, the sun a thin line along the distant horizon, the light still dim around us. A vehicle passes us on the highway, its lights still on, leaving an empty road in its wake.

Lasinha turns around in his seat as he sees that I am awake. "Everything all right?"

"Yes," I say, swallowing, my throat dry.

"You were dreaming," he says. It is a question of sorts.

"Yes," I say, not elaborating. I can't explain the Aurellano dreams to people I trust, let alone to Lasinha. Was I saying anything in my sleep? Suon always said I did, so it is likely. I can only hope I did not inadvertently reveal anything important. But I will have to assume that I have and be on guard. I have forgotten how exhausting being in Lasinha's presence is.

He turns back to face the front, accepting my refusal to say anything further. Hopefully he assumes I am suffering guilt for the murders I have just committed. That will come soon enough, I am sure. In some ways it would be better than whatever these other visions are, the parts of

113

me I cannot contain or control. At least Aeida is no more. There is only one monster within me.

"We're almost to Strathmore. We'll find somewhere for breakfast there."

I don't reply, glancing from Lasinha to Gloria, wondering what they have been talking about while I was asleep. If they have dared to say anything of consequence, or if they will wait until they are truly alone for that. Gloria feels me looking at her and finds my eyes in the rearview mirror. There is triumph in them, as though she has the upper hand now. Which she does. I close my eyes in response and listen to the road.

We found her on the edge of town, after Lasinha and I fled the school, trying to jump-start a car that was abandoned some weeks or months earlier, likely because it would go no further. It was convenient that she was on the main street heading out of town, though there were few other options available to her. Most of the other streets we drove down were lined with houses in various states of disrepair, with overgrown yards. There were no vehicles on them, but for the odd heap, people not willing to leave anything useful out in the open.

Lasinha insisted that we bring her with us. I objected, though halfheartedly, knowing that he would not relent. We had acquired a vehicle at the school. There were two in the parking lot outside, and I wondered why Gloria hadn't tried to break into one of them. They were high tech, and anyone who touched it without a key would receive an electric shock, though there were ways to bypass those safeguards. Maybe Gloria didn't know what those were. She wasn't of this universe, that much I was certain of. Lasinha might have told her to wait on the outskirts, where he could easily find her on his way out, while he made his play with me.

Has it turned out the way he expected? It certainly hasn't for me. Suon is dead, and I am left unarmed and defenseless, trapped with these two wolves.

I play over the scene again in my mind. There was something wrong with it, though I can't say what. Suon was wrong. Something in her movements, her lack of affect. It was as though the Acolytes had worked on her, erasing everything down to the foundation. Even Morris and Ana had something of themselves left after the tamps were put in place. Which suggests that whatever happened to Suon was something else entirely.

But what? It doesn't matter now, I tell myself. Suon is gone, and whatever ignominies she suffered at their hands are over.

The other question that remains is Lasinha's relationship to our captors. My assumption before our breakout is that they were in league together, my imprisonment with Lasinha just another attempt to apply leverage. But now I am not certain. Lasinha may be far more willing than I to sacrifice people's lives for his cause, but he would never let a situation like that, where he held all the cards, spiral out of his control as it did. Yet it was still far too convenient for him to be detained at the same time and place as me, along with someone else he knew in Gloria. That she tipped off our captors and Lasinha to where Suon and I were going nopw seems obvious.

We arrive in Strathmore, coming from the east along the old TransCanada highway. During the night we stayed to the backroads, making our way north and east, not wanting to go straight to Calgary on the off chance someone was watching those roads. The highway through Strathmore is empty, but for a few early risers, and the only place open is an all-night diner at the truck stop. Inside are a few lone men scattered at tables throughout, drinking coffee and eating breakfast.

We find a booth with a clear view of the door and the kitchen and give our orders to the waitress. Gloria disappears to the bathroom after, giving Lasinha and me a chance to talk.

"What's your plan?" I say, unable to keep the

accusatory edge from my voice.

Lasinha smiles at the waitress as she brings our coffees. "Go back to the Church and see what's left. Try to track down Molijc, I guess."

"How do you know he's here?"

"He wouldn't go far. That is the Church for him. The Grand Regent's tower, all that. He couldn't just leave it. He'll be waiting for his chance to take it back. Once the smoke with the Society clears."

I frown. "He can't really expect anyone in the Church to follow him after what he's done. The whole point of the Watchers was to keep the Society out. You think they'll just go along with this?"

"Oh, I think so," he says. "You know the man as well as I. He's compelling as hell. People will follow him regardless of what he does."

"This is different, though," I say, even though I know he is probably right. The thought sickens me. "The Travelers are our greatest enemy. Anyone who works with them is an apostate for the Order to deal with. Now it turns out he's been working with them, using them to get rid of his own enemies in the faith when convenient. And who knows what else."

Lasinha waved a hand at me, laughing. "You think that matters. It won't. He'll come up with some half-assed explanation. Or maybe he'll just totally deny it. Doesn't matter. The people who have followed him this far will follow him forever. Anywhere."

His utter confidence in this, and the ease with which he contemplated the idea, tells me this was the plan all along. The Order, for that would be all that is left of the Church aside from a few stragglers and all the half-things, will follow Molijc wherever he leads. They have proven as much. But there has to be a point where he goes too far, even for them. What would that be? I cannot even contemplate it.

"What about you?" he says. "What were you coming

back for?"

"Who says I was coming back here?"

He snorts and shakes his head. The waitress arrives with our plates of food as Gloria returns from the bathroom. I add ketchup to my hash browns and stir them around, still contemplating the implications of what Lasinha said and left unsaid. He is returning because he expects to resume his place at Molijc's side. Because there is still work for the Order to do, even now that they have purified the faith. What can that be?

"You think you can leave the faith. That's your delusion," he says, between mouthfuls of egg. "But we both know why you're back here."

He means my body. I wonder what he knows about it, but decide to leave that question aside for the moment. The real reason I am here is that the Seekers want me to be here, so that Molijc or the Society, or whoever is conspiring in this universe against them, is exposed. They have told me the reason for it, but I don't believe them, and it doesn't matter anyway. None of this matters, except that I am doing this for Ana.

"What about you?" I say, turning to Gloria. I don't feel like going over old territory with the man who is responsible for my predicament. It disgusts me and would leave me enraged, if I had any more anger to give. "Going your own way?"

"Something like that," she says, giving me her approximation of a mischievous smile.

"So following me, then," I say. "Don't worry. I'll keep you apprised of my movements."

Lasinha chuckles. "Probably wise to stick together for the moment anyway. We'll all want allies in the event whoever was holding us before sends more people after us."

"And it'll make it easier for them to track us down if we're all in one place," I say.

His smile doesn't slip, but I can sense his irritation.

About time. I return his smile with one of my own until he looks away. We finish our breakfast in silence.

Little has changed on the Church grounds in the weeks since I fled this place. As we drive along Thirty-Second Avenue and turn onto the road that takes us near the Grand Regent's tower, we encounter no Watchers or Travelers, and no signs that anyone has been there in a long while. The grass on the lawns is tall and littered with dandelions gone to seed, while the windows are all dim. There are no vehicles anywhere, no movement but the tree branches in the breeze.

"Welcome to the Church of the Regents," Lasinha says to Gloria in a mocking tone. Is he making fun of the faith or Gloria? On the way here he peppered her with questions about her own beliefs, much to her discomfort, after I told him she was a follower of another cult.

"Nothing but a dead cult now," Gloria says, rolling down the window to sniff at the air as though she expects to smell carrion.

"I'm sure Laila agrees with you," Lasinha says with a laugh. "But I can assure you the faith is not dead yet. Its heart is still beating."

Lasinha ignores the roads, driving over grass and sidewalk, to reach the Grand Regent's tower. The windows are still shattered where the Travelers attacked. We enter through the main doors and find a man in ratty jeans and hoodie passed out on a winter jacket that he has spread on the floor.

"Is this the Grand Regent?" Gloria says.

I laugh, and this seems to provoke Lasinha, who goes to sleeping man and kicks him awake. "Get out, scum. This is sacred ground."

The man scrambles away from Lasinha's blows, looking up at us in terror through bleary, drink-filled eyes. "What, man?" he says. "Just tryin' to sleep." He mumbles something more unintelligible.

"Get the fuck out," Lasinha says, lunging at him again.

Before he can land a further blow, the man gets to his feet, heading for the door. In his haste, he stumbles, crashing into it headfirst, momentarily stunning himself. He rolls around, clutching at his head and moaning. Lasinha moves to attack him again, but I step between them.

"Let him go," I say. "He's obviously just passing through your sacred ground. Lucky half the city hasn't moved in here."

Lasinha glares at me. I have never seen him so angry; I did not know it was possible. Though he looks like he wants to shove me aside and continue his assault, he lets the man regain his senses and scramble outside onto the Church grounds. Lasinha exhales slowly, trying to regain his control. Have I finally seen the true man? After all that we have gone through these past years, a homeless man hoping to steal a few hours of sleep is what causes the mask to slip.

"What a welcoming faith you have. No wonder you have so many adherents." Gloria's voice is acidic, mocking. Even I want to snap at her, to defend what we were, though that was all a lie.

Lasinha whirls around to glare at her. "What do you know of faith? All you have is third-rate communist bullshit masquerading as belief. You know they were all anti-religious."

"They were atheists. That doesn't mean they weren't religious. They believed."

"What did they worship?" I say, torn between laughing at her and hoping she eggs Lasinha, who is still seething, into doing something foolish.

"What all faiths do whether they realize it or not," she says with the infuriating serenity of true belief. "The future."

"The future's murder," I say, echoing a song I heard somewhere. Lasinha looks at me as though I have said something revealing that is making him reassess what he knows about me. I smile at him, as if I know what he is thinking.

Gloria's face twists at my words, and she struggles to find something to say in response. I ignore her, heading to the stairs to go up to the second floor. The others follow, and I sense rather than see a shared glance between them. It may all be in my mind, given what has just transpired, or it may be that this was all played for my benefit.

I brace myself as I arrive at the top of the stairs, half expecting to find the rotting corpses of Osahi and De Vroes, though the stench below would be awful if that was the case. There is no sign of them, though, and nor are there any remnants of Osahi's encampment. Someone has been to clean everything up, taking all the Acolyte equipment and other detritus. Was it the Church or the Society?

Lasinha is watching me for my reactions, while Gloria is looking around bored. I wonder what he knows of what went on here, both while I was here and after I left. It seems obvious he will still have allies in the Watchers' Order, who may be laying the groundwork for his return. That he is here now suggests the ground has been readied.

"Was this where Osahi set up shop?" he says.

"I'm sure you have friends who can give you that answer," I say, not even looking at him.

He smiles. "You haven't changed at all, Laila."

"Neither have you," I say. It is an accusation.

He holds up his hands, nodding and grinning. "Shall we head upstairs?"

Neither Gloria nor I reply, but we follow him to the bank of elevators. All three stand open and dark. The generator has either failed or been shut down. Lasinha mutters a curse and heads for the stairs, and we follow him up. At the sixth floor, where Osahi's team was making their preparations and where the Travelers launched their raid from their airships, the door has been blasted off its hinges and lies on the landing. Each of us pokes a head in to look.

There is shattered glass by the broken windows, while the rest looks like an unfinished construction zone. From what I can see, it appears Osahi was constructing a second throne room—to be the true seat of power, once he established himself. The man was more delusional than I ever realized. But he still had the sense to know he could never occupy the top floor. Not while the Watchers were still a power in the Church.

We next exit the stairs at the twelfth floor, where I am overcome by memories, thinking of Suon insisting on rescuing me over De Vroes' objections. She gave everything to me and wanted so little in return, but I couldn't even manage to give her that. My trust and feelings. Those I placed in Meredith, who never deserved them and who I knew would betray me. That is all she is.

Without realizing it, I have wandered over to her door, poised to enter. Lasinha and Gloria are watching me from the entrance to the audience chamber.

"Going somewhere?" Lasinha says.

"I'll be right behind you," I say, and go into Meredith's room. No doubt he knows whose room it was and is wondering at the hold she still has over me. That makes two of us. The room looks unchanged from the last time I saw it, revealing nothing about its former occupant. Not that I expected it to. I stand and breathe in the stale air, smelling only dust, and let memory wash over me.

Suon deserved so much better than I gave her.

When I have wallowed in misery for long enough, I leave the room and go to the audience chamber, where Gloria and Lasinha are looking things over. The secret entrance to Molijc's hideaway has been closed and the throne returned to its place on the dais. All the stolen antiquities still line the walls. Someone has returned to clean things up, as with downstairs. And evidently no strays have made their way to the top floor of the building, or, if they did, they've decided that nothing here is worth enough to bother stealing.

Lasinha studies the objects, almost sorrowful, before heading into the rooms behind the audience chamber. I am surprised he does not go to Molijc's hidden study, but the Grand Regent and Meredith wouldn't have left anything of value behind. We pass to the quarters, Lasinha proceeding directly to the Grand Regent's. There he finds the safe opened and empty of its contents. I note with some curiosity that whoever returned took the bills from the other universes that I left.

"The hard drive is gone," Lasinha says.

"Yes," I say.

"We never did find what you did with the missing files, you know," Lasinha says.

His tone is light and conversational, but I know he is anything but. This has consumed him since he kidnapped Ana. What is on them that I missed? I may never find out now. They are with the escape route the Seekers gave me in Ana's bag, somewhere in that school. Those working with our captors will have returned and discovered it by now, which means it may soon be in Lasinha's possession.

Yet again I curse myself for allowing him to lead me from the school before I retrieved them. I was so distraught at all that happened—numb with it—that there didn't seem any point. The future was empty again, and I wanted only to flee from it. To go to some world where I could live in peace, out of time, away from these battles that are no longer mine. It is a naïve hope that this will ever happen. This is my punishment for the wrongs I have done. I will never be free.

"I know," I say, and smile at him.

He returns my smile and walks from the room, heading down the corridor to my old quarters. There he pokes around, though I have no idea what he expects to find. I stand in the doorway, resisting the urge to shudder, and watch him. Gloria has wandered off somewhere, clearly bored with what is a trip down memory lane for the two of us.

Lasinha begins to dig around in the closet nearest the doorway, hidden from my view by the doorframe. What can be left here that might possibly interest him? The ruins of my life. Lasinha lets out a grunt of triumph and emerges, holding up a modem. Not a modem; Ana's dead man's switch. He holds it out to me, smiling, his eyes cold.

"Just a reminder of the price paid."

I stiffen, as though he has struck me with a blow, refusing to take the object. "One of us still has to pay it."

He laughs, tossing the switch over his shoulder and slipping past me out the door. It bounces on the carpet, the plastic shell around it cracking. I linger in the doorway, staring at its broken form, until my body stops shaking.

21

Gloria returns from her excursion breathless, unable to contain her excitement and fear, which dance across her face like some strange exultation. "There's someone coming," she says, leading us from the throne room past the elevators to the alcove that overlooks the north of the campus. Looking below, we can see two vans parked behind our SUV, blocking its escape. People exit them, pulse weapons in hand.

I glance at Lasinha, who is watching expressionless. "There's a way out. I don't know if it's still working."

"I know," he says. "I built it. It will be."

The people below check the vehicle before heading inside. There are enough of them that they can check several floors at once. It won't take them long to reach us. They don't appear to be Travelers—at least, they are not wearing the uniform, but I know that doesn't mean anything.

"What do you want to do?" I say.

"I'm waiting for them," he says. "What you choose to do is up to you."

He looks from Gloria to me. I shrug, deciding to wait as well, guessing they are Watchers and that he is expecting them. It is time for me to fulfill my duty to the Seekers, and the only way I can do that is to get closer to the Acolytes and whoever is secretly working with them, be it Lasinha or Molijc. They are the conduits between the Acolytes and their allies in the Society. Though the Seekers have never adequately explained why a conduit was necessary, or why the Acolytes left the Society in the first place. Perhaps they do not know, and they hope I will find out.

I look at Gloria for a moment to see what she is thinking. Her face is still torn, moving from apprehension to eagerness from one moment to the next. She makes no move to flee, or to ask what the escape route might be, apparently resigned to whatever happens to us. I almost ask her why, but there is no point belaboring the obvious.

We hear them on the stairs, a group entering the tenth floor and the eleventh. Footsteps approach the door to the twelfth, and we step away from the alcove and move back down the hallway to face the intruders. They emerge, three women, one after the other, casting their weapons up and down the hallway.

"We've got something," one of them says over their comms. Two approach, the other training her weapon behind them in case we have an ambush planned. "Three people. Unarmed."

They come closer, not lowering their weapons. We hold our hands out, making clear our peaceful intent. "Welcome back," the woman says.

Lasinha smiles and points at me. "I believe he's been looking for her."

I am bundled into the back of the one of the vans, while Gloria and Lasinha are placed in another. By all appearances, I am being treated no differently than they. I am not placed in bonds, and there are no weapons trained on me, though the three people in the back of the van with me keep a close watch. They treat Gloria and Lasinha with the same wariness, not viewing any of us as a threat but not trusting us either.

No one speaks as we drive away. My eyes are intent on the road, watching where they take us. The vans came from the north, and that is the way they return, heading across Thirty-Second to what was once the research park of the university. The Church never bought this land; the companies that existed there folded and were replaced by others, while De Gofroy built his empire of lies.

As the vans turn toward one of the buildings, taking a road that swings back around the structure to where there is a parking lot, I recognize it immediately. This is where I followed Meredith to when I was feeling the worst effects of the dampeners. I did not recognize it, because I had never been there before.

It was empty then, abandoned looking. Now it is a hive of activity. There are at least a dozen vans similar to the ones we are in, all anonymous and with tinted windows. As we drive past the building entrance with its many glass doors, I glimpse the stairway that I sat upon, where Meredith found me. There are people with rifles visible behind the doors, standing guard. To protect against some incursion, or to make sure those who are held inside remain there? Probably both.

The three of us are emptied out of our vans and hustled up a ramp and through a loading dock door, which closes behind us. They are worried about being seen, I realize. I don't have time to linger upon that thought, for we are separated, guards dragging us in three opposite directions. The last I see of Lasinha is him grim-faced, watching me.

I am led down a hallway, up two flights of stairs and down one, with various twists and turns through corridors along the way, all in an attempt to obscure where we are in the building. But I have been here before and retain a good sense of its layout, despite the addled state I was in previously. It has three wings, each converging at the entrance with all the glass windows. I know we have not left the wing we first entered, the central one, because it would require passing through that vast entrance.

They take me to a room on the fourth floor and lock me within. I guess that I am somewhere toward the center of the wing and at least a floor or two from the top, so about as far from any exit as they can manage. The room is in the middle of the floor and has no windows. It was clearly once an office. There is a desk built into the far wall that my captors have not bothered to remove. Aside from that, there is no other furniture.

They leave me alone, though I only hear one set of footsteps walking away, so someone is presumably on guard. They've left the light on in the room, and when I try the switch, it doesn't work. There is what I am sure is a small camera disguised in the corner of the ceiling, and I stare up at it for a time, contemplating taking it down.

In the end, I decide not to provoke whoever is holding me here. At least not until I find out more about what is going on. Instead, I lie on the desk and try to sleep while I wait for whatever is to come next.

I am unable to sleep, though I am utterly exhausted. My brain will not let me. It keeps playing over the scene of Suon's death again and again: Agathon shoving her roughly to the floor and raising her weapon to fire. Her hair is lifted by the force of her descent, and I catch a glimpse of her face for only a fraction of a second. My mind plays through that fraction, slowing it down so that it is a frame that holds still. Sometimes I see Suon's face, sometimes some other woman. An imposter.

But none of that is real, I know. There was no moment where time stopped and I could see her face clearly, whatever face was truly there. There is only the nagging sense that something was wrong with all that happened there. My eyes saw it and identified what it was, but my mind, as yet, cannot determine what was actually amiss.

I am saved from further torturing myself with questions, guilt, and doubt by the door being unlocked. Meredith enters as I stand up from the desk. She looks at me with a possessive smile and glances at the guard. "You can stay outside. I'll be fine."

The guard looks doubtful, but she closes the door and resumes her position. Meredith takes a step toward me, crossing her arms. "You should have just come that day. It would have been much easier. Without the price you've paid."

"You've been talking to Lasinha," I say.

"He is an old friend of Molijc's."

"That's not what Molijc was saying the last time I saw him." I sit on the edge of the desk and cross my arms, matching her gaze. It is hard to admit that I am excited to see her again. What a fool you are.

"Lasinha put himself before the needs of the Church, as he now understands. The Order is not his to do with as he pleases," Meredith says with the disdain of the favorite pupil for her recalcitrant schoolmate.

"And now you're all friends again. How convenient. Just like it's so convenient Lasinha came across me in Black Diamond."

Meredith allows herself a thin smile. "You were never truly faithful. A faithful vessel would trust their fates to the universes."

"Spare me that bullshit. We both know you don't believe. Let's cut to the chase. Why am I here?"

"Don't presume to tell me what I believe. I've proven my faithfulness, unlike you."

I laugh. "Is that so? Do you think anyone believes that? Do you think Molijc or Lasinha or whoever is watching this charade actually believes that? They know what you are. They've relied on it. They know you'll sell them out in a second if you thought it benefited you."

"Really, you're going to say that to me?" Meredith says. There is color in her face, and I know I've touched a nerve, which gives me pleasure. "You sent me away so that you could stay near the Grand Regent. For what? So you could betray him too. You didn't love me, and you didn't love him. You used us both. I've always done what I've done for the faith. Can you say the same?"

That I could say the exact same about her is pointless, I know. "You two have had a lot of time to talk about all this, I'm sure. I guess I shouldn't be surprised that you'd both see yourselves as the wronged ones. Need I remind you that I'm the one in someone else's body, who you used as your fuck toy for a year, on the orders of that madman. But I suppose you did that for the faith as well."

Meredith flinches at my wrath. I wonder if she feels guilt at what she's done, but I expect not. How is it that I've allowed myself to fall for her again and again? What spell of attraction does she weave over me, and will she be able to do so again? I am fearful that she will. What I need is Suon's sour expression to remind me I am being a fool.

The thought of Suon, still dead, for nothing, brings me back to myself. I will not waste any more time bantering with Meredith. This is all we do: trade barbs, try to put one over on the other, and get in each other's pants. It always ends the same.

"I'll ask again," I say before she can reply. "Why am I here? Why are you holding me? I am no longer a member of the faith."

"You expect me to believe that?" Meredith snorts. "You're like Osahi. As soon as you think you have a chance, you'll be back, ready to take whatever you can."

"What's left? The only thing you have that I could possibly want is my body."

Meredith interrupts me with a scornful laugh. "If only."

I shake my head. It is pointless to talk with her at all. All she will give me is lies and barbs, and I will be left no wiser. Silence would be the better option.

"Why am I here?" I ask again. The last time, I promise myself. "Is the Church holding me, or are you working for the Society full-time now?"

Meredith smiles, her manner changing, her usual armor of scorn and disdain evaporating. "You just don't understand what is happening, do you? You always thought you had a special insight into the nature of the universes, but you can't see beyond this cell. What we are doing will see that everyone is set free."

Something of what she says reminds me of what Tingco said to Josefina Aurellano in my dream. There is some strange echo there: the cell and breaking free. I want to ask Meredith what she means by that, if she too is talking about destroying the universes, whatever that might mean, so that we can see what lies beyond them. Something holds me back from doing so, a wariness I cannot quite explain, except that it seems unwise to reveal that I know about the universe-destroying plans of some man in some future universe I cannot possibly have met. Any questions they ask me about I may not be able to answer without revealing the still fractured state of my mind.

"Everyone but me," I say instead, hoping I haven't revealed any of my thoughts.

She doesn't reply, uncrossing her arms and knocking on the door to let the guard know she is ready to leave.

"Be seeing you," I say as the guard unlocks the door. Meredith doesn't answer, nodding at the guard and leaving without a glance back.

22

I'm left alone in my cell for hours, the only interruption to my solitude the guard outside bringing me a plate of food and leaving a bucket for me to see to the demands of this body. I do that first before turning to the plate of food. Potato salad and beef on a bun, still cold from the fridge. There are even a few pickles on the side. An actual meal, so at least they don't intend for me to starve. The plate is paper and the fork is plastic. Even the cup of water they've provided is disposable, so there is little chance I can fashion a weapon or a means of escape.

I eat the food and drink the water, though I know I should be wary. This is Molijc and Lasinha and Meredith, after all. The Acolytes will be here somewhere as well. At some point they will want to go delving into this mind. Or worse, tamping my mind or removing me from it. I am somewhat curious as to what will happen in the event they try. Aeida is not there to be restored. The false construct Aurellano is there, though what it is becoming is still to be determined. Something far realer than any Acolyte could have anticipated.

As soon as I am finished, the guard returns to take the plate, cutlery, and cup. She glances at the bucket. "You still need it?"

"Eventually," I say, following her gaze.

She picks it up, letting the contents slosh around. "Knock when you do."

The door bangs shut, leaving me alone again. I lie on the desk again, trying to sleep, and finally manage to, escaping even visions of Suon falling and Agathon shooting her. Just as I enter a deeper state of sleep, there is a loud knock at the door, jarring me awake. My guard enters and jerks her head for me to leave.

"You've been summoned," she says, as I blink away the sleep and confusion.

I get to my feet sluggishly and go out into the hallway, where another guard is waiting to escort me. The first closes the door, and they each take me by the arm, leading me down the hallway. We go to the stairs and descend five floors to the basement, no attempt made to disguise where we are going. They deposit me in another cell-like room, much like my previous prison, except it is about twice the size. The two of them assume positions on either side of the door and stand at attention, staring at the wall over my shoulders.

I pace from one end of the room to the other, trying to better wake myself and orient my mind. The guards track me with their eyes, otherwise not moving, their faces betraying nothing. Summoned, my guard said. By that I take it that whoever interrogates me next is more important than Meredith, though why they felt it necessary to bring me here is unclear. Unless they think the stale odor of dust and mildew is more amenable to whatever comes next.

The door opens without preamble as I ponder these thoughts, and an Acolyte enters, followed by Molijc. The unmistakable rasp of an Eye accompanies them, and I am unable to resist a shudder as it floats into view behind Molijc's head. The Acolyte moves to stand in one corner, near the door but away from the guards, touching the screen he holds in his hands. There is a camera above him, I note, recording the proceedings, whatever they may be.

Molijc comes before me, trying to stand tall and authoritative, but somehow looking ridiculous in the process. I know him too well for any display to threaten me. His eyes cannot seem to focus on me, darting to and fro with a barely contained mania. By some force of will, he stills his eyes and lowers his gaze to look at me.

"Are you going to tell me who you are?"

"A faithful vessel," I say.

He laughs, a barking grunt of thing, most unlike his normal laughter, ending it abruptly. "You think this is a joking matter. The last we met, you were Laila. You were Aeida. And at no point were you honest with me about your intentions. I demand that you reveal yourself to me."

"Demand away," I say.

Molijc seems temporarily at a loss for words, as if he is expecting me to follow the same script as him and I have gone off it. I look past him to the Acolyte, who is intent on his screen, preparing for the Eye and the real interrogation to come. He is not someone Aeida or I ever encountered. His head is shaved, and he has something of a monk's reserve, though perhaps it is just his dark clothes and stillness. The startling blue of his eyes stands in contrast to the darkness of his skin. I would not have thought such a combination possible.

"If you won't answer, we have other means to learn what we need to know," Molijc says, having recovered himself. There is sweat on his forehead, as if just standing here takes an excruciating effort.

"You know what's in this vessel," I say. "You had them put it here."

I point at the Acolyte in the corner as I speak. Molijc whirls around, seemingly surprised to see the Acolyte standing there. The rasping of the Eye intensifies, drawing everyone's glances, before subsiding.

"I will give you one final chance," Molijc says. "If you

don't have any loyalty or affection left toward me, I will understand, but you must have some feeling left for the Church. The faith. All that we have worked for is at stake, you must understand. We are set upon at all sides. By Seekers and worse. You cannot know. That is why I must ask you who you are."

I stare at Molijc, who seems to quiver under my gaze. "The Church is dead. You destroyed it. And the faith is a lie. Surely even you can see that now."

"Apostate," he screams at me, his eyes bulging. The sweat beads down his face. "Apostate. You've betrayed the faith and you betrayed me."

I shrug in response, dividing my attention between him and the Acolyte. He is looking up from his screen, but he is watching Molijc and not me.

"You will answer for what you've done. You will finally answer. I'll see to it. Do you understand? I am still your Grand Regent."

"Don't you get it, Dejian?" I say. "There's no more Grand Regent. There's no more Church. That's all done now. That ended the moment you called the Society down on Osahi. Who's left to follow you?"

Molijc opens his mouth and closes it, shuddering slightly. "Do with her as you will," he says, turning to the Acolyte.

"Of course," the Acolyte says, not stepping from his corner. He nods for Molijc to move away, allowing the Eye to drift toward me.

I take an involuntary step back and find myself pressed against the wall, before forcing myself not to panic. The Eye comes closer and closer, rotating and rasping, until I can barely see the others in the room. To my surprise, they don't strap me to a table and inject me with any drugs. That is the usual procedure, but no one is bringing in any Acolyte implements, and the Acolyte himself is not straying from his corner, his eyes intent upon the screen only he can see. The Eye will judge me alone.

As it watches me, the depth of its breathing changing, I feel a tingling in the back of my head, as if some current were running through my nerves. My hands begin to twitch in response, and I have to clench them tight to keep them still. There is a deep-seated itch that forms somewhere in my head, neck, and arms, below the skin, where no amount of scratching will reach. I want to throw myself about and scream with frustration, but I hold my emotions at bay.

My reactions seem to excite the Eye, causing the Acolyte to glance up at it with some interest. Again I am reminded of Tingco and Aurellano in the cell with the Eye, how Josefina feared the Eye could see into her despite the guards she put up, whatever those might be. I have no such defenses, but I try to force those images from my mind on the insane chance that the Eye can see them as well.

"Who are you?" the Acolyte says.

"David Aeida and Laila Johar," I say.

The Eye's breathing shifts to an elongated hiss. The Acolyte looks at me and smiles. "No, you are not."

"Apostate." Molijc is unable to contain himself. One of the guards steps forward to hold him back so he doesn't interfere.

"Who are you?" the Acolyte repeats.

I clear my mind, maintaining my gaze upon the Eye. "Laila Johar. And I want my body back."

The Eye's breathing returns to normal, and the Acolyte purses his lips. Molijc, realizing the import of what I have said, cries out, "What have you done with Aeida?"

"What should have been done a long time ago."

"Murderer. Apostate."

I ignore Molijc, watching the Acolyte, who is considering his next question. "Who helped you remove his consciousness from this mind?"

"The Society of Travelers," I say. It is the truth, though not the truth they are looking for.

Molijc makes a strangled sound in his throat and bursts free of the guard's grasp. The Eye barely avoids him as he lunges, seizing me by the collar of my shirt. "How could you, Laila? How could you?"

"You think I had any choice in this?" I say. "You put me in this body and created a monster so unstable that I'm worried there's not going to be any of me left if I ever get back in my body."

Molijc doesn't seem to hear me. "I should have known. I shouldn't have let my feelings blind me like that. Lasinha was right. You were always with the Society, from the beginning. You and Ana and her father. That's why you wanted to send Ana to them."

"That was Lasinha's idea," I say, but Molijc continues as if I haven't spoken. He is mournful, slumping against me, all the strength gone from him.

"The two of you arranged for the Society rendition when you thought enough time had passed and that things would be safe. The tech to cross the universes was just a cover. You expected us to be so excited that we had it that we wouldn't question what you and Ana were doing. And you were right: there were no questions at all. We never doubted you after that. You had delivered the universes to us. When you were ready, you brought Ana back, so that the two of you were positioned to destroy the Church and do the Society's bidding."

He is almost weeping by the end. One of guards comes, gently pries his hands from me, and leads him from the room.

"I should have seen it. I should have known," he says as he is taken away.

I stare in amazement as he disappears from sight. Does he really believe what he said, or has he convinced himself that was how it had to be, since the Grand Regent couldn't possibly be the author of the Church's infiltration and destruction? It was Lasinha who suggested we send Ana to the Travelers as an agent to protect her from Osahi.

Lasinha and Molijc were also the ones who insisted that Ana be returned to the faith, because Lasinha had his own agent within the Society.

But I have no proof for any of this, beyond my own hearsay, whereas my contacts with Ana and the Society were well established. Lasinha had people following me, and he has Ana's interviews after he had the Acolytes and the Order interrogate her. Molijc knows all this. He knows the truth even if he has allowed himself to forget as a way to justify all that has befallen the faith.

But maybe that's not what this is about. A chill runs through me at the thought. They have all the proof they need to hang this version of events on me if they so choose. Is this what this whole farce is about? To set me up? But who are they trying to convince? Not themselves. Not the Society, or at least the Acolyte faction of it, who will know the truth of whom they were conspiring with. The Seekers and their allies, then? They cannot possibly believe this will fool them, though. The idea is ludicrous.

"Who in the Society helped you?" the Acolyte says as the guard who led Molijc away returns. His expression and tone are unmoved. It is as though Molijc's outburst didn't happen.

The Eye moves back into position, rasping with more intensity again. By force of will, I clear my mind of all the questions that Molijc's outburst has raised. "I didn't get their names. And they didn't help me."

"You expect me to believe that?" the Acolyte says with a particular disdain.

"I don't particularly care one way or the other," I say. "I'm telling the truth. I don't know their names, and they didn't help me. Helping me would mean getting me out of this body. It would mean getting me away from all you fuckers. I want no part of this."

The Eye's rasping doesn't change, and the Acolyte raises an eyebrow. "You are a part of this whether you wish to be or not."

"So it would seem."

The Acolyte quirks his mouth, somewhere between a smile and a grimace. "What did they ask of you in exchange for removing Aeida from this consciousness?"

I smile, staring directly at the Eye. "Nothing." It is the truth. What the Seekers did to me, they did without asking my permission and without expecting anything in return. They did it because I was useless to them otherwise.

The Eye spins in its orbit and rasps some more, and the Acolyte frowns in response, staring at his screen as though hoping it will reveal something other than what the Eye says. He senses he is asking the wrong question, but isn't sure how to frame it properly. He lowers the screen and looks at me.

"This will go much easier for you if you cooperate. We'll get the answers we want eventually. You're familiar with our means, of course."

I laugh, and he blinks in surprise. "How do you know that isn't what I want you to do?"

The rasping of the Eye changes, its pitch deepening, and the Acolyte quickly looks at the screen. He looks up after a moment, his eyes narrowing. "Very well," he says. "You'll get what you asked for."

He stalks from his corner, muttering something to the two guards before leaving. I don't catch what it is. The Eye hovers before me for several seconds, as if waiting to see if I will let my guard down for an instant. I smile at it, and it floats from the room, following the Acolyte.

The two guards remain, both of them staring straight ahead, their stances unchanging. I don't move either, still leaning back against the wall, though I allow myself to relax a little. The first part is done now. It will only get worse from here, as the Acolyte said, but for the moment, the danger has passed. As the thought crosses my mind, the two guards stiffen, hearing some message I cannot, and leave the room, going a few paces down the corridor. I stay where I am, waiting for what comes next.

It is Lasinha who walks through the door, a smile upon his face.

23

Lasinha gently closes the door, as though he wishes to do it no harm, and moves to the corner where the Acolyte stood. Using all of his height, he stretches up, pulls the camera down, turns it off, then throws it to me so I can see for myself that we are not being watched. It is off, but I am certain there are others in the room. Microphones, at least. The Watchers' Order does not do half measures.

Lasinha approaches, coming to stand close, almost intimately, gazing down as though he is considering whether to pull me into his arms for an embrace. "We don't have much time," he says, in the barest of whispers, his lips hardly moving. "Someone will be along to see what we're doing."

"What are we doing?" I say, not bothering to match his whisper. Does he really believe the microphones won't pick up what we're saying? Does he expect me to believe it?

"You've seen him," he says. "He is not well."

"I could've told you that," I say.

"It's worse than you could imagine."

"I've lived through the worst," I say, gesturing at my false body.

Lasinha smiles. "No, you haven't. He's desperate now. The Church is in shambles, and he doesn't see a way out. But he's going to do whatever he can to keep his hold on the Order."

I shrug. "Not my problem, Lasinha. You created that monstrosity with him. Surely you have friends there still."

Lasinha winces. "Some, but not in positions of influence. Meredith has been busy since I was…sent away. She's got her people everywhere."

"How unfortunate for you."

"No. How unfortunate for you. She hates you. She wants to destroy you completely."

"You and Molijc did that already."

Lasinha puts a firm hand on my shoulder. I resist the urge to push it aside, though I am repulsed by his touch. "I understand why you feel that way, but there are fates worse than this. Believe me. And Meredith is setting you up for that."

I return Lasinha's insistent gaze with what I hope is skepticism, though I don't doubt the truth in what he is saying. "And what is that, exactly?"

"You heard the questions they were asking. About who you really are. Meredith has been talking with people in the Society—whoever she and Molijc used to deal with Osahi—and she's told them that you're not just Aeida and Laila. There's something else in there."

I feel faint and almost have to catch myself against the wall. Aurellano. She couldn't possibly know that. But she was with me for so long in Aeida's world, when my state of being was in such flux, that it's possible she knows something.

Lasinha is watching me, so I force a smile to my lips. "Why would they give a shit about that?"

"She's telling them that the Acolytes put something in there. A weapon to destroy the Society."

"That's ridiculous."

Lasinha shrugs. "Probably. Although I wouldn't put it

past the Acolytes, would you? Not that you alone could, but if they put it in a dozen or so people? I know what they told me about what they were doing, but I also know it wasn't everything. Molijc was the only one they trusted. You and Morris tried to get inside. Did you find out anything?"

I don't answer, wondering how much he knows about the truth of the Acolytes and the Society, that they are fractious parts of a whole. That much, at least, of what the Seeker told me I believe. And I suspect that Lasinha knows a great deal more about this than he is letting on, given how closely he worked with the Acolytes in setting up the Watchers' Order.

When I don't reply he shrugs again and continues. "Anyway, the point is that she's convinced the Travelers that it's true, and she's going to give you to them so they can take you apart and see for themselves. She's convinced Molijc that you're responsible for his downfall, so he'll go along with it, even though he still loves you. He can't let himself see the truth of it."

I feel cold inside, a glacier expanding and edging through my soul. It is just possible and would make as much sense as anything. It would also explain the Seekers' interest in me. If I am an Acolyte weapon, why not send me back to them to see what they do? All the talk about needing to expose the conduit between the Society and the Acolytes may just be that. Why do they need a conduit if they are one and the same?

"It's still ridiculous," I say, stalling, wondering how much of what I'm thinking he can see on my face. "And Molijc doesn't need Meredith to convince him he's done no wrong. He didn't need you either, but you did all the same. What do you think now?"

Lasinha hesitates, not meeting my eyes, just for an instant. "I don't deny that things…went awry. The Watchers. We lost sight of what we were doing and why we were doing it. I accept my part in that failure. We gave the Travelers exactly what they wanted in trying to fight them. Well, unless we do something about it now, they will destroy the faith entirely, and you along with it."

"Whoever's coming to check on us is sure taking their time," I say.

Lasinha smiles. "Joke all you want. I'm taking a significant risk being here with you. Meredith may try to send me to the Society with you."

"You'll forgive me if I shed not one tear."

"Look. I don't blame you. Not one bit. I'm asking you to set aside whatever's gone before—and I know that's asking a lot. Maybe too much. But I'm asking it anyway."

I cross my arms, brushing the hand that is still on my shoulder away. "Just ask what you want to ask."

"We need to work together. To stop Meredith from selling you and the faith to the Society. We need to get Molijc back in his right mind. Or, if we can't do that, we need to figure out just what the hell the Acolytes are up to."

"Do I need to remind you I'm a prisoner here? What the hell do you expect me to do about any of this?"

"You're the only one I can really trust." He holds out his hands almost as if he is begging me. "Strange as that may be. Everyone here now might be Meredith's. So I'm going to get you out. We'll take Molijc and get through to him somehow."

There is a soft knock at the door. A warning.

"Doesn't sound like much of a plan." I make a show of studying my fingernails.

"It isn't. It's all we've got. Laila, I don't know how much time we have. You especially."

"Hmm," I say, still looking at my foreign hands. "What happened to Gloria?"

Lasinha is left momentarily speechless. "I thought you said you weren't friends?"

"We aren't. What happened to her?"

There is a pause where Lasinha weighs what to tell me.

"The Order is interrogating her. She's spouting some nonsense, so they don't trust her. They think she's connected with you somehow."

Another knock at the door follows, this one louder and more urgent. Lasinha glances over his shoulder and takes the camera from me, replacing it in its corner.

"Think about what I've said." He glances at me in warning before turning the camera on. "I'll come to see you tonight."

I don't bother to reply, and he doesn't wait for one, retreating out the door. The guards return, taking me by the arms and leading from the room. On our way back to the stairs, Meredith emerges glaring at me.

"What is she still doing here? The session with the Acolyte ended."

"Lasinha stopped by for a chat," I say before either of the guards can speak. One of them elbows me in the ribs.

"Is that right?" Meredith's eyes burn with anger, and her jaw juts out as she grinds her teeth. "What did he have to say to you?"

"We were just talking about old times." This gets me another jab from the guard.

"Explain yourselves." Meredith glares at the two of them.

The guards go still beside me, neither wanting to answer and neither daring to look at the other. The one elbowing me finally summons the courage to speak. "He asked to speak with the prisoner."

"And you let him?" Meredith crosses her arms and fixes the guards with a glare that is equals parts disdain and disbelief.

"He is still the head of the Order," the other guard says. "Technically."

"Technically." Meredith waves the guards past her. "I'll deal with your insubordination later. For now, take our guest back to her cell. She needs her rest. She has a long day ahead of her."

144

She stares at me, daring me to say something. When I don't comply, she adds, "You're going to get what you've deserved after all these years. I've seen to that. You like playing games with me, with the Grand Regent, with the Society. Well, tomorrow, you're going to answer for all of it."

My stomach twists at the thought, even as I still believe this is all some ruse she and Lasinha have cooked up. I attempt a brave smile. "I look forward to it. I hope we all get a chance to answer for what we've done."

Meredith doesn't reply, jerking her head at the guards. They lead me away, upstairs and back to my cell, where I am left alone to contemplate all that has taken place and what awaits me tomorrow.

24

Sleep eludes me, the minutes stretching on endlessly in this cell. Even when I lie on the floor under the desk and close my eyes, I can see the lights above my head glaring down at me, trying to pry into this mind to see what is there. After so many questions about who is in here, I am almost afraid to sleep and to dream, because it might reveal to someone that Aurellano is there.

Outside I hear the shift change, one guard replacing another, and my pulse quickens at the sound. Is it Lasinha coming to break me out or Meredith summoning me to my doom? The two women share a few whispered phrases I cannot make out before the one who has been spelled goes on her way. I am left both relieved and disappointed, waiting for the next footfalls down the corridor.

It is a long time before they come. While I wait, my mind plays over the conversations with Molijc, the Acolyte, and Lasinha, trying to make some sense of them, to fit them with what the Seekers told me. They sent me here, expecting me to be captured by the Acolytes, or their faction within the Society of Travelers, so that I might reveal the conduit between the two. Then I was to make my escape, but Suon is dead and the transfer unit is lost.

I accepted what they told me then, not particularly caring about the details, which I knew the Seeker would never entirely reveal to me. It didn't matter to me who the conduit was, or why it was so important that this person be unmasked. When I consider it now, I realize that it makes no sense. They are involved in a universe-spanning struggle—what difference does it make whether it is Molijc or Lasinha who is acting as their secret agent in this particular world?

It doesn't matter at all. That wasn't the reason I was sent here. I don't know that I believe Lasinha's story, but there is clearly something about me that has everyone interested. It has to be connected to these dreams of Aurellano. That would explain the endless questions about who I am. Lasinha knows something, because he always does. He sent Gloria and Hazim to look for me, though the details of their connection are still obscure. Is their faith a put-on, or is Lasinha deep in playing yet another game?

And is he also working with both Meredith and Molijc? Molijc, I cannot tell. He seemed even more unhinged than the last time I saw him. But with Meredith, it seems clear. The whole act after the Acolyte left, with Meredith appearing only after Lasinha was gone after telling me all he needed to, was obviously scripted. The coming breakout, just like the escape in Black Diamond, is similarly a setup. To what end I don't know, but I have no choice but to go along with it for the moment.

Footsteps interrupt my thoughts, and I sit up, preparing myself. The guard says something to the newcomer, sounding deferential to my ears. A man replies, and the guard unlocks the door, throwing it open to allow Molijc to enter. He steps within and nods at the guard imperiously. She looks reluctant but goes, closing the door.

Molijc glares down at me, his face suffused with emotion he can barely control. His hands, I notice, are trembling. He glances over his shoulders, as if remembering there are cameras watching us, before dropping to his knees before me. His whole body is shaking as he reaches out to take my hand. There are tears in his eyes, which are not as clear, not nearly as wild as they were earlier.

"You have to help me, Laila. Please. We have to get out of here."

It takes me some time to summon a response from my brain. Part of me wants to laugh hysterically. You're the reason I'm here. But I don't. Is this another in the series of ruses everyone has been trying to play on me since I was arrested with Suon and Gloria? Everyone pretending to be what they are not, in the hopes of what? It is hard not to think I might be going mad. As mad as Dejian.

I pull my hand free of his. "What are you blubbering about? If you want to go, then go. You don't need my help."

Molijc chokes back a sob, snorting mucus. "You don't u-u-u-understand. That wasn't me before. That wasn't me in the tower either. I didn't call on the Society to get Osahi. I would never... The Acolytes. It was them. They betrayed me."

He is unable to stop himself from breaking down, piteous, gulping sobs bursting from him. I grab him by the shoulders and give him a good shake. "Get yourself together. She's going to hear you."

Molijc nods and swallows his sobs, taking a deep, steadying breath. When I am certain he has control of himself again, I say, "From the beginning. What the hell are you playing at here?"

"I'm not playing at anything. I swear it, Laila. I swear it on De Gofroy."

I roll my eyes but allow him to continue.

"I haven't been myself for months...maybe longer, I don't know. It's hard to remember. The details...come and go, I guess. I remember you—Aeida, I guess—coming back at the tower, but that wasn't me. The Acolytes did…"

"To you exactly what they did to me."

Molijc swallows loudly and is unable to meet my eyes. "Yes…yes."

"Why should I help you, then?"

At the mention of help, his desperation returns in full force. "Oh, you have to. You have to. I can't go back like that. I can't. The Acolytes aren't what I thought they were. You were right. What you said before. There's no Church left. There's nothing. We just have to get out of here. There's no telling what they intend to do to us."

I give him an annoyed smirk. "You still haven't answered my question, Dejian."

He hangs his head, deflated again. "I have no right to ask this of you, I know. But you're the only one I can trust."

"Seems I'm the only one anyone can trust anymore. So convenient for me." I glance up at the ceiling, wondering if anyone is observing us right now. Someone must be, so why haven't they done anything?

"We don't have much time," Dejian says, following my thoughts.

"No." He still doesn't seem himself, but I never knew a broken thing like this. The wildness in his eyes is gone, but they are still not steady. It is just possible to believe he has emerged from behind the wall the Acolytes put up. I know too well how dislocating that can be. That they would do something like this to the Grand Regent surprises me, even as I know it shouldn't. Ana and Osahi both suspected they did something to De Gofroy in his last failing years.

If Molijc is nothing more than a puppet, then Lasinha must be the conduit the Seekers tasked me to find. But I am not certain of anything here yet. Molijc's reemergence now is far too expedient, just as everything else has been to this point. A puppet show to test me, to see what happens. To see what else lies within. That must be what this is all about.

"Please, Laila. You have to. You can't leave me like this."

I am about to tell him that I am in no position to go anywhere, but footsteps, coming down the hall, urgent and quick, cause both of us to go still. Molijc looks at me, a smile tinged with sadness on his lips. A smile only he could make. I feel a rush of familiar emotion that I haven't felt in so long. He nods, as if he understands.

"Are you ready?"

He gets to his feet and turns to face the door, and I join him. Meredith orders the door open, and the guard fumbles with the keys as she tries to comply. When it is unlocked, Meredith shoves past the guard to step inside, the defiance on her face tinged with fear that she is trying her best to hide. Behind her, the guard and two others crowd the doorway, looking nervous, though they haven't drawn their weapons.

"What are you doing here, Grand Regent?" Meredith's smile is sickly sweet.

Molijc crosses his arms and tries to look authoritative. He speaks in a loud, booming voice, as though he wants to let the whole building know where he is. "Why would you presume to think I need to explain myself to you?"

Meredith winces. "It's just...we had agreed how we were going to handle things with Laila. And now you're here with her. We don't know why."

"I've changed my mind." Molijc is dismissive, but there is a slight quaver to his voice, revealing his nerves. His hands, I can see, are trembling.

Meredith notices it too. "I see," she says, and glances at the guards behind her.

Before they can draw their weapons in response, Molijc reveals a stun grenade in his hand, which he must have secreted somewhere on his person. Everyone, including me, takes a step away from him.

"Now, wait." Meredith holds up a hand.

Molijc does not, tossing the grenade into their midst.

The three guards run into each other trying to get out of the doorway, while Meredith snarls in rage at them. I dive under the desk, tucking my head into my body and covering it with my arms in the vain hope that it will help protect me against the pulse. The last I see of Molijc, he is standing, doing nothing to protect himself and grinning like a fool at the chaos he has created.

25

Someone is knocking at the door. Loud, now soft, and loud again. I listen to it, trying to discern the pattern, but there is none. The knocking continues, and there is no one to answer it. Except me. I force my eyes open and slowly push myself up from the floor. My head aches from the pulse blast and a wave of nausea overwhelms me as I try to sit up, so I retreat back to the floor. It is tiled and cool, not the floor of the cell where I was kept, which was carpeted.

That intrigues me enough that I ignore the pain and discomfort and get unsteadily to my feet. I have to lean on the counter beside me for support, the room swirling with colors. When my vision resolves enough, I notice a sink at the edge of my fingers and realize that I am in a bathroom. Not just any bathroom—the one in Joseph Aurellano's apartment in Vancouver.

I look up in the mirror by reflex and see my own face staring back at me. That is enough to tell me I am dreaming, but still I weep at the sight of it. My own face, me. I feel whole for the first time in so long.

The knocking intrudes on my consciousness again, and I head out of the bathroom down the corridor to the door, leaning against the wall for support as I go. The knocks grow louder, more insistent, the closer I get. It seems to take forever for me to get down the short hallway. I fumble with the lock, opening my mouth to say something curt, as I pull open the door.

It reveals not the hallway of the apartment building, but a view of ocean, vast and seemingly still from this distance. I step through, and the doorway and the apartment are gone, and I am standing in the middle of a tulip garden on a terrace overlooking the sea. Behind me are the buildings of the university campus. The distant hum of traffic on unseen roads from the city reaches my ears.

There is an ornate metal bench, with a faux-medieval design, set against a wall beneath a set of stairs that lead up to the one of main avenues of the campus. I go to sit on it, dividing my gaze between the ocean, which glimmers in the sunlight, and the tulips at my feet. They are purple, pink, and yellow, some with petals of each color on a single blossom. As I marvel at that, wondering if such alchemy is possible in any universe, let alone the ones I have inhabited, someone approaches, their shadow falling across me.

I look up to see who it is, but I know. Aurellano. Their face is shifting as they sit beside me. Now Joseph, now Josefina. Now a colonial administrator, now a Seeker or an Acolyte, face hidden by their biological armature. There are others as well I don't recognize. Hundreds, maybe thousands. I sense that my face will join them soon. But which one?

Aurellano leans back on the bench, favoring me with what I think is a smile. It is hard to discern amidst everything else. I turn away, unable to stomach what I am seeing, feeling very afraid. Though the sun is bright and warm I am cold, and it feels as though a shadow has fallen across this small garden. Aurellano doesn't speak, letting the silence linger, seemingly lost in a reverie as they stare out at the ocean.

With reluctance, they rouse themselves. "We have a lot

to discuss."

"Yes."

Molijc is slapping my face, one cheek and then the other, gently but enough to sting. "Come on, Laila. Wake up. Come on."

I surface slowly, a behemoth coming up through the waves, my breach only hinting at what lies below.

"Thank De Gofroy." Molijc sighs with relief, sitting back on his heels.

I lever myself up and assess the situation. We are still in the cell. I am underneath the desk and Molijc is beside me. Just beyond the doorway, I can see the prone forms of Meredith and the guards.

"We have to go." Molijc stands up and holds out a hand to me.

I don't trust him—how could I?—but I take his hand anyway and allow him to lead me out the door past the still bodies. Part of me wants to check if Meredith is alive, but I don't. There is no time, and if I survived the blast, so did she. We come to the end of the corridor where the stairwell is, and Molijc hesitates.

"What's your plan here?"

He looks at me in a panic. "I don't know. I didn't think I would get this far."

I roll my eyes and head to the opposite side of the building, where I am certain there will be another stairway. If I am right, it will lead us to a door exiting to the south. There are trees on that side of the building—I remember from when I was brought here—which should provide something in the way of cover from whoever might be standing watch in the parking lot or the main entrance.

"Do you have any more of those?" I say over my shoulder as I rush down the stairs. There's no telling whether they will have someone watching every exit. I am their only prisoner, that much seems clear, and the slowness of their response to Molijc going off script suggests they are either undermanned or complacent.

"No, but I have this."

I turn back to see Molijc waving a pulse pistol at me, and hold out my hand. Reluctantly, he passes it to me, fear in his eyes, but he knows that I can make far better use of it than he can hope to. I check to make sure the setting is low before resuming my descent.

"How many people do you have here?"

"I don't know. Thirty, maybe." Molijc sounds breathless. "There's been so many coming and going since you and Lasinha came. He's gone tonight with a bunch of them."

"Where to?" I pause at the second-floor landing to listen. There is still no other sound within the stairwell and nothing to indicate any response to Molijc setting off a grenade. If there are cameras set up in the stairwell, then no one appears to be watching them. I still don't trust it entirely. This is far too easy. Lasinha and Meredith are not this careless. Neither is Molijc, for that matter.

"I don't know. Somewhere close. They must have transfer equipment set up there. It's not the same crew here all the time." He hesitates—struggling to recall something or deciding whether to reveal it to me? "Harith, I think, has something to do with it."

"Harith?" It is a name I have not heard before, at least as it relates to the Church.

"You know. He was the Acolyte who cared for De Gofroy. We worked together on…everything."

We reach the first-floor landing, and, as I hoped, there is an exit. The door has a sign saying a fire alarm will sound if it is opened, and I wonder if that is still true. Across the landing is another door leading back into the building. I glance between the two, clenching the pistol tight, knowing I have to go somewhere but expecting a trap no matter which door I choose.

"The one with the scars?"

Molijc is following my shifting eyes, gulping nervously

as he does. "Ye—es. All the help I had from the Acolytes came from him. I wouldn't be Grand Regent without him. And now…"

"Now he's friends with Lasinha."

Molijc lets out a mournful sigh. "Was I ever truly Grand Regent? I wonder."

His self-pity infuriates me and raises my suspicions again. He was not some pawn in others' games. If Lasinha or the Acolytes were truly the ones who wanted the Order and its horrors created, Dejian needed no pushing to create it. And he had no issue with what it did in his name all those years. Only now that everything has crumbled to dust and all his dreams of being De Gofroy's anointed have been proven false has he come to regret what he did, because now some of the consequences have returned to him.

I swallow my anger and the harsh words on my lips— now is not the time for them, as satisfying as that would be—and push open the exit door, just enough to peer out. No alarm sounds, and no one is standing guard outside. I am surprised to see it is still light out, though it is clearly dusk, the shadows long and the sun gone from the sky. I was certain it was two or three in the morning, but it seems to be no later than ten at night, which is somewhat disconcerting. To my relief, though, my memory is correct, and there are two large pine trees on either side of the door, each with branches near their base that must be several meters across, heavy with needles. Between that and the dim light, we are mostly shielded from anyone on the road, as well as the entrances on either side of the building.

I push the door open wide and step out, beckoning for Molijc to follow me. As he does, I notice there is a camera above the door, and I detach it from its mount and turn it off. If anyone is watching, or reviewing the video later, they will know which door we used, but not where we went after.

Molijc is looking around frantically and continuing to make that odd gulping sound. I don't have time to check on his state, nor do I care to, so I just squeeze his arm and force him to meet my gaze. There are tremors vibrating through his whole body, and I am certain I will have to abandon him somewhere before too long. I know what he is going through, though it seems worse with him, and at a certain point, the body and mind need time to recover.

"Stay with me," I say, and he nods, looking scared. He must know I will abandon him if he falters at all.

I listen to the traffic, tucking the pistol into my pants and covering it with my shirt. Once I have confirmed there is no one approaching this side road, I dart between the trees and across the road, not glancing back to see if Molijc is following. There is a small parking lot for a one-story building on the opposite side, which looks to be some kind of service building to a nearby office complex. I head to the service building, walking in its shadow, being careful to stare straight ahead.

Behind me, I can hear Molijc gasping for air. It is so loud that I almost wonder if he is being deliberate about it, making sure that someone will be able to track us. I refuse to turn around to check on him, though the temptation is strong. My pace is quick but deliberate, which I hope conveys that I am someone on my way to somewhere, not an escaped prisoner on the run.

"Wait, Laila. Wait." Molijc's voice is desperate and pitiful, and seems to carry far through the evening's quiet calm.

I don't slow down or glance back, giving no sign that I have heard him. "Shut the fuck up. And don't use my name." I keep my voice even, trying to move my mouth as little as possible.

Only once I am past the service building do I pause to look back, using it as cover and dropping down to pretend I am tying my shoe. Molijc is far behind, his steps painfully slow, as if he is relearning how to walk. But there is no one behind him and no sign of anything stirring in the Order building. The roads are quiet, no vehicles on them—hardly a surprise, given the time of day.

I allow myself a quick survey of my surroundings before resuming my flight. The office complex looks empty for the most part; the parking lot beyond has only a scattered few vehicles. Though it is tempting, I reject any thought of stealing one of them. I would be too exposed, and the last thing I need is to bring the police into the mix. I have a feeling I would end up back where I started.

Instead I decide to proceed in the same direction, staying parallel to the street, but somewhat hidden by the line of trees that runs alongside it. Past the office complex and its parking lot, there is an undeveloped lot that is overgrown with shrubs and weeds. That is where I head as Molijc catches up to me. There are tears in his eyes. "Wait. Please. I can't go any further."

I don't bother to answer, keeping walking, wanting to put as much distance between me and the Watchers as possible. Molijc comes to a halt, and I can feel his eyes burning holes in the back of my head.

"Fuck, you fucking bitch. Come back here."

He is irate, his voice echoing across the parking lot and beyond. I stop and turn to glare at him, touching the front of my pants where the pulse weapon is, not saying anything. He flinches when I do, going pale and still. I turn back, heading toward the overgrown lot, on the other side of which is the campus.

It pulls at me like a center of gravity from which it seems I will never escape. Today, though, it may be a sanctuary. If I can get there, get into the buildings and tunnels, I can hide from the Order. They don't seem to have the people necessary to do a full-scale search, and, with a few key exceptions, I feel confident I know the grounds better than they do. From there, I can find my way as necessary.

The sharp squeal of tires makes me stop. I look around

wildly, but all I see is Molijc making his ungainly way toward me. I can hear the vehicle on the road between the Order building and office complex. There is another screech of rubber on pavement, and they are in the parking lot, still out of sight on the other side of the building. I look around wildly for somewhere to hide, but I am out in the open, too far from any of the cars in the parking lot, with only the line of trees to hide behind, their trunks and branches now looking pathetically narrow.

Before the vehicle comes into view, I start to run. Molijc curses and yells at me for abandoning him. I go through the line of trees and across the street to the sidewalk, where I resume walking. There is a small knoll running along the street, with a line of trees atop it. On the other side there will be another office complex like the ones I have just wandered past. Maybe I can find an open door and a place to hide, or a vehicle to steal.

As I start up the knoll, I hear the vehicle hurtle across the parking lot, drowning out Molijc's enraged cries. If I am lucky, they will stop and collect him first, if only to determine where I have gone. It might give me enough time to get myself hidden somewhere.

Before I reach the top the knoll, one of the Order vans comes crashing through the trees and down onto the street, its bumper and underside grinding against the sidewalk. I glance back, in time to see the van coming up the knoll, careening toward me. I start to run, but find myself on the edge of another vast, empty parking lot, the nearest building a hundred feet away.

The van bounces off the lawn and onto the pavement, racing around to cut off my path to the building. It skids to a halt in front of me, and Gloria leaps out of the driver's seat, a malevolent look upon her face.

26

Gloria kicks the door of the van shut and strides over to confront me. I watch her impassively as she glares at me, quivering with triumph and hate. "Going somewhere?"

"Just out for an evening stroll with the Grand Regent."

Gloria snorts. "The Great Hoohaw seems broken."

"I wonder why that would be."

Gloria shifts on her feet, unconsciously flexing the fingers on her right hand. There is no weapon on her I can see, but there is no doubt she has one on her person somewhere. I look closely at her pants and shirt, realizing for the first time how anonymous they are. Like the clothes those of us in the Church adopted, so that we could slip from world to world without standing out anywhere. Jeans and blank t-shirts. Button-up shirts with solid colors. Blouses and skirts that weren't too tight or revealing. Nothing with any labels visible.

"You like what you see?" She waves a hand up and down her body.

Her clothes do accentuate her curves, which I admit does stir something within me. But it also makes it hard to disguise a pulse pistol. I smile. "You're crazy. Just my type."

"Don't get cute. You've no idea the danger you're in right now."

"Everyone here is big on threats, but there's no follow-through, I notice. Makes me think you don't actually want to do anything to me. Like I might be more valuable alive and in one piece."

"Don't be so sure. The situation is not what it was."

"Clearly. You're out and about. Lasinha told me the Order was questioning you, same as they were me. I guess you busted out too."

Gloria blinks, momentarily uncertain, but she is saved from saying anything by Molijc's arrival. He comes up the hill with an awkward, limping trot, his forehead glistening with sweat, his breathing ragged. She turns to him. "What do you think you're doing?"

Molijc swallows loudly. He looks as though he might collapse at any moment. The tremors are now running up his whole left arm, though he tries to disguise it by clenching his fist. He puts on a brave face and returns Gloria's glare. "Is that any way to speak to your Grand Regent?"

"Grand Fool is more like it. And I'm no Regent. I know the real truth of the universes. I'm no pawn in the Society's game like you idiots."

Molijc opens and closes his mouth, unsure of the situation and looking very tired.

"Means and ends and all that, right?" I say, hooking my thumb into the pocket of my jeans near where I have the pulse weapon tucked away.

"That's right." Gloria is staring at my hand.

I wiggle my fingers, and she blinks and braces herself, her hand moving up to her shoulder. She tries to hide the motion by rubbing her arm, but I now know her weapon is over her shoulder. "Spare me that bullshit. Poor Hazim may have believed whatever nonsense that was, but you don't. That's why you're running around out here thinking you can tell us what to do."

Gloria narrows her eyes, looking from Molijc to me, deciding whether to set aside this charade or try to keep it going. Her nostrils flare, and I know the decision has been made.

"That's right. It's all bullshit. Just like this is all bullshit." She points at Molijc, who blinks and looks as though he wants to protest. "The Watchers, or whatever you call them, they're pretending too."

"De Gofroy's protocols are proven…" Molijc starts before I shoot him a withering look. He falls silent and looks at his feet, his lips quivering.

"But for who?"

Gloria smirks. "The Society, of course. We need to keep the Church looking active for them."

"Even though there are no faithful left."

"Well, there's him." The look of disdain on Gloria's face as she says those words and stares at Molijc makes me angry. I loved him once, idiot that I was. Gloria laughs at my tortured expression. "But you're full of shit yourself, aren't you now?"

"What do you mean?"

Gloria rolls her eyes. "If we're going to stop playing, let's stop playing. You're Aurellano. I've known enough of them. I ought to know."

"That was just the name they gave me when they exiled me." I look at Molijc for confirmation, and he nods miserably. "I've always been Laila, more or less."

"But it wasn't just a name, was it, Grand Pooh Bah? Who chose it?"

It takes Molijc a moment to answer. "Lasinha, I think. I don't know the origin of it. We just needed a name. And that's what he came up with. Nothing more to it than that."

"Nonsense. Pure crap." Gloria laughs again, but there is no mirth in it. "You were putting her in this Aeida's body. In his universe. Just keep his damn name. Fewer questions that way if anyone ever started snooping around."

Molijc is affronted. "We didn't want Laila's people to be snooping. Certainly not the Society. We couldn't be certain if they knew about Aeida. Better to keep his name out of it."

"Is what Lasinha said. What he was really doing was tipping off those who needed to know about who he suspected the Aurellano was."

"The Aurellano?" Molijc's confusion echoes my own.

"You know, don't you?" Gloria is looking at me with an arrogant grin. "Lasinha's still not sure, but I know. I'd know an Aurellano anywhere."

I don't speak, hoping that my face betrays nothing. There is no question of admitting that there is someone, or something, inside me. An Aurellano, I suppose. If I understood what this all meant, how I can just have been talking to them in my head, I might be in a position to use that knowledge to my advantage. But, as always, I am left blind, fumbling my way forward.

"I'm tired of this nonsense," Molijc says, summoning all the haughtiness that remains in him. "This ends now. I am the Grand Regent of the Church of Regents. I am returning to the Church. Do not attempt to stop me. You have no authority to do so."

Gloria sketches a mocking bow. "Please, go, your majesty. Sit in your empty tower."

Molijc doesn't move, sensing a trap. Gloria sneers at him. "Go. Get out of here. You're no use to us anymore."

Molijc remains where he is, all the vitality drained from him, the void of his future visible now. I almost feel pity for him. How many days did I yearn for a moment like this where I treated him as Gloria is, dismissing him from my life? Rage consumes me. He stole my body, left me with nothing—and for what? For this pathetic end.

I turn to Gloria. She is right, after all—Molijc is irrelevant now, and my focus should be on her. "You don't need the illusion of a Church anymore?"

"It's too late for anyone in the Society to stop us now. Everything has begun. And now that I've found the Aurellano…" She shrugs and reaches behind her back, pulling out a sword like the one Hazim attacked us with. It seems to grow in length as she lowers her arm, forming to a pointed end. I think of the walls in my dreams and in the place the Seekers took me, forming and re-forming.

Gloria levels the blade at Molijc, its colors changing from turquoise to a kind of violet in the dying light. "Run along, your regency."

Molijc's lip quivers, and he clenches and unclenches his hands. He looks to me for help, but I have none to offer, and he bows his head in surrender, walking between Gloria and me in the direction of the Church. When he is just past us, he turns abruptly and charges at Gloria. With the aftereffects of emerging from the tamp still heavy upon his limbs, he isn't as quick as he normally is, though even if he was, I don't think it would matter.

Gloria flicks her wrist, a casual movement, and the sword enters and exits Molijc's midsection. The blade cuts right through him—I am certain I see its tip protruding from his back before Gloria withdraws it. Molijc falls to his knees, looking up at her. Blood and other things puddle on the ground around him before he collapses entirely.

He gurgles and twitches for thirty seconds or more, and when it is done, I go to him, kneeling gingerly and trying to avoid the blood that is spreading along the pavement. I check his pulse at his neck and can't feel anything. Gloria watches me, a smile on her face. I straighten up, and she points the sword at me.

"Lose the weapon," she says. I start to move my hand toward the pistol, murderous thoughts on my mind, and her smile broadens. "Slowly. Slowly. Don't try anything, either. You don't want to find out what I can do with this sword."

I want to issue a cutting retort, to pull out the gun and

blast away, but I don't. That is what she wants me to do. She is looking for a reason to cut me to ribbons. "Lasinha won't be happy if you kill me. Especially if you're right about the Aurellano." It is a stab in the dark, one I fervently hope is correct.

Gloria's smile fades a little. "We're done pretending, are we?"

"I don't have a goddamn clue what you're talking about. But I know Lasinha. If he suspected I was a threat and that killing me would solve that problem, I would have been dead in Black Diamond."

Gloria flicks her wrist again, and the blade is somehow at my throat, its tip piercing the skin by my jugular. "Lose the gun. Or try it. I dare you."

Moving slowly, and not taking my eyes from hers, I pull the gun from my pants, making sure to keep my fingers away from the trigger. I toss it on the ground at her feet, but not before squeezing the butt end. She smiles, though it is clear she is disappointed. The sword retreats from my throat. I reach up to feel where the blade nicked me, and my fingers come away with blood.

"Just a taste of what you've got coming. Now, come on." She motions with her sword toward the van. "And no funny stuff, or I'll cut a lot deeper than that. Just remember, I may need to keep you alive, but I don't need to keep you in one piece."

"You're not from this universe, are you?"

She looks at me. "Why?"

In answer, I dive away from her to the ground as the pulse weapon erupts, its charge bursting up, the wave catching Gloria unaware. She collapses to the ground, the sword falling from her hand and clattering to the ground. The blade disappears back into the hilt as soon as it does.

The outer edge of the pulse reaches me, not strong enough to knock me unconscious, but sending my head spinning and leaving my whole body tingling and numb. Movement is agony, a thousand points lancing through each muscle, but I force myself to get to my feet. My legs won't support me, and I collapse back to the ground.

I groan and start massaging the feeling back into my legs, watching Gloria for any signs of life. She took a direct hit from a pulse wave at close range. People have died or suffered severe trauma from contact with a wave that close to the source, even though it wasn't at full power. I would be unconscious now if that were the case. But Gloria is not most people, of that I am sure, and I don't know how long she will remain unconscious. Or how long it will be until someone comes looking for her and me. I have to get the hell out of here now.

When the feeling in my legs has been reduced to mere pins and needles, I succeed in standing. Walking gingerly, I approach Gloria and conduct a quick search. There is nothing in her pockets, which is no surprise. Underneath her blouse and wrapping around her shoulder there is a strap for her sword with a small scabbard. I lift up her shirt and loosen the strap, wondering how this will look to anyone who chances upon us. Not good. But if there is anyone in the office building, they don't seem to be watching.

When I have the strap free, I put the sword in the scabbard and collect the gun Molijc gave me. I climb into the van and head out of the parking lot. There is only one way in or out, which takes me back to the street leading to the Order building. I head the other direction and take the first side street I come to, going east. At the next intersection, I turn right and find myself back at the Church campus.

I avoid it, assuming Lasinha has cameras and alarms set up, and make my way toward downtown. As soon as I am certain there is no one on my trail, I pull over on a side street off Kensington Road. Lasinha may have a way to track the van. If nothing else, he will have the police out looking for it. I leave it, though not before conducting a quick search to see if anything useful turns up, and putting the sword on underneath my shirt. It feels uncomfortable and obvious and I have to fight the urge to keep adjusting the strap.

I wander from the side street back onto Kensington Road, which is bustling with people moving among the restaurants and bars. I ignore my misgivings about the sword and slip into the crowd, making my way to Tenth and the bridge across the river to downtown. From there, I follow the river path for a while, wandering up onto quiet streets filled with office towers and darkened stores, circling my destination while I make certain I am not being followed.

When I am, I make my way to a tower with circular balconies that bulge out of the side of the building, giving the appearance of flying saucers docked for the evening. There is a concierge at the front desk, and I give him the lockbox number for the keys to an apartment I secured for meetings with Morris and others. The Order will have this apartment if they questioned Morris closely or looked at the Church financials in detail. They could have sold it to raise funds, though funds never seemed to be an issue for the Watchers and the Acolytes, even as the Church hemorrhaged faithful.

If they do know about this place, they could easily have changed the lockbox number, in which case I am about to sent back out into the night. As I watch the concierge painstakingly go through the files on his computer to confirm the number, I have my doubts. But I am betting they've done nothing with the place. After Morris was captured, they may have kept watch here to see if I, or some of my allies, returned to use it. In all the chaos that followed, with the collapse of everything, it will have been forgotten. I hope.

The concierge finally looks up from his screen and nods. Relief and exhaustion flood through me as he goes to the mailboxes that line the wall behind him, digging through his keys until he finds the one he's looking for. He opens the box, pulls out an envelope, and hands it over to me. I check to make sure there is a key inside, my hands shaking, before scurrying to the elevators. Once inside the apartment, I do a quick search, but find no cameras or bugs. All the blinds on the windows are closed and the place smells stale. There is a heavy layer of dust covering everything.

It is safe enough, I decide. I am too tired to care if it isn't. Now that I am able to relax a little, the after effects of two close range pulse blasts return with a vengeance. There is still a tingling in my arm, running from my elbow to my shoulder. A twitching nerve that won't quiet. My head feels like it's been rattled around in my skull and my mouth is dry.

I can't stop seeing Molijc, the light going from his eyes, while his guts spilled out on the pavement. Sometimes it is Suon I see impaled by Gloria's sword. The sword that is upon my back. Nothing feels real about these last days. Nothing feels real at all.

Though I am so exhausted I can barely keep my eyes open, I force myself to go through the cupboards in the kitchen to find something to eat. There is a kettle and some instant noodles, so I boil some water and make some soup. When I am done, I feel whole again—as whole as I can ever feel, anyway. I go to bed, not bothering to get undressed and putting the gun and sword under the pillow, where I can easily reach them. As soon as I close my eyes, it seems I am asleep

27

I open my eyes to darkness. When I move, there is a gentle sway and the groan of rope straining against wood. Fumbling about, I come to understand I am in a hammock. I climb out of it, and my bare feet touch the floor, which is made of woven bamboo. As my eyes adjust to the darkness, I see that the whole room is made of bamboo, the roof thatched with leaves. I remember Doña Pía's house, where Tingco had her murder me, and understand what is going on.

A figure materializes from the darkness outside, standing in the doorway. "Good. You're here."

"Sorry to keep you waiting."

They shrug. "You needed the rest. I gave you as much as I could, but our time is short and we have a lot to discuss."

I look past them into the darkness beyond, which teems with stars. The house seems to float in a void along with them, no world near us. I feel I am looking at the same vastness that greeted Josefina Aurellano when she emerged to the observation deck while fleeing the other Seekers. "Yes, we do. First we have to get you out of my damn head."

A long silence follows, and a mournful sadness emanates from the Aurellano. "That isn't possible."

"What the hell do you mean?"

"I've always been here. From the moment you were born, perhaps. I don't know. I can't pretend to understand it. For all intents and purposes, we are one. I am you, but not. Not evident, either. I am there, but I only emerge after a time. When I am needed."

"I don't need you."

"No. I'm the burden you must carry, just as the others did. Most of them died before they became fully aware. But you have not. Things have taken their course, so to speak. And now we must make sure we make it count."

"I don't want to be a part of whatever stupid war this is. I'm done with all that. I'm through with being a fucking plaything." I am shaking as I speak, emotion gusting and twisting through me. None of this is real, I tell myself. I am asleep on a bed in a safe house. If I am lucky, I won't wake up and all these problems will disappear. "Let the Seekers and the Acolytes fight it out amongst themselves. I just want...to live my life."

The Aurellano nods. "Like trillions upon trillions of others in all the universes. I know. But all their lives are at stake now. That is why I am here. Why I am in all the universes at some time or another. We must protect against those who seek to destroy it all."

I shake my head. "How could anyone possibly destroy all the universes? I mean, according to you Seekers, any change in one creates another and another. There are infinite possibilities."

"But the universes are still contained. Each of them is a closed system, a...program following its logic to an end."

"What end is that?"

They shrug. "Who's to say? I've never been at the end of things. Or the beginning. Who's to say why the universes are even here to begin with? But there are those who believe that there is something beyond even the universes. Reality. That this is only a kind of simulation, played out again and again in its infinite varieties."

"Is it?"

Another shrug and a smile. "What if it is? It's real enough to all of us who are in it. But not to them. They want this reality they think is out there, even if it means murdering trillions upon trillions and ending these universes."

I put a hand to my head, which is aching. "Let me get this straight, then. My life—everyone's—is just some simulation, played out again and again?"

"It may be so, yes."

"And these people—the Acolytes—"

They shake their head. "Not the Acolytes. Or the Seekers. What the Seeker told you is true, more or less. The Seekers and Acolytes are Sojourners, people who discovered the nature of the universes. The code behind the simulation, if you will. Please understand that is a poor analogy, but I know it is something you will understand. The Sojourners grew drunk on their power in the early days, so they created what you call the Society of Travelers. It has many names in many universes, but it is the same people, always."

"Wait." I exhale, frustrated and feeling more confused. "When the hell did these Sojourners figure out the nature of the fucking universes?"

"Many lifetimes after you have lived. But understand as well, the universes do not proceed along the same timelines. Just because your Church went from universe to universe along more or less the same timeline does not mean that transferring to different points and time isn't possible."

"Those sons of bitches. The Society came from the future. And just took over the whole goddamn planet."

The Aurellano smiles. "Yes. The ones you call the Society and Acolytes did this to many universes."

"Why?"

"Because they could, at least at first. Even after the Society was formed, they still did it for power, though they dressed it up with high-minded justifications. The same sorts of things colonizers and conquerors always say, if you remember your history at all. The Seekers are those in the Society who became disillusioned with these justifications and came to believe what they were doing was wrong. They have been fighting across time and universes forever since this for control of the Society.

"Your Church became part of this battle. A proxy war, in effect. But hidden within the Society is another group. The majority are unaware of its existence."

"These ones who want to end the universes," I say, running a hand through my hair. I am momentarily left dislocated as I realize that my hair is long, that I am myself here in whatever this place is.

They are watching me, something like concern on their face. "Yes. They are few, but they have managed to figure out a way to destroy the universes." They hold up a hand to forestall my next question. "Think of it like a computer program that is running. Again, the analogy isn't perfect. A virus can alter what the program does, take it over and make it attack itself."

"But that won't destroy the program. It just repurposes it."

"It will if the repurposing is to unwrite all the code."

"That's what they intend to do?" I shake my head. "Won't that just write them out of existence too?"

The Aurellano smiles. "They don't believe so. They believe they can transcend the universes to whatever is out there. Perhaps they can. If there is anything beyond this. That they can unwrite the universes, there is no doubt, though. The code undergirding everything can be rewritten to null. But there is a fail-safe."

"You."

"Us," they say.

They move from the doorway to come near me,

standing close in the darkness. They reach out and take my hand. I look at them and see myself staring back. And I understand everything with a terrifying clarity that makes me want to race out into the void, to dissipate into nothingness. They tighten their grip, closing their eyes, and my eyes close too.

"What do we have to do then?" I say, not opening my eyes. Neither of us do.

"I'm not certain. We've never come this far before. They've been finding us and murdering us before we can take form, thinking that would stop the fail-safe. But of course we just reappear. So they've waited here, trying to make certain that you are what they think you are. And now they will try something else. Unwriting the fail-safe code. That is our first concern, avoiding that. So long as we do, if they start unwriting the universes, the fail-safe will be enacted."

"We'll know what to do."

"I believe so."

"Fuck me. We're going on belief now for the fate of everyone alive."

"It's all we have, I'm afraid. Belief, hope, and perhaps a few friends to help us."

"That's our first step," I say with authority.

They don't reply, and I open my eyes to find my hand empty and them gone. Not vanished, exactly. A part of me. They are us. I go to the doorway and look out at the darkness. There are stars all around, above and below. I watch them for a time, imagining that each one is a universe caught in the ebb and flow of all others, pushed and pulled by distant and unimaginable forces. From my vantage point in this hut, I will have to navigate among them, finding a way to keep them all alight.

FOUR:

THE AURELLANO

28

I wake up feeling more rested than I have in months, and more myself than I have in forever. This false body feels irrelevant, something I will transcend. Perhaps that is true. It may have to be, for I fear my own body is gone forever. I feel alive to myself, to the universe, to everything, in a way I never have before. I am ready to begin.

After a breakfast of instant noodles and tea, I spend some time figuring out how to use the sword I stole from Gloria. Like the pulse weapon, it responds to pressure on the hilt, extending or contracting depending on my grip. When I have a good feel for the weapon—at least to the point that I'm not worried about impaling someone by mistake—I have a shower and ponder my next move.

I am faced with two tasks: avoiding Lasinha, Gloria, and their compatriots, and finding allies of my own. The obvious choice is to make contact with the Seeker again, but I am not so sure that is wise. He may be one of them—though few in number, the Aurellano said they have converts throughout the Society. It would explain his continued interest in me and the laughable mission he sent me on. Likely I am just being paranoid, and he hoped I could shed some light on what Lasinha's people were up to. The Seekers had to suspect something was up with the efforts made to keep what was essentially a zombie Church looking viable long after its utility.

Once again, I feel Suon's loss keenly. I could trust and rely on her, as I never truly appreciated until she was gone. She did not deserve what happened to her. If she were here now… There are a great many things I need to say to her. Too late, always too late.

In the end I decide I have to risk making contact with the Seeker. There seems no other choice at the moment. All those I knew in the Church are gone. They will want nothing to do with me or this anymore, and I cannot blame them. The question now is how to let the Seeker know where I am. One would think he would know—isn't that what Seekers are capable of doing?—but thanks to the Aurellano I now have a better understanding of their skills and their limits. I will need to let him know where I am.

I could march to the nearest Society outpost and try to turn myself in. That would garner some attention. But it would also alert Lasinha's people. If I could get access to transfer equipment, I could perhaps send myself somewhere where I could draw his attention. But any effort I made to break into some transfer site would expose me to the same risks.

As I ponder how to reach out to the Seeker, I realize I don't need to. I just need to know someone who can.

The downtown public library first thing in the morning is filled with transients and elderly, along with a scattering of children and their mothers. I make use of one of the public computers there to see if I can find any trace of the person I'm looking for. My expectation is that the Society will have scrubbed all remnants of him from this world, but to my surprise, I find him very easily. The address where he is living now makes me laugh, drawing a dark stare from the teenager beside me, who is busy looking up recipes for homemade methamphetamine.

I steal a car from a parking garage not far from the library. A calculated risk, but I have little time to spare and need to know if the person I've found is the one I'm looking for. I drive out of the city, south and west, to Turner Valley, a small town only a few minutes down the road from Black Diamond. They even look similar, the same broad streets lined with buildings with false facades. Turner Valley doesn't have quite the same sense of desolation. There are only a few empty shops with boarded windows on the main street, and the cars parked there appear to be in good enough shape to be driven away.

Was it only a few days ago that I was near here? It seems impossible. It feels like months have passed. I have the irresistible urge to drive through the town and on to Black Diamond. To go to the school and see if Suon still lies in the hallway there. Look for the transfer box, my escape route. But there will be nothing left there, no traces at all. Lasinha will have seen to that.

The place I am looking for is just a block and a half off the highway, which doubles as main street in town. It is a distillery and bar in a cavernous old building that looks in need of a coat of paint. Out front there is a small patio with mismatched metal tables and chairs. A sign out front promises distillery tours and happy-hour pricing until six.

I step inside the building to a dimly lit bar, as empty as the patio out front. There is a long counter on the far side of the room, with lines of bottles running along shelves of the wall. I sit on one of the stools by the counter, swiveling around on it to look at the various animal heads mounted on the wall. This is not at all what I was expecting.

On one end of the counter there is an open door, presumably leading to the distillery itself. I can hear noise coming from there, but I decide to wait. After a minute or so, someone emerges from the back, blinking in surprise.

"Sorry. Didn't hear you come in. What can I get for you?" It is a familiar voice. And a familiar face, if aged, his dark hair streaked with grey and cut short to try to hide the fact it is thinning. But there is no mistaking who it is.

"Gabriel Arajuano," I say, and smile.

"Yes. That's my name." He returns my smile, but he is on guard now.

"Laila Johar." I extend a hand to shake. "It's been a long time."

"Shit," he says, taking a step back. "Who sent you?"

"I brought myself. It's Laila, Gabriel. Despite all appearances."

He squints at me, a look of revulsion on his face. "I don't know who you are, friend, but I have nothing to do with the Church anymore. I want no part of it. So why don't you just head out that door back to wherever the fuck you came from."

"I'm not leaving, Gabriel. But don't worry; this is nothing to do with the Church. I've lost the faith. That's what happens when the Acolytes take your mind and put it in another body."

"Impossible," he mutters, looking me up and down. "Look, I don't know what you're playing at here, but it's not funny. I told you once to go. I'm going to tell you again. And then I'm going to call the cops."

"Let's not get excited now." I pull the pulse pistol from my pants and place it on the counter. "Now why don't you pour me a negroni, and whatever you like for yourself, and we'll talk."

Arajuano swallows, staring at the gun. "What happens if somebody walks in here? What's your plan then?"

I make a show of looking around the empty bar and then fix him with a mocking glare. "Pour the damn drinks, Gabriel. I'm thirsty."

He does, moving with care, making sure to keep both hands visible at all times. I watch, my hand resting on the pistol, but my finger away from the trigger. What is he thinking about me, I wonder? He must be trying to decide whether I'm just some madman, broken by the faith, who has tracked him down, or someone from his past come to settle debts. Both are true in their way.

When he hands me the negroni, I take a sip and let out an appreciative sigh. "Good gin."

"Thanks," he says, mixing himself something.

"I was surprised to find you here, so close to the Church. Did they ever tell you what happened to Frederik?"

He stiffens at the mention of Frederik De Gofroy, but continues making his Tom Collins. "No. But I never asked. This is my father's place. I didn't know where else to go when it was over. There was nowhere, really. This was all I had left. But no one has ever come looking for me."

Until today, he doesn't bother to add, turning around to come stand near me. Close enough that he might be able to grab the pistol, should the moment present itself. I smile at him and raise my glass.

"Not surprising, really. We disappeared up our own asses after you were done with us."

"I heard a little. Didn't like most of what I did. I'm glad I got out. I'm just a simple distiller now. Nothing to do with all that anymore."

"Oh, I know. I'm not asking you to get involved. Well, only a little. I just need you to get in touch with an old friend of yours."

Arajuano studies me warily. "Who might that be? All my old friends who stayed in the Church are dead or worse."

"Not in the Church, Gabriel."

"The Society cut me loose when I was done. Didn't care what happened to me. Didn't give a damn what I'd done for them. I was no use to them anymore."

"Do you remember the night you left Montreal? After leaving Frederik in jail? We followed you to the airport, Lasinha and I. Saw you get on. There was a Seeker there. I couldn't see him, but I could feel him watching us."

"Jesus." Arajuano takes a step back, flinching. "Laila."

I grimace in frustration. "What have I been telling you?"

"Jesus." He shakes his head and takes a long drink. "What the hell happened?"

"Molijc and Lasinha happened. Can you get in touch with that Seeker?"

"Maybe. I don't know. I mean, it's been years. I could try my handler. She might be able to. Though I don't know where she is in the Society now. Or if she still is."

"Let's track her down and give her a call."

Arajuano shakes his head. "Why should I help you, Laila? I mean, I don't want to get dragged into this again. I don't want my life ruined again. Besides, in my experience, the Seeker will find you. You don't need to find them."

"They're not what you think they are."

Arajuano snorts. "Of course not. This is why I don't want any part of this. I'm sorry, Laila."

I lift my glass, studying him over the rim. "The Seeker has Ana."

"What?" He shifts uncomfortably, suddenly unable to meet my eyes.

"They have Ana. Lasinha and Molijc—well, they did what they do." I point at myself. "But I got her out, and now the Seeker has her. They promised to restore her so long as I did something for them. Well, I did it. Now I need to get back there and make sure they pay their debts."

"Jesus." Arajuano shifts on his feet some more, looking very old. "Look, things didn't end well between Ana and me. The last time…"

"I'm sure I don't give a shit, Gabriel. She needs friends now. She needs her father to help her."

Arajuano sighs, looking up at the ceiling. He drains the rest of his drink. "Fine. I'll help you. I just hope to God this doesn't go wrong."

I smile my thanks at him, though I am fervently hoping the same.

29

"Hester? Glad I caught you. It's Gabriel Arajuano. We need to talk."

Arajuano has closed up shop for the afternoon, and we are sitting on opposite sides of a cluttered desk while he tries to reach his handler. I sip at some tonic water, legs crossed, resting the pulse pistol on my thigh. A reminder to Arajuano not to try anything. He seems subdued for the moment, word of his daughter and what she suffered clearly disturbing him.

"Look, I can't really discuss it on the line." Arajuano looks at me and grimaces. "I've got someone that Ngurawan is looking for. Do you have some way to let him know?"

Another grimace. He looks at me and shakes his head. "I won't do that, Hester. I'm out and I'm not getting back in. I'm just doing this as a favour to Ngurawan, nothing more."

He puts a hand over the receiver. "She won't do it unless she knows who it is."

"Tell her I'm willing to meet with her. No one else. We'll confirm this. But it has to be tonight."

Arajuano relays my message, looking doubtful. "In

Calgary, I assume," he says in answer to her question. I nod confirmation. "Look, I already told you I'm not getting involved. I'm making the call here, nothing else. I understand, but…"

He listens, his face getting grimmer by the moment. "Fine. She wants to know where you want to meet."

I think for a moment and give her an address. Arajuano shakes his head. "I hope you know what the hell you're doing." He ends the call and looks at me, shaking his head again. "It's set up. She wants me there to do the introductions. You better not be fucking us over."

"Let's take your car," I say, smiling.

The strip mall is along Fourteenth Street, just south of downtown. A laundromat and Chinese delivery place occupy the main floor, as before, though the names and signs are different. The barbershop and pizza place are absent. In their place is a donair shop, where Arajuano and I have supper, and a tattoo parlor. The space on the far end, near the door to the office upstairs, is vacant, a faded lease sign taped to the window.

It has been over a decade since I was last here. This was where I did my first pre-screening, while fighting off the itch of withdrawal. I left unsure, not quite believing what Opal and Hector told me. Within a month, less, the Church was my entire life, consuming me. Now there is nothing left. How did I let it happen?

"Is it still a pre-screening site?" Arajuano says as we leave the donair place and head to a door leading upstairs. Nearly his first words since leaving Turner Valley.

"The Church is dead."

I try the door, hoping it is still open, though it is almost nine and offices should be closed upstairs. To my relief, it is, and we head upstairs. The carpet is the same as before, though even more worn and sad looking. I pause at the directory to see if anything is still listed. That the Church is still renting the space, I have no doubt. To my surprise, it is still there: 214 Regency Services Limited. A strangled sound comes out of Arajuano's throat. I look back at him, raising an eyebrow in question.

"Sorry. Just never thought I'd be back here again."

Neither did I, but I don't bother to say it. I chose this place because when Arajuano's handler does her checking and passes it on to the Seeker, or his people, they may recognize the significance of it. It is also another place where Lasinha and his people are unlikely to be watching. I hope.

We head down the hallway to room 214. The corridor is brightly lit, but quiet, just as it was all those years ago. I try the door when I come to it, but it is locked, and I step aside for Arajuano. He sighs and pulls out the lockpick kit I made him bring along. It takes him a while, but he manages it, and we go inside.

"You're out of practice," I say, flipping on the lights.

The rooms look the same as before. Anonymous office décor in the outer room to greet prospective Initiates and a few framed motivational posters with quotes from De Gofroy are the only obvious signs of the Church. The inner conference room is unchanged as well, three chairs sitting around a table. In one corner there is a box of books. Arajuano pulls one out while I go to the next room, which functioned as workspace and kitchen for the Regents who worked here.

"I didn't know Molijc wrote books as well."

I glance at the book Arajuano is holding as I return from the back room, to check that all the blinds are down and closed by the front desk. It is something called Regency and the Mayan Codices. Molijc wrote several books, most cribbed liberally from De Gofroy's works. Hardly a surprise, given De Gofroy wrote variations of the same book his whole life, plagiarizing himself endlessly.

"He wanted to be De Gofroy." It is intended to be flippant, a dismissal, but as I say it, I realize it is true. Molijc wanted to be his hero, and everything he did led from that.

We turn off the lights in the office and take up positions where we can observe. Arajuano stays in the offices, peering through the blinds, with a view of the parking lot and Fourteenth Street. I return to the stairwell, propping open the door with a wooden stopper left in a corner by the caretaker. The stairwell has windows on each floor, which give me a view of the parking lot's other entrance. I will also be able to see anyone approaching the door. The only risk is leaving Arajuano alone, but I have no choice now but to trust him.

At ten, just as the light begins to dim enough to make watching difficult, someone approaches the door. I catch a glimpse of a woman wearing a dark blazer and pants, looking as though she is just coming from the office. She tries the door, but it is locked now that it's past nine. Before she steps into the shadows against the building, I see her pull a phone from her pocket. I step out of the stairwell, back into the hall, and Arajuano emerges moments later.

"It's her."

I go downstairs, checking the sword on my back and pulling the gun from my pants. Standing off to the side of the door, against the wall, I push it open a crack. Just enough to allow Hester to pull it open. She steps within and finds herself face to face with the muzzle of the gun. I motion for her to move against the wall, putting my foot out to stop the door from closing all the way.

Her pale face goes flushed, and she holds up her hands. For some reason, I notice the wedding ring on her left hand. "I don't know who the hell you are, but do you really think it's wise to be pointing a gun at—"

"Save it." I pat her down and find a pulse pistol in the inner pocket of her blazer. Tucking it into my pants, I point my pistol up the stairs. "Go nice and slow. Keep your hands where I can see them."

She looks as though she wants to argue with me, but

she turns and heads up the stairs. Before following her, I take a quick peek outside, just to make sure there is nobody else lurking out of the line of sight of the windows. There are only a few cars parked across the street, but they were there when we arrived. Arajuano is waiting in the doorway to the Church offices. He nods a greeting at Hester and gestures for her to follow him.

"I can't believe you went along with this, Gabriel."

"You'll notice who has the guns." Arajuano takes her into the conference room while I make sure the door is locked. We leave the lights off in the outer room, turning on the ones in the conference room only when the door is closed. Arajuano sits beside Hester, and I sit across from them, resting the gun on my knee, my hand still on it.

"What the hell do you think you're doing, Gabriel? Got tired of your shitty little life?" Hester is nervous, which is why she is on the attack.

Arajuano holds up his hands. "I'm only here at your request, to make the introduction. And to guarantee your safety." He looks at me, and I give what I hope is an enigmatic shrug. Arajuano sighs. "Hester. I'd like you to meet Laila Johar."

Hester stares at us, dumbfounded. "No. That's impossible."

"It's true. It's her."

I don't speak, letting Gabriel do the convincing for now.

"It can't be."

"It is. I've talked to her. She knows things only Laila could. And I knew her, remember. This is her—in another body, maybe, but her."

"It can't be. We found her body. I found it. This can't be her."

"Where did you find my body?" I ask, hoping my voice doesn't sound as unhinged to them as it does to me.

Hester looks at me and then down at the floor. "I can't say."

I raise the gun. "Where. Is. My. Body?"

Hester swallows. "Incinerated. We found it, like I said, in some house in Vancouver. You'd been shot. We did all the tests to confirm it. It was from this universe. It was you."

"When was this?" My voice sounds very calm now, but my entire body is shaking. The gun is trembling in my hand and I have to press it down into my leg to steady myself. Up until now, I always assumed that I would find my body and get it back. I would be whole again. Molijc would never be able to destroy it, because he still loved me in his own terrible way. That was true, but it seems it is still gone forever, and I am lost.

"Six—eight months ago. I guess."

That would put it right around the time I managed to come across from Aeida's universe. Lasinha must have been worried that I would somehow make contact with Molijc and he would agree to return me. So he created a new puppet Laila for Molijc and got rid of my body, trying to throw the Society off my scent at the same time.

Why do all this, why put me in another body when they could just as easily put a more stable tamp in me? But would a tamp be more stable with the Aurellano present? Killing me was out of the question, for then the Aurellano would just crop up elsewhere, in another place or another time, and they would have to begin again.

All of this, these last weeks—the charades in Black Diamond and here—has just been about buying time until they were certain the Aurellano was within me. Are they now? Am I? I reach out for it and find something there in my thoughts that isn't me, but I shove it away before anything can happen.

Hester and Arajuano are watching me nervously and I am suddenly aware that I am hyperventilating. Gloria said to me that they were ready to enact their plan. It may have been all bluff and bravado, but now that I am to the winds Lasinha will certainly be putting everything in motion, while at the same time looking to recapture me.

What is abundantly clear is that, what I am, whatever this thing inside me is, I am not ready. All I can think about is that I will be left in this rapist monster's body forever. It sickens me and fills me with such hate that I worry about the fact I am holding a gun.

I force my attention back to Hester and Arajuano, pushing aside all my thoughts, all the despairing questions that I dare not entertain. "What did you find out?"

"Nothing. We chased our tails for months. They made it look like it was someone in the Society, acting on behalf of Molijc. We spent weeks trying to find a double agent that didn't exist."

I sit back in my chair and force myself to breathe. "Do you believe I am Laila Johar?"

Hester looks from Arajuano to me. "I guess I do."

"Good. The Seeker, the one Gabriel mentioned."

"Ngurawan," Arajuano says.

"Right. He asked me to do something. To find something out. I've done it. Now I need to get in touch with him. Can you do that?"

Hester goes still. "If he's working with you, he must have left you a way to get in contact with him."

"It was taken from me."

Hester purses her lips. "I need to know more before I reach out to him. What were you doing for him?"

I try not to let my impatience show. "To find out who the Traveler mole in the Church of Regents was."

"We had many moles in the Church." Hester looks at Arajuano.

"You had assets. I was one too. We had our own assets in the Society. But that's not what we're talking about here. Arajuano can tell you what I'm talking about. The conduit. The Seeker told me he narrowed it down to three people. I was one of the three. Lasinha and Molijc were the other two."

Hester shakes her head. "I don't know. Why would he

still care about who the conduit was? It doesn't matter anymore. The Church has collapsed. Molijc and whoever's left is on the run. We know Lasinha was kicked out."

"Do we?" I ask. Hester looks at me sharply. "The Church isn't on the run. It's dead. There's nothing left. It has been for over a year. The question you should be asking yourself is why someone has gone to such lengths to make it seem like a living thing, with agents in the Society killing apostates like me. What are they really up to?"

I have her attention now. "I don't suppose you'll tell me," she says.

"His ears only."

She considers me, worrying at her bottom lip with her teeth. At last, she relents. "I'll make the call."

I try not to exhale in relief. No one would have heard it anyway, for just as Hester finishes speaking, a battering ram splinters the door to the office.

30

We all freeze, looking at each other and waiting for someone to act, while a second barrage from the battering ram finishes the office door. We can hear footsteps of people entering the reception area and starting down the hallway toward the conference room we are now trapped in. I am the first to spring into action, moving my chair in front of the door to the room and making sure it is locked. Outside, I can hear Gloria issuing orders for a search.

"Make that fucking call," I tell Hester, while Arajuano and I move the table in front of the door as well.

She nods, mouth open, and scurries to the corner, phone to her ear. Arajuano and I move the other chairs, the box of books, anything we can put our hands on in front of the door. It will not stop the ram, but may buy us a few seconds. Hester is talking to someone in a low voice, but I cannot make out what she is saying. I pass my gun to Arajuano and pull out the sword from behind my back. His eyes widen as it extends.

Someone tries the handle to the door, and I hear Meredith shout, "They're in here. Bring the ram."

"Careful. She's armed," Gloria says, causing me to smile.

Arajuano and I take up positions on either side of the door, ready to attack as soon as they do. Hester comes over, and I toss her gun to her. She nods, I hope indicating that she got through to the Seeker. We all brace ourselves for the ram and the attack to come, but on the other side there is only the shuffling of feet. It sounds like people moving away from the door.

Hester and Arajuano reach the same conclusion as me, and we all back away from the door. As we do, a new idea occurs to me. I go to the wall between the adjoining offices and this one and plunge the sword in. It cuts through the wall like paper, making hardly any sound as it does. I carve a person-sized hole and push the chunk of wall out. It falls with a dull thud, a cloud of dust from the drywall and insulation drifting back into the conference room.

There is a shout on the side of the door. "What was that?" A woman, Gloria, I think, responds, but I cannot make out what she says.

I don't wait to hear the rest, ducking through the hole into the other offices. Arajuano and Hester are right behind me. We find ourselves in a small, darkened room with a desk and computer facing a door, which I go through, closing it behind us. Outside, we find ourselves in a darkened corridor, with only an exit sign at the far end providing any illumination. I head toward it, assuming it will lead to the entrance, and choose an office at random to enter, waving for Arajuano and Hester to follow me.

I close the door and flick on the lights, heading behind the desk, where the floor will not be immediately visible from the doorway. Hester and Arajuano watch as I begin to carve the floor, confusion and fear on their faces. As I hoped, the sword cuts as easily through the concrete of the floor as it did the wall. I have a moment to wonder what will happen if there is someone below us, before an explosion shakes the building, its reverberations sending dust spilling down from the ceiling. It pushes any doubt from my mind, and I finish cutting.

The floor falls away before the blade completes the circle, nearly causing me to topple in after it. The slab lands with a resounding crash, but no screams of agony, to my relief. I duck my head through the hole and make out through the shadows that it is the tattoo parlor, which is evidently closed for the evening. There is a barber's chair immediately below us, which the slab of concrete has fallen on, but otherwise our path is clear. I motion for both of them to go through the hole.

Arajuano goes first, lowering himself down tentatively. There are exclamations from what sounds to me like just down the corridor, though I suspect they have just entered the conference room. It won't take them long to cross over to these offices and begin searching. Hester goes through the hole next, and I follow on her heels, after turning off the lights and sheathing my sword.

Arajuano is already looking for the way out of this room. The strange gleam of my sword provides enough light that we are able to make out the door, and we slip out of the room and down a corridor, emerging to the main room of the tattoo parlor. We are facing a wall of windows, fortunately tinted so that no one can see in, for several members of the false Order are milling about in the parking lot, along with customers and employees who are evacuating the restaurants following the explosion.

No one is looking our way, but I retract the sword, just to make sure its glow doesn't attract any attention. I head to the back of the store, the others following, hoping that there is another entrance there. All I find is a storeroom, a washroom, and a wall displaying pictures of the tattoo artists' work.

We all freeze as we hear muffled cries from above, though they grow fainter rather than louder, suggesting they have not located where we descended. But they will figure out what we are about soon enough and try to surround the entire building, rather than just the exits, if they haven't already. I unleash the sword and cut through the exterior wall.

We step out into the dusk of the back alley. Someone steps around the corner, attracted by our noise. Before he can do or say anything, Arajuano shoots him. The sound is covered somewhat by sirens in the distance. Police and the fire brigade are no doubt on their way, which means we need to get the hell out of here. The alley leads in both directions, but Hester starts back toward the side entrance of the building, saying under her breath, "My car's this way."

"No," I say, waving her in the opposite direction. "They may have it."

Arajuano nods in agreement, and, reluctantly, Hester accedes. We head in the opposite direction, with me in the lead, staying close to the building. The sound of the sirens grows louder. At the building's edge, I step over the body of the man Arajuano shot and peer around the corner. Another man is standing watch there, in the narrow gap between the building and a retaining wall that separates the strip mall from a gas station.

The man is looking toward the parking lot at something that is happening. I look at Arajuano, who nods and steps around the corner, shooting the man, before ducking back again. There are no shouts or cries from anyone. No one has noticed the other man is missing yet either, though it won't be long. He was likely supposed to go around the building to the side entrance to confirm we hadn't made our escape that way.

One by one, we dart across the gap. On the other side there is an eight-foot fence extending the length of the alley, presumably to keep traffic from the gas station out. The alley doesn't connect to the street, ending at another fence to someone's backyard. There is a second alley, running perpendicular between the houses that line the rest of the block west of the strip mall though and we sprint down it. At the end of the block, we cross the street and run down the next alley, before pausing to catch our breath and see if anyone is following.

"Where is the Seeker?" I return the sword to its sheath, not wanting to draw any attention should we encounter anyone. The others hide their pulse weapons, and we move out of alley down the sidewalk, so that we are out of sight of anyone who might happen to be following us.

"Coming," Hester says. "He can find us. We just have to give him time."

"How much?" Arajuano says.

The sirens have gone quiet, suggesting the police and fire departments have arrived on the scene. Hopefully Gloria's team is delayed with having to explain what is going on, though I have no real hope in that regard.

"I don't know," Hester says. "I gave him the address of that place. He knows which universe. He'll be here. We just need to keep moving."

"Right," I say. "Let's head to the river. We'll stay apart. You two on the other side of the street, so maybe they don't think we're all together."

The others nod, and I go first, crossing the street and heading north a block before turning west. Hester and Arajuano follow, staying on the opposite side of the street and walking hand in hand. Just a couple out for an evening stroll. We walk at a steady pace, quick but not hurried, working our way northwest.

A car turns onto the street behind us, its headlights illuminating the three of us. I just manage to stop myself from freezing, forcing myself to look ahead and keep walking as it drives by. A red Accord, with only the driver in it. The vehicle doesn't slow, crossing to the next block before turning right. The sound of it gradually disappears, absorbed into the general hum of traffic on distant streets.

We end up at a strange intersection beneath a freeway. To the west are the on-ramps and off-ramps to the freeway—it is not lost on me that this is likely the way that Gloria's team came and will leave to return to the Order building. To the north are four abandoned-looking warehouse buildings, all in the shadow of the freeway. In the middle of the four buildings there is a small loop for drivers to turn around, behind which there is a broad patch of gravel connecting to an alley that runs behind the entire street.

There is also a path that goes over a set of railway tracks, running parallel to the street and alley. A broken and rusting chain-link fence separates the tracks from the street, except for the crossing where a gap has been left. The tracks, and what was once the path across them, are overgrown with trees and grass up to the waist, but I know that on the other side there is a way to the river pathway. I used to come here for a quiet place to get high, where no one would bother me, several lives and bodies ago.

We are just over the tracks, following the trampled grass and weeds to find our way through chokecherries and caraganas, when a voice reaches us through the darkness, carrying far in the quiet of the night. I stop as soon as I hear the first speaker, recognizing the voice, nearly causing Arajuano to run into me. He looks at me, knowing who it is as well. We both crouch in the grass, using the trees and bushes to hide us from the street and the buildings.

"We have to keep going," he whispers, touching my arm.

I nod, knowing he is right. Gloria and her people will be able to track us; it is only a matter of time. A race between her and the Seeker to see who finds us first. But instead of continuing on to the river, I creep back through the trees, staying low to the grass, until I am close enough that I can just make out Lasinha and the scarred Acolyte through the darkness. They are standing in the alley behind one of the warehouses, looking in opposite directions.

Fear seizes me. Have they followed us here? Are they trying to see where we have gone? If they are, they have yet to notice us on the tracks. Still, I crouch lower, checking behind me to see where Hester and Arajuano are. I can just make them out through the darkness and underbrush, kneeling behind trees where I left them, heads together as if in discussion. No doubt trying to decide whether to leave me or wait.

I turn back to the warehouse and the two men. Their faces are now in shadows as they move beyond the circle of light shining above the door to the warehouse. Did they come from that warehouse?

Lasinha is on the phone, his back to the Acolyte. "Don't stop until you've found her. We can't let her slip free now, of all times. And remember. You can't trust Meredith."

He ends the call and turns back to the Acolyte, shaking his head. "The Aurellano got away again."

"You're certain now?"

"There's not a doubt in my mind."

"But you have no proof."

"The proof is that she's managed to survive this long."

"I don't know." The Acolyte kicks at something on the ground. "She was always resourceful. She was your equal in that regard."

I cannot see Lasinha's expression, but have the strange sense that he feels insulted by the comparison. "We took her out of her own body and put her in another with somebody else still in there. Let them both fight it all out. It was inherently unstable. You even said so yourself. She survived that all without losing her mind. That's more than resourceful, I think."

"Maybe she is mad. How would we know?"

Lasinha shakes his head and lets out a long sigh. "No, Harith. I know her. I've spoken with her. She hasn't lost her mind. That much I can say for sure."

They lapse into silence, both of them staring out toward the verdant railway tracks. The Acolyte, Harith, seems to be looking right where I am crouching. Sweat trickles down my forehead to my nose, and I fight the urge to brush it away, not wanting to move at all. If they could see me, they would be reacting already, I tell myself.

"There's something else," Lasinha says, and the Acolyte turns to look at him. "She has an unbinding sword. Took it when she got the jump on Gloria."

"She didn't tell you?"

"No. Apparently that's how she made her getaway tonight. Cut through walls in the building."

Harith shakes his head. "Does she know its full potential?"

"She's the Aurellano. We have to assume so."

"Why didn't Gloria tell you?" There is an edge of accusation to the Acolyte's voice.

"I don't know. She's always followed her own path."

"You mean she's been impulsive. She's never been able to control her emotions."

"Her value to this enterprise is without question," Lasinha says. "Whatever her faults may be."

"She may also cost us everything if the Aurellano escapes, which will be much easier to do with that kind of weapon in her hands."

"Gloria knows what the consequences of failure will be." I can almost see Lasinha's smile. "She'll stop at nothing to get the Aurellano back. The question is: do we evacuate?"

The Acolyte considers the question. "We have to. If the Aurellano's escaped, there's no telling where she's gotten to. She was only ten blocks away. She could easily come here."

"She doesn't know about this place."

"Are you willing to take that chance?"

Lasinha looks up at the night sky. "No. But we're not ready."

"We have to be. If what you say is true, the Aurellano is active, or will be soon enough. We need to initiate things, and we can't do that from here."

"She is the Aurellano. There's no doubt in my mind."

"Then the decision is made. Let's get everything ready."

The Acolyte stalks back to the warehouse, ducking inside. Lasinha follows after him, but not before taking one last look around, as if he has the sense that someone, somewhere, is watching him.

I count off the seconds until I reach sixty before daring to move from my position. That last look from Lasinha tells me something has made him wary. Is it just intuition, or did he see a shadow in amongst the trees that might be more than a shadow? I stay low to the ground, moving with care, as I back away, just in case someone is still watching from the warehouse.

To my surprise, Hester and Arajuano are still waiting for me, standing on the remnants of street that once led to a work yard. There are a few pieces of abandoned equipment left there, no doubt already raided for any usable parts and metal, along with a warped stack of chain link. Trees crowd its edges, and beyond that, I know, is the river. There is a pathway there, and a pedestrian bridge across it. That is where we should be heading now.

Arajuano looks at me nervously. "Do they know we're here?"

I shake my head. "No. Apparently that's their base of operations."

"Jesus. And we just about walked right into it."

"Keep your voice down. They just got word we slipped the noose and they're worried we might come by, so they'll be on alert."

"What are we waiting for?" Hester says. "We should be going now."

"Where's the Seeker?" I say. My other questions I keep to myself, though I would dearly like to know whether she had anything to do with Gloria being able to find us. How many people did she let know about this meeting aside from the Seeker? I don't think Arajuano betrayed me. He was with me almost every second from the moment I walked into the distillery to when Gloria and her team arrived.

"I don't know." Hester looks scared. "I didn't talk to him, just his people. They said he would be here. I just don't know how long it will be. He will be here, though." She says it like a mantra.

I turn to Arajuano, who is looking concerned, probably wondering, as I now am, whether the Seeker will even appear. "I'm going back," I say. "I need to see what Lasinha is up to."

"There's no way in hell I'm going back there." Arajuano shakes his head fiercely.

"I'm not asking you to. Or you." I glance at Hester. "These people are only after me. They don't care about either of you. So keep running and stay safe."

"What about you?"

"When the Seeker finds you, you tell him where I am. Tell him I've found his conduit and more. He'll understand."

Hester and Arajuano look at each other and shrug. He offers me his pistol, and I shake my head. "Keep it. I need you both safe so the Seeker can find you. You need to tell him where I am, because he can't find me."

"He can find anyone," Hester says.

"Not me, he can't. Or he'd be here already."

Hester looks as though she wants to argue with me further, but Arajuano grabs her by arm, motioning with his head toward the river. She swallows and nods, and they turn to go.

"Gabriel," I say before they go any farther. "Tell the Seeker who you are. Tell him I said you're to make sure he keeps his end of the bargain, because I've kept mine."

His eyes widen. "I'll make sure she's okay, Laila," he says, his voice heavy with emotion.

I nod and turn away, not bothering to see them off. Not wanting to be tempted into going with them. This may be my only chance to discover what Lasinha and his false Order have planned, and perhaps my only chance to stop them. If I am to be the fail-safe for all the universes, as the thing in my head claims I am, now is my time to act.

31

There is no one standing watch outside the warehouse, no vehicles arriving or leaving. Gloria and Meredith and the rest of the team have yet to pass by in pursuit of our trail. They must be going block to block, or talking to their contacts in the Society to see if they can track Hester down. Hopefully that will keep them away from me and give me time to see what Lasinha and Harith are up to. The fact there are no vehicles on the move here suggests that the evacuation will be across universes, which means I need to move quickly if I'm to find out where they're going. Where they plan to end the universes.

I stay nestled in the grass beneath a chokecherry tree, studying the warehouse, wondering how to get in. Aside from the door that Lasinha and Harith used, the entrance at the front is the only way in or out. The only windows are on the second story of the building, suggesting that the building only has one floor. So even if I could get to the windows and break them with no one noticing, I would be stuck dangling above for someone to pick off with a pulse blast.

I get to my feet and move further east from the warehouse, staying under the cover of the trees and stopping only when I come to the edge of the next building. It is three stories tall with windows on all levels, suggesting there are three floors. There also appears to be roof access from inside the building. If not, I can cut a hole in the ceiling and get there. I also try to gauge the distance between the buildings. They look close together, but are they close enough?

They are, I decide, and anyway, there are no other options. Before I have time to find any more doubts, I duck through a hole in the chain-link fence and jog across the alley, feeling terribly exposed. I hide around the corner of the second building, listening to see if anyone has noticed me. There is no sound; even the surrounding streets are quiet. The nearest door is behind the building, where I will be exposed to any of Lasinha's people who happen to step out into the back alley. I decide to risk it anyway, reasoning that the chance of them seeing me will be the same at the front or the back, but at least in the alley I will be hidden from any chance passersby.

Regretting that I didn't think to get the lockpick from Arajuano, I step around the corner and draw the sword. I extend it a short distance, hoping to diminish its ethereal glow, and cut through the deadbolt on the door. The door handle stubbornly refuses to budge. Telling myself not to panic, I cut a hole above the handle large enough for me to reach through. The metal from the door lands on concrete within, making a wince-inducing clatter. Frantically, I reach through and open the door, getting inside as fast as I can.

I keep the sword out, using its glow to help guide me through the building, and make my way from the loading dock to the stairs. At the top, there is a door leading to the roof. It too is locked, and I am forced to cut the entire handle and lock out before it gives way. This time I manage to catch the pieces before they fall to the stairwell.

Before I step out on the roof, I retract the sword. I don't sheathe it, wanting to keep it at hand, though I don't know how much good it will do me if someone starts shooting from below. When I go out onto the roof, I try to stay low, hopefully out of sight of anyone below. Gravel crunches underfoot. I tell myself it is not that loud, but I know how much the sound will carry in the night with the city growing quiet around me.

There is nothing for it but to keep going, though, so I make my way to the edge of the roof. I don't know what is more daunting, the distance between the two buildings or the drop below. The air goes from my chest at the sight of both. At least, I tell myself, there is no one in the alley looking to find the cause of the earlier noise.

As the thought occurs to me, I hear something, though I am not sure what. The scrape of metal on concrete, perhaps, as if someone opened the door below and kicked at the piece of it that I cut away. I wait, trying to hear more. The darkness seems to swallow all sound, leaving me with doubts and questions, to which the only answers I can provide are fevered imaginings.

I take a deep breath and tell myself to get moving. There is no other choice. I need to be in the other building, and I can't afford to delay. They may already be crossing over. Taking another deep breath, I back away from the edge, giving myself a bit of a runway. I charge across the roof, heedless of the sound. In my attempt to get as close to the edge as possible, I almost overstep. It puts me off balance in the air so that, though I am able to make it across easily, I cannot stick the landing. I tumble across the roof, sending gravel flying.

My shoulder aches from where I land on it, and my face stings from where it was scraped by rocks. The sword is no longer in my hands and it takes me a few frantic seconds to find it. Only when I have found the sword do I go still, hushing even my breathing, to see if anyone has come outside to investigate. Hearing nothing, I hide myself behind the roof access, which is just a hatch door, lying flat and clutching the sword tight. From what I can see across the way, the door to the other roof remains closed.

No shadows move there.

I exhale in relief and shift my focus to the next problem: how to get to where I can see what Lasinha and Harith are up to. Now that I am here, that seems impossible. If I open the hatch to the roof, I might as well announce my presence with trumpets and fanfare. Anything I might do to cut the roof with the sword would also surely draw attention. And I am certainly not capable of scaling down the side of the building to look through one of the windows.

Why did I think it was a good idea to come up here? Because all the other alternatives were somehow worse. I curse under my breath and look at the sword.

Does she know its full potential? That was Harith's question, and Lasinha's answer was that, as the Aurellano, I must. But that is not the case. I do not have access to a storehouse of new knowledge. All I have is the presence of a multitude of others within me that terrifies me beyond measure. I want them gone. Perhaps if I am able to stop Lasinha somehow they will leave me. There is an ache in my chest that tells me that is not the case.

What good is a fail-safe that knows sweet fuck all? I slam my fist in frustration against the hatch.

The distant cacophony of the voices within me grows louder. One voice, in particular, is insistent on being heard. Josefina. I close my eyes and find myself in the cell where I last saw her trading barbs with Tingco. She is sitting on the floor, as she was then, and I am standing where Tingco stood. I look around for the Eye, but it is not there.

"An unbinding sword doesn't just cut," she says, looking up at me.

I open my mouth and close it, unsure whether I will be speaking aloud to the night or only in this place, which must be somewhere in my mind. It has to be.

Josefina continues. "It unbinds molecules. No different than an unbinding pulse, which I think you are familiar with."

I nod.

"That is a crude weapon, though effective. The sword isn't so crude. It can cut through everything, as you have seen. But not only that. It can find a path through the particles of the wall. Let you pass right through, so long as you are holding it. It will find a way through. If you let me, I can get you in there."

I swallow, wanting to refuse, but knowing I have no other choice. I need to get inside. What happens after, though, will I have a thousand other voices insistent on their opportunity to walk around and do whatever they wish?

Josefina smiles at my reluctance. "This is not like Aeida. I can't take control of this body. I exist as part of you. We are one. All of us. You have our experiences to draw upon, to guide you, but you will have to do what needs to be done. I am dead, a long time from now in another place, and I am not coming back. Tingco murdered me in this cell."

Her words don't reassure me, but I nod my agreement anyway. There is no other choice. She stands up and walks toward me. When I open my eyes next, I am back on the roof. She is there with me. We move as one—we are one—crawling back from the access hatch toward the middle of the roof. The sword handle warms in our hand, though the blade does not extend, and somehow we can see through the roof, through gravel, tar, and concrete to the inside of the building.

Our view is clouded and grainy, the figures within the building paused in the midst of whatever they are doing, suggesting that what we are seeing is a snapshot in time. As I suspected, the warehouse is one vast room, except near the front of the building, where there are what appear to be offices on two floors. Transfer equipment is set up in the middle of warehouse, the largest I have ever seen, though not the largest Josefina has. There is other equipment set up nearby, which we recognize, intended to mask the transfer signals or the other equipment's activity. There are others, whose purpose even Josefina is unclear on.

We crawl toward the front of the building where the offices are. From what we can see, everyone is busy in the warehouse, shutting equipment down and moving it into position to be transferred. There are no more than half a dozen people present. We think we see Lasinha in amongst them, though it is hard to make out individuals from this vantage point. The Acolyte doesn't seem to be present, though we are unsure on that. Maybe he has already crossed over to manage the transfers on that end.

When we reach the offices, we look through them to make sure they are empty. We cannot see through to the ones on the bottom floor, but the one immediately below us is dark and vacant. The sword warms in our hand, growing hot enough to burn. My instinct is to drop it, but we don't, gripping it tighter despite the pain. The roof seems alive, particles of it moving in swirling waves. They are clumped close together, almost impenetrable, but slowly the space between them opens up, a gulf through which we can swim.

We step inside the current of the particles. It isn't one current but many, all of them interacting, so that it is impossible for us to tell where any particle will be at any given time. The sword guides us, pulling us through the countervailing currents to the office on the other side. We land on carpeted floor in a darkened room, the ceiling unchanged above us and the sword cool in our hands.

I let out a breath I didn't realize I was holding, looking around to get my bearings, still not quite believing that I have passed through a wall of concrete. Be careful. We are here if you need us. These are Josefina's last thoughts to me before she rejoins the cacophony. Reluctantly, I don't push it aside as I did before, letting it wash over me, listening to what all of us have to say. As disturbing as it is, it gives me an odd sort of comfort and lets me believe I am not stepping out of this room to face Lasinha, Harith, and their conspirators alone.

The office door is open, and I step out into a corridor that runs the length of the building, feeling a renewed urgency. Before we stepped into the current of the wall, I am certain I heard the door to the roof of the other building being opened. I wonder if someone saw me pass through the wall. If they did, and I have to assume that is the case, I won't have long before they alert the other conspirators.

The upper floor of offices is empty. There is a stairway at either end leading down to the lower offices and the warehouse floor, but I use the sword first to check that the offices below me are also vacant before heading below. Downstairs, I find myself in a similar corridor, stretching the length of the building with offices on either side. The line of offices is broken by the front door on one side and the entry to the warehouse on the other. Starting from the stairs, I go from office to office, looking for one that might have a window that looks out on the warehouse.

The only one I find is in a conference room near the entry to the warehouse floor. A set of Venetian blinds covers it, slats closed tight, light from the warehouse bleeding around the side into the room. I close the door and crouch beside the window, lifting up one of the slats to peer out on the floor. It offers me a clear view of the transfer engines, where Lasinha and his people are moving equipment and boxes into position to send across.

As I watch, a transfer takes place. I can feel the pull of the other universe even from where I am crouching. I am able to see the other place taking shape in the warehouse, the walls fading away. A new world emerges, an unrecognizable one. I see the walls of a broken building where everything will be transferred. There are already stacks of equipment sitting in the shadows against one wall. There is a gaping hole where another wall has been eaten away down to the foundation, and beyond I can see further ruined buildings, many of them overgrown with tropical plants or flooded with swampy water.

The channels close as I try to memorize every detail in the desperate hope I can find some clue to as to where they are and in what universe. The image vanishes, far too soon, and the half-dozen people begin gathering the next load of equipment for transfer. I am looking at them again, trying to see if the numbers are the same as before, when a hiss erupts behind me.

I whirl around, jumping to my feet, the sword leaping from the hilt, all in one motion. Facing me is Harith. His face seems even more broken than I remember from before, as if it has been taken apart and stitched back together many times. He fixes me with a hate-filled glare and snarls. "I see Gloria has failed in her duties again."

A sword extends from his hand, and he raises it, pointing it toward me. "You've stayed hidden long enough, Aurellano. Let's see what you are truly capable of."

32

Harith takes a step toward me, and I back away, bumping into the blinds. The Acolyte smiles, a terrible thing to see on his marred face. "You should be afraid, Aurellano. The hour is getting late for the universes and for you. If I strike you down now, it will be too late for you to regenerate in some other body."

The voices rise within me, and in my fear I allow one of them to speak. "Are you so sure you're right? There are more means in the universes than you will ever know."

The Acolyte's smile doesn't fade, though he tightens his grip on the sword, its colors shifting with the pressure of his hand. "In that case, we'll just have to keep you alive and incapacitated until the end. Or I can just leave you here. Once the transfers are complete, there's nothing you can do to stop us."

"You underestimate me at your own peril," I say, though I share none of the confidence of the voice that speaks.

Harith's eyes glaze over, growing distant. "The Aurellano is here in the building. Complete the transfers. I will hold it here."

As he finishes speaking, he flicks his wrist, and the

blade leaps toward me. I just barely manage to parry his blow, gasping with fear. Harith chuckles to himself, taking a confident step into the room. Josefina returns from the multitudes, and suddenly I am attacking, my sword moving with a blur I never thought possible. Harith parries each of my blows, seemingly with ease, though the smile has gone from his face and there is sheen of sweat on his forehead.

"No," he says, slightly out of breath, in response to a query. "Get everyone across. I will join you when I can."

"If you can," I say, attacking him again with a lunge for his knees. "What happens if you don't make it across? Will you die with the rest of us?"

He dodges it easily, slapping my blade away. "That won't happen. I'll see what lies beyond the universes. And I'll know what your kind have denied us for so long."

He says the last with a furious shout, launching himself at me. I jump out of the way, stumbling a little on my feet. By the time I regain my balance, his blade is lashing out. I move to parry its edge and do, but not without the blow knocking me back on my heels. Harith moves with frightening speed, flicking his wrist so that the flat of his blade snaps at me. I raise my sword to defend myself, but it is too late.

The blade strikes me in the shoulder, the force of the blow lifting me off the ground and sending me into the wall. I crash through the drywall, catching my hip against a stud so hard that it goes numb. There is dust and insulation everywhere, and I am seized by an overwhelming urge to sneeze and scratch at myself.

I get unsteadily to my feet, moving my hip to try shake the numbness from it. Another voice in my head tells me that the blades respond to the approach of edges, automatically shaping themselves to protect against a cutting blow. But they can be fooled, as I was, by an attack from the flat of the blade struck fast enough. It suggests another trick that perhaps Harith doesn't know. Josefina steps aside, and this new voice takes command.

I stand my ground, making sure to favor my hip, shifting the weapon from hand to hand. Harith approaches, coming in slowly, a predator sensing the kill. I squeeze the hilt, holding it tighter and tighter. It grows warmer, as hot as it was when I passed through the ceiling. As Harith is about to begin his attack, I drive my blade into the floor. It dissolves, leaving nothing beneath his feet. He drops into the hole I have created, a cartoon character come to life, crying out in pain as he lands awkwardly. The sword is still in his hand, but the blade has gone from it, and he looks up at me, fear in his eyes, crouching so that the floor comes up to his shoulders.

I level my sword at his throat, the tip of the blade breaking the skin. "Tell me where you're going," I say. Harith grimaces, but he refuses to speak. "Tell me, or you won't live to see this through."

"The unmaking will happen whether I'm there or not. If it's not for me to see what lies beyond this prison, then so be it. I'll die happily knowing that others can."

I laugh, pressing the blade harder against his throat. Blood begins to trickle around it. "You expect me to believe that bullshit?"

Harith opens his mouth, but doesn't speak, trying to formulate some sort of reply. He doesn't get a chance, for the Seeker bursts through the door, surprising us both. Harith seizes the distraction provided by the Seeker to duck away from my blade, sending his own out to attack me. It puts me back on my heels, ducking and parrying, giving him just enough time and space to scramble out of the pit.

He doesn't bother to attack, the chasm between us providing enough of a defense. Instead, he turns and runs for the wall to the warehouse, where he frantically cuts an escape route. I move to intercept him, my sword raised for a killing blow. But before I can unleash my blade, the Seeker steps between us, holding his hand up sternly.

"We must go."

"I'm not leaving until I find out what he knows."

I move to shove the Seeker aside, but he grasps my shoulder and holds me back with impossible strength. "If you stay, you will die, Laila Aurellano. They have set an unbinding pulse to go off. We have to go now."

Harith glances back with a malicious grin on his face, so I know what the Seeker is saying is true. He darts through the hole he has cut toward the transfer engines, where a channel is beginning to close. I catch a last glimpse of the ruined building, overwhelmed by foliage and swamp, as it begins to fade, the connection between the universes breaking down. There may not be time for him to make it.

My gaze shifts past Harith and the transfer point to what looks like a massive spotlight set up near the back wall. It is pointed at an angle toward the roof. The multitude within me begins to scream as one to leave, but I still don't want to. There is still time. There is still a chance...

The Seeker pulls me by the shoulder, dragging me out of the conference room toward the front entrance. "Live to fight another day, Laila Aurellano."

I want to argue, but the chorus within me agrees with the Seeker. At last I relent, running with him out the door and across the street. He doesn't stop, and I follow, both of us picking up speed as we go. We are half a block away from the warehouse when I feel the air begin to change behind me. The hairs on the back of my head all seem to rise, pulled by some form of electricity. Next, my legs and arms seem to drag with each stride, caught in some gravitational field. As soon as I begin to feel that inescapable pull from the warehouse, the Seeker turns around and tackles me to the ground, holding me to the pavement.

The gravity of the pulse gets stronger and stronger, feeling as though it is going to tear my joints from their sockets. Litter, loose twigs, and stones along the street begin to tumble haphazardly in the direction of the warehouse. A few hit me in the face, but I don't dare move to brush them aside. It feels important to keep my hands on the ground and clutching the sword.

The Seeker doesn't let go, holding me down, seemingly unaffected by the force. He looks back down the street toward the warehouse, until the gravity reaches its pinnacle, when he buries his head beside me on the street. The force shifts in that moment, expelling everything it drew to it, sending a shower of detritus outward on a blast of wind. It rains down on us, some of the particles striking hard enough to leave a mark. Only when the shower has passed does the Seeker release his grip on me. We both sit up looking back down the street.

The warehouse is gone, with only a hole in the ground remains to mark where it once stood. The building beside now looks a ruin, with massive chunks of its wall and roof just gone. Its foundation must have been weakened grievously, for it is already beginning to lean. Though I cannot be sure in the darkness, it seems there are chunks of concrete missing from the freeway above as well.

I cannot take my eyes from the site of the explosion and the gaping maw that is left. We get up, both of us a little shaky on our feet, and I start to walk toward it before the Seeker stops me again.

"The ground may be unstable there."

"We need to see if there's anything left. If there's any clues to where they went."

The Seeker shakes his head. "There's nothing left. That's why they turned on the pulse."

I take another step forward, reluctant to acknowledge the truth in what he is saying. "We have to find them. They're trying to destroy the universes."

The Seeker cocks his head, a faint smile on his face. "It seems we have much to discuss."

I turn to look at him. "We do."

"Then we should go. The others who were after you

have likely crossed over as well, but they may return. We shouldn't be here when they do."

I nod, still reluctant to go, though he is right. There is no more to be gained staying here. The Seeker is still smiling slightly, reminding me of Lasinha for some reason, and raising my suspicions.

"What the hell is going on Ngurawan?"

His smile broadens. "As I said, we have much to discuss."

33

We return to Jakarta—a Jakarta of some future, I now understand—at Ngurawan's insistence. It feels like a waste of time, though none of the multitude protest. I still forget that time is not linear with the transfers. No matter when and where Lasinha and the others have gone, we should still be able to transfer to a moment before they enact their plan and give ourselves a chance to stop it. Of course, they know that too, and they will be prepared now that I have slipped through their fingers.

The building we return to is the same one the Seeker brought me to before. The room he has left me in may even be the same, though all the rooms in this place look similar to my eyes. Gleaming and blank surfaces that can sprout furniture, visuals, and who knows what else. Nano-walls, I now know they are called. The Seeker has gone to get me a change of clothes, leaving me to my impatience and all these questions and doubts.

"I thought it wasn't safe for me to be here," I say as the wall dissolves behind me.

"It wasn't."

I whirl around from the viewscreen of the city to find Suon facing me, holding a change of clothes.

"It's good to see you too, Laila," she says, handing me the clothes. I take them awkwardly, afraid to touch her and discover that she is but a specter of my imagination. "But we don't have to worry about that anymore. Evidently the ones who were after you have disappeared."

"They have." My mouth is dry, and I find it difficult to speak. Can it really be her? "I watched you die."

She blinks and laughs nervously. "Well, it wasn't me. When we were separated they asked me all sorts of questions about who you really were. I figured it had to be the people the Seeker warned us about, so I used the emergency transfer. They left it with me. I just thought they were amateurs. That's what it seemed like, anyway. I only realized after that they wanted me to use it. They wanted you stranded there with them."

"I watched you die. It was you. It looked just like you." Even as I say the words, I know it isn't entirely true. I had my doubts in the aftermath of the moment. The charade at the school always felt like it was a play put on solely for my benefit. And yet, my mind keeps insisting that she is dead, that she cannot be standing before me, that this is some sort of trick. The Seeker must be in league with Lasinha and this is another charade to distract me from what needs to be done.

Several voices give me potential explanations. An automaton, printed from a 3D rendering of surveillance footage while she was imprisoned, seems the most likely. Faces are difficult, though, the voices tell me, particularly expressions and reactions. As are movements. They couldn't trust that the automaton would fool me, even at that distance, so they made sure her hair obscured her face and shot her as soon as possible. Even then I still had doubts, though I didn't trust them.

I wince at all the voices, putting a hand to my head. It is hard to deal with. Before, they were just a distant din that I could safely ignore. But now they want to be heard. Part of me thinks, despite Josefina's reassurance to the contrary, that they want to take control. That they don't trust me to save the universes and want to see it through for themselves. Why wouldn't they?

Suon has her usual expression of concern, which used to infuriate me and now leaves me aching with guilt. "I don't know what to tell you. I'm sorry. I panicked in the moment. But I thought it would be better to go back to the Seeker. I thought he would be able to find you and extract you."

I shake my head ruefully. "But he couldn't find me. Not without the transfer device."

"No. He wouldn't even look. We could have picked up your trail somehow, though. At least the trail of the others with you."

"Maybe he could have. They were very careful, though. They didn't want anyone tracking them. Anyway, I made it out alive." I touch a finger to this face as though to confirm the matter.

Suon studies me carefully. "He said you would. I wasn't sure. I thought you wanted to die."

I'm unable to answer her, so I turn to look out on the future Jakarta. An afternoon storm is passing through the city, the clouds moving closer. Soon they will engulf our tower. It is thrilling in a way to watch its approach, to wonder if we will be consumed.

The Seeker enters the room, so I turn away from the viewscreen. Suon is watching me, unable to hide her hurt. There are many things I want to say, but I have no words to say them. Someday soon I will have to try. But for now, there are more pressing matters.

"You've let her know that I've kept my end of the bargain?" The Seeker looks from Suon to me.

Before she can speak, I say, "I'll want to see for myself. When all this is done."

"Of course. I have returned Gabriel to his world as well. My people are watching him, in case someone managed to connect him to what happened there. But I don't think any of those people will."

"They're all gone," I say, nodding. "Getting ready for the unmaking."

"Unmaking of what?" Suon says.

"The universes. And all of us with it."

The Seeker looks at me with the full force of his eyes. They don't frighten me now. He cannot see within me. Voices in the multitude show me how to see to that.

"You've learned a great deal since we last met," Ngurawan says, giving me an appraising look.

"I have. But not enough to make a difference. We have to find them and stop them. I'm going to need your help." I look at both of them, feeling vaguely ridiculous about my pronouncement.

"I don't understand," Suon says. "Why do they want to unmake the universes? Are they suicidal?"

"They're like we were with the Church. Ideologues. They think they can unbind the universes and, in doing so, escape them. They think this is a prison, a simulacrum of the real universes, or whatever might be out there. And we are condemned to live our lives here again and again."

"They may not be wrong." Ngurawan looks at both of us for our reactions. "The Society, as you call us, has a similar understanding of things. The universes began with what we call the big bang, though we cannot seem to go back to that beginning in our crossings. Some have tried. Regardless, the universes multiply from there, propagating themselves into infinities.

"But the laws of entropy always apply. The propagation reaches a point where too much energy is lost. The expansion is too great. There are two theories on what happens when that point is reached. One is that the universes keep expanding, gradually dissipating into nothingness. That is the end, so to speak. The other is that the underlying system doesn't allow that to happen. When the propagation reaches its tipping point, it ceases. The universes snap back to the beginning of things, and we begin again. Of course, even then, entropy must hold. The system can only repeat itself so long before too much energy is lost. The engine must eventually run out of fuel and burn itself out."

"That's why you're fighting the Acolytes," I say. "You're trying to slow down the propagation of the universes."

"In part, yes. We've seen things begin to break down, and it seems that the pace quickens the more universes we infiltrate and propagate alternatives to. The universes are connected, of that there is no doubt, but that doesn't mean we should be crossing between them. It is also not our place to rule over whole planets and timelines. Those should be your futures to live as you choose."

Suon pinches the bridge of her nose, frowning deeply. "So what you're saying is: the universes are fake."

"That's what the Unmakers believe. And it is true that the universes may be constructed. A simulation that runs its course, so to speak. There are some in the Society who believe this to be the case, which is why they think it doesn't matter what we do here. Others disagree." Ngurawan says it as though these are mild disputes hashed out over a drink in a bar.

"It doesn't matter whether it's all a simulation, or whatever you want to call it," I say. "We're all alive in it. It's real to us. It's life. What happens to the universes happens to all of us. That's what Unmakers don't understand."

Suon still looks perplexed. "Who are these Unmakers? The Society? Acolytes?"

"Yes. And others too. Lasinha is one. Gloria too. Meredith seems to be along for the ride." I turn to face the Seeker. "Why did you send me back to them? What do you know about the Aurellano?"

"Very little, I'm afraid. That's why I sent you back. To see what they would do. If I had known you were so central to their cosmos, I would have proceeded differently. But I know very little about them as well. They've hidden themselves in the Church and the Society. Made it look as though they are taking part in our wars, but in actuality using it as cover to achieve their own ends. Which, if you are correct, are unimaginable."

"I am," I say gravely.

His answer reassures me somewhat, though the voices within me disagree. You cannot trust him, they say. He may be an Unmaker. I cannot deny the possibility. He has yet to tell me the whole truth in any of our encounters. The first time we spoke, he did say that we would be there together at the end. What end was he referring to? The Church or the universes?

The multitude stirs with different answers, and my sight goes blurry. Suon comes over to take my arm, worried that I am going to fall. I wave her away, shaking my head, though I am terrified. The Aurellanos are trying to take control. I cannot get the thought from my head no matter how hard I try.

I blink and focus of Ngurawan. "When did you begin to suspect something was going on?"

If the Seeker realizes I am interrogating him, he doesn't acknowledge it. He is relaxed, his face betraying nothing. "You were the clue, once I realized something of your true nature. Why bother putting your mind with another in a body? It is inherently unstable, yet the Acolytes were quite good at keeping someone like Ana or Morris passive and under control. Why not just do that? So there was something about you they were scared of.

"When we began to investigate, I knew they had given you the name Aurellano to try to hide you. Yet the more we looked into things, the more we heard about an Aurellano. But they didn't make sense, because it definitely wasn't you they were talking about. It was many people in many universes, and yet one individual all the same. Or so it seemed. So I sent you back to the Church. I figured whoever had done this, whoever feared what you were, had to still be there."

"The conduit," Suon says. There is anger in her eyes, which gladdens me. Still protective, Suon, after all I have done to her.

"Yes. At the same time, I conducted my own investigation of the Church and its activities. I discovered what you did: the Church was a shell. A façade. So the question became, why bother? Someone wanted the proxy war to continue. But I didn't know who or what they were trying to hide. I just knew you were the key, because this Church that wasn't a Church had one activity they were solely focused on. Getting you back, no matter the cost."

"That wasn't their only activity," I say. "It was just the only one you could see."

The Seeker nods, and Suon looks at me for an explanation. "He cannot see me the way he can you. He can't see any of the people the Acolytes played with. That's why they did it, to be able to hide people from the Seekers. To hide what they were doing."

"And so that the people themselves didn't know what they were doing." Suon lets out a low whistle. "No wonder they could keep all this hidden. So what do we do now?"

I smile at her, feeling relieved. My greatest fear was that she would turn her back on me. Especially because I am no longer Laila. That person is gone, along with that body. I am another thing now, though I don't know what. The thought makes me tremble.

"We need to find them and stop them."

"How?" Suon says. We both look at Ngurawan.

"I cannot find them," he replies. "They are small in number, and they've hidden themselves too well. They know our techniques, and they know, better than anyone, how to frustrate them. If we knew what they were planning to do, it might help. Also, why it matters that you not be there."

I sigh with frustration. "I don't know what they're trying to do. Just unmake the universes. But I don't know how. No one does. All I know is that I'm the only one who can stop it."

Suon lets out a sigh, somewhere between disbelief and laughter. The Seeker does not appear surprised.

"It's true," I say. "I am the Aurellano."

When I am done explaining to them what I am, what I have become, I am met with silence. I wait to let them absorb it all, though I am impatient to forge ahead. But though it is easy for me to understand—the multitude lies within me, a roiling mass that is never silent—for them it must seem impossible. Ngurawan especially, since I am the proof that he is wrong, that the universes are a construct. Things that evolve and are natural do not have fail-safes built in them.

Suon is the first to speak, looking up at me hesitantly. "How will you know what to do when the time comes? Assuming we can find them."

I shrug, though she has pinpointed my greatest fear. "I don't know. There are many Aurellanos within me. With our shared experience, we will know what to do."

"You hope."

"I hope." I attempt a smile. "Anyway. We have to find them first for any of this to matter."

Ngurawan goes to one of the walls, and a screen emerges, showing a model of the universes and how they might interact. He studies it, putting a hand to his chin. "If I were trying to unmake the universes, I would break the connections between them. All of them are connected causally, even if it is at a great remove—that's why we can cross between them. If they have found a way to sever those connections, the consequences would be grave. I don't know if it would unmake the universes, but it might."

"Can they do that?" Suon asks. "I could see breaking apart two universes. But all of them at once?"

"You do it in the crossing channels," I say, though it is

not me who says it.

"Perhaps." Ngurawan looks at me closely, as though what I have said surprises him. "They would have direct access to the connections there."

"All of them?"

"When you cross the universes, it appears seamless, going from one directly to another. But there are always a few seconds when you are in neither. That is the crossing. From there, theoretically, you can go anywhere, to any universe. The equipment doesn't allow that, of course. It's too dangerous. You could be stranded in the crossings and…" The Seeker gestures with his hand.

"That's that," Suon says, and Ngurawan nods.

"But the equipment could take them to the crossing?" I ask.

The Seeker considers my question. "It would take some reprogramming, but yes, it could. The question is how long someone could remain there to do anything. We have no idea. People who get stranded in the crossings tend not to come back to report on their experiences."

"And if they set off an unbinding weapon of some kind in there?" I ask, but I don't even need to hear the answer. The chorus within me has already told me. This is what they are doing.

"I don't know what the consequences of that would be," Ngurawan says. "No one has ever done it before, to my knowledge."

"I bet people have," Suon says grimly. "The half-things the Acolytes made. You can bet Lasinha sent some of them in there to see what was possible."

"Perhaps. Though they would need a way of seeing if their tests were successful."

"I think we can assume they've managed that," I say.

"They will still need someone to go into the crossing to do whatever they have planned. Assuming we are correct." The Seeker shrugs. It is the first I have ever seen him being uncertain, but I find it oddly reassuring. He seems human as he never did before.

"If we're right, and this is how they're going to do it, then they could do it from literally anywhere," Suon says, sounding defeated. "All they need is the transfer equipment."

At her words, something clicks in my mind, a thought that has been lingering half-formed taking sudden shape. "You're right. They can do it from anywhere. So the answer to where they are isn't how, it's who."

Both Suon and Ngurawan look at me blankly, clearly not following.

"You said the Church has only been focused on one thing," I say, looking at the Seeker. "Me. But that's not quite true. There's one other thing they've spent a lot of time looking for, even before they put me in this body. For the longest time, I thought that was why they were after me."

Ngurawan frowns. "I'm not sure I understand what you're referring to."

I smile, feeling hopeful in a way I have not before. "Do we still have De Gofroy's files?"

34

When I first read Lasinha's file on the hard drive we stole from De Gofroy's study, I did not give it much attention. There was little there that I didn't already know, after all, given we had come up together in the Church. He was there before me, of course, but both of us had cut our teeth with Osahi and the Protectors. We carried out the same kinds of missions, made the same dubious compromises, and could be kept in line because all those details were there in our files to be used against us if the need arose.

Even our backgrounds were similar. I grew up in Medicine Hat and he in Calgary, both of us in seemingly happy homes that were anything but. We both left our families as soon as we possibly could, leading itinerant lives that somehow brought us within De Gofroy's orbit. So many of us who came to the faith were the same. Aeida. Gabriel Arajuano. Molijc.

That was the story I recall from Lasinha's file, but it was not the truth. At least not all of it. I suspect that the details of his early life are more or less as he recounted them when he underwent the pre-screens and Protocols under the Eye. They would have to be in order for him to escape suspicion and rise through the ranks. But the story of his conversion, of his coming to the faith and becoming a Regent, happened much earlier than his arrival at the Church. He became an Unmaker, as the voices in my head have taken to calling them, and they sent him to the Society and the Church to prepare the way for the end of the universes.

I remember well the day I removed his file, along with Molijc's and Ana's. I was acting on instinct, thinking only that it might prove useful at some point down the line. Later, when things went bad between us, I studied both Molijc and Lasinha's files intently, looking for anything I might use against them. There was nothing I saw then that struck me as revelatory.

But there was something in there that he feared. Why else would he spend so much time trying to recover it? Why else would he tamp Ana, when doing so would only bring more scrutiny of him from me? It never occurred to me that he was worried about exposing himself. I always assumed it was something to do with Molijc that they wanted hidden. Aeida thought much the same. But then, he would. Harith and Lasinha were the ones guiding him.

Suon still has the hard drive with her, having carried it back when she used the emergency transfer engine. All those weeks after Aeida stole it from the Grand Regent's safe, following an unconscious impulse put there by the Seeker, I never bothered to look at it. There was only the past there, a past I was trying my best to avoid.

"What do you think you're going to find in there?" she says after retrieving it from her quarters.

"I don't know." My belief, hope, really, is that what is in the file will lead me to where Lasinha and the rest of the Unmakers are now. It seems likely there will be some clue held within those reports that indicates who he really was. I can only hope it will also shed light on where the Unmakers might go. They will want it to happen someplace significant, I tell myself, a place to begin the journey from these universes to whatever lies beyond.

"It's all we have to go on," I add. Which is true. It is also terrifying.

It takes some time for Ngurawan to find equipment that will allow us to access the drive and do what I need to do. "The primitive and the advanced sometimes talk past each other," he says with what passes for a wry grin.

In the end, he finds a portal that will connect the drive to his systems. When we connect them, a screen materializes from one of the walls, the image appearing just as it would on one of the screens in my universe. The familiarity of that is a little unnerving. Ngurawan gestures for me to sit in front of the screen, and as he does, a chair emerges from the floor. As I sit down, a small desk with a keyboard and mouse form out of the wall at the level of my hands.

Feeling self-conscious, I begin to enter the commands that will give me access to the drive. Though it has been so long since I did any coding, and even longer since I hid the files, I have no trouble remembering what I need to enter. It all flows back as if I did it yesterday. I can see myself sitting in Molijc's quarters in the tower, surrounded by darkness, the screen illuminating my desperate face. A face that will never be mine again.

"What are these?" Ngurawan says, interrupting my thoughts.

I blink at him in surprise. Suon is looking at me with concern. "These are De Gofroy's files. It's what you sent me back to the Church to find."

He shakes his head. "We sent you back to find the conduit. To find out what was going on. That you responded to that by recovering the files…"

"Suggests I'm on the right track," I say.

"Perhaps," he says. "But how did Lasinha not realize the files he was looking for were here?"

I smile. "Because I deleted them. Cleaned the hard drive. I kept copies for myself, and he knew that. But he didn't seem too concerned. Until Ana was meeting with someone who knew what he was. Then he must have realized there was something in here that could reveal that too." I tap the screen, which is now filled with lines of code.

"By then, I'd already hidden them. I could have made a million copies and put them in a million different universes, but I was worried that if they ever decided to turn the Acolytes loose on me, I'd reveal the locations. And I was right, because I did reveal where I'd hidden them when the time came. They just didn't believe me."

Suon's eyes widen. "Because you hid them on the original hard drive."

"Last place they'd ever look, I figured." I wink at her and return to the screen. It takes some time to call them up. I embedded them deep in the drive's infrastructure, to protect against someone coming and looking for them. They are also encrypted, and only I have the key, which I memorized. Thirty-two random characters, which I now enter.

"Here they are," I say when I have them, leaning forward in my chair. Suon and Ngurawan peer over my shoulders to read what is there. I feel a twinge of excitement as I click on the folder for Lasinha's pre-screens and first Protocols. That excitement quickly dims as we read through page after page of tedious and extraneous detail about Lasinha's early life. Did anyone ever read any of these reports? Over my shoulder, someone sighs.

"How many reports are there?" Ngurawan asks.

"You don't want to know."

"Do we have time for this?" Suon looks at the Seeker, who shrugs.

"Unless they are destroying the universes right this moment in this universe, time is not the issue. Although I'm not entirely certain of the impact destroying the universes would have on the nature of time within them. It is hard to say. Will all the universes end at exactly the same moment in time when they destroy the universe they are in? If that's the case, then we may already be far too late. Or we may have millennia to arrange things. There is also the fact that time proceeds differently in different universes."

"Forget I asked," Suon says dryly.

I am ignoring them both, scrolling through the transcription of one of Lasinha's final Protocols, the words barely registering. Something catches my eye as it goes past, and I quickly go back. I read it through twice to make sure I am understanding what it says correctly. But there can be no mistaking it.

"This is it," I say, highlighting the text. Both Suon and Ngurawan turn their attention back to the screen. Suon leans closer, putting a hand on my shoulder, not even realizing she is doing so. I hold my breath and close my eyes at her touch, opening my eyes to read the words again:

My family goes back centuries in Calgary. We were part of the fabric of the place, or so it seemed. Yet I never felt a part of it or of them. It was all so broken by the time I was born.

"I don't understand." Ngurawan puts a finger to his lips, his doubt plain.

Suon realizes the significance immediately. "A black man would not have family going back centuries in Calgary. Not in my universe, anyway."

"Mine either," I say. "Two hundred years tops. And none of those people would feel their families had been part of the fabric of the place. Hell, I was still dealing with racist shit when I was growing up."

"So he is not of your universe," Ngurawan says. "That would certainly have exposed him as a Society agent if anyone ever noticed. But I don't see how it helps us now. We already know he is one of these Unmakers. What it doesn't tell us is what universe he is actually from. And when. If you're right and that's where they've gone."

I swivel my chair around to face them. "It is. When we went back to the tower after Black Diamond, he noticed the hard drive was missing. It set him off. He was still worried about it. If we find out where he's actually from, we find the rest of them."

Suon shakes her head. "Even if we can figure out where and when he's from, how do we figure out exactly where in Calgary and when they've actually gone?"

"Once we know the universe, that will be easy," Ngurawan says. "You cannot remove all traces of a transfer. You can only obscure it. But if we know which Calgary they've gone to, we'll be able to find them. The question is how do we find out which Calgary it is?"

They both turn to look at me. I sigh, putting a hand to my head. This is a moment I have both dreaded and longed for, but it is not the circumstance I would have chosen. "We need to speak to Ana."

35

Ngurawan makes the arrangements, sending us and Ana on a series of transfers through half a dozen different universes, until we meet in the same one. When we leave, we will each go through another series of universes to obscure our connections and our crossing. Though he assures me that the precautions he has taken will hide our trail from anyone who might try to follow me, I am not reassured. I still have doubts about his true loyalty. Yet again I am putting Ana in danger. What price will she pay this time?

The place the Seeker has chosen for this encounter is a grass-covered plain under a vast and vivid blue sky. A sky like home, except there are no buildings on this prairie, or any signs of human habitation nearby. Ngurawan leads us forward through the thick grass, which comes up to our knees, until the plain drops away, revealing the confluence of two rivers. Though the shape of the rivers and their confluence are different, because it is another universe at another time, I recognize where we are immediately. The joining of the Bow and the Elbow.

"Where is Calgary?" I feel ridiculous saying it. The wind rises, coming hard from the west.

The answer is both obvious and yet isn't, given we could be here at any time. "It hasn't been built yet."

"What if someone sees us here? Aren't you worried about distorting another universe?"

Ngurawan glances back at me with his unblinking eyes. "No one will. The nearest people are at least a day's walk away. It doesn't matter, though, whether we encounter them or not. We have already distorted the universe and created an alternate. I judged it worth the price, given the alternative."

"How generous of you," Suon says. I shoot her a quick look, and she makes a sour but apologetic face.

As we approach the riverbanks, Ana emerges from the tangle of willow and poplar trees, making her way toward us. A Black Robe follows, keeping her distance, signaling to Ngurawan that all is well. Ana flinches at the sight of me, coming to a halt, before taking a deep breath and coming forward to meet us.

"Thank you for agreeing to meet us." Ngurawan inclines his head.

"Didn't feel like I had much of a choice." Ana cracks a bitter smile, glancing at the Black Robe who lingers behind her.

"I apologize. There was some urgency in the matter." The Seeker glances at me, and Ana shudders. Seeing it is like a knife cutting into me.

"I'd like a moment alone with her." I look at Ngurawan, who nods at the Black Robe. Both of them move to stand together, though they don't speak, their backs to the river. Suon joins them after squeezing my arm and giving me a knowing look that makes me want to weep.

Ana shifts uncomfortably and opens her mouth, as though she wants to call everyone back. She struggles to keep the emotions from showing on her face. "Is he still in there?"

"No. They removed him. He's…gone for good."

Ana crosses her arms, holding herself close, looking down at the grass dancing in the wind, unable to look at me. At this face that is not mine. "That's good. It's the least of what he deserves."

"I'm sorry that you still have to see…this." I hold up my hands that are shaking with revulsion. The voices have gone quiet. I almost wish they would return, take over, and drag me away from here. "It's the only body I have left."

"I can't believe Molijc would ever destroy your body."

"Lasinha did." The reality of it seems to descend upon me with the words stated out in the open. A black cloud threatens to swallow me, to send me spinning deeper and deeper. The other voices within me cry out against it, pulling me away from that inky tidal pool.

There is no future there, they say. There is no future anywhere, I want to reply. But there may be if I can somehow stay strong now.

Ana is quiet and still, staring out at the horizon. She will not look at this. She will not meet my eyes.

"I'm sorry I wasn't able to help you, Ana." The words feel so hollow. Inadequate.

"Not as sorry as I am, Laila."

"I know. I'll never forgive myself for that. For any of this, really. It was all so wrong, and I should have known better. But I didn't want to see it. I wanted to believe in what De Gofroy said."

Ana bites her lip, to stop herself from saying something or hold back her feelings. I let out a sigh heavy with my own emotions. "Anyway, you probably want to be done with all this. I'm sorry for dragging you back again. He promised me that he would restore you and send you to whatever universe you wanted to be in. I'm going to make him keep that promise."

"You can't trust him, Laila. You can't trust any of them." Her voice is so low that I can barely hear it over the wind.

I look over at Ngurawan, who is ever watchful, his face

expressionless. It is likely he can still hear us, I realize, with his various enhancements. "I know." I smile halfheartedly. "But I have something he needs." And I need his help, though I don't say that.

"It's not worth it. None of this is worth it. Look what happened to us." She reaches up to brush the tears from her eyes.

"It's all over now. The Church is dead."

"It was never about the Church, Laila. They used us for this war of theirs. They ruined our lives, and for what? The Society is still here. He can still go wherever the fuck he wants and do whatever he wants to whoever he decides." She turns to direct her harangue in the direction of the Seeker and the Black Robes.

"Ana, you're right," I say, my tone gentle. She looks at me with fury in her eyes, ready to fight. "You're right. But after this, you're free. I promise, Ana. Go wherever you want. Live the life you want."

"None of us is free, Laila."

"No. I guess not." I put my hands in my pockets and shrug. "I saw your father."

There is a sharp intake of breath, and she turns her back to me, facing the river. I go to stand beside her, watching the flow of the water. "He seemed happy. At peace." Until I got there. But I can't say that. "They've let him be, Ana. With the Church over, they'll let you be too. You can find a place to be happy."

She is quiet a long time, the wind rising and falling, rippling across the grass. "What about you, Laila?"

"I'll never be free of this. It's a part of me. Who I am now." It is hard to admit. The multitudes will always be there, always. It is too much to bear.

"I don't understand."

"Better if you don't."

Ana looks at me for the first time, really looks at me. I want to turn away, but I force myself to meet her gaze. "I'm sorry, Laila."

I smile, though my heart is breaking. "Don't be. Live your life. You have that chance. It's just what I am."

She swallows, turning back to face the river. "I hope you find your peace too."

"I'm going to try," I say, meaning it, though I have no idea what peace for me could be. "But first I need your help."

"What do you need?"

"The woman you were with when Lasinha and Aeida took you. Who was she?"

"You're going after Lasinha, are you? What's the point now? Molijc exiled him. But you know that."

"Molijc is dead," I say. Her eyebrow quirks with an unspoken question, and I shake my head. "Lasinha is responsible for that. He's responsible for all of this, really."

"So you're out for revenge? Why bother now? It will never end, Laila. It never does." She points at Ngurawan. "Ask him how long he's been fighting this war."

"I can't make right what was done to us, Ana. I know that. Nothing I do to Lasinha will change that. But I can stop him and all his people from harming anyone else. That's what I have to do, but first I have to find him. The woman who was with you, she was from his universe, wasn't she?"

The wind swirls, sending Ana's hair into her face. She brushes it aside. "Yes, she was. I was trying to discover who the conduit was—I'm sure our mutual friend has told you all about that. I started digging into everyone's pasts. Lasinha's didn't make any sense at all. He had no family in Calgary. There was no trace of his past anywhere that I could find.

"That told me all I needed to know, but it didn't feel like enough with him, you know. He would just smile and come up with some bullshit explanation to wave it all away. I wanted him dead to rights. I wanted to destroy the Church. I didn't care what the Seeker wanted, and I sure as hell didn't trust him. I just wanted to make sure I destroyed the three of you, like you destroyed my life and Dad's."

Ana goes quiet, letting out a soft breath of air and closing her eyes, as if saying this has wounded her. She glances over at the Seeker. "If I'd trusted him, maybe this all would have been different. But I didn't."

"Don't blame yourself," I say. "He doesn't make it easy to trust. None of them do. And you couldn't know which of us was the real threat. All of us were a little mad. We destroyed the Church and the faith. I can see that now. I couldn't then."

She begins to speak and then stops herself, shaking her head. "I started to go through the Society, looking for hints that Lasinha was a member. I figured there had to be something somewhere. They can't remove all traces. I found someone who remembered him. They'd gone through some sort of training together. Right after that, you tried to bring me back to the Church."

"Lasinha wanted you there," I say, confirming her suspicion.

"Once I was back in the fold, I couldn't make contact with the guy again. Lasinha was watching me far too closely. I should have told Ngurawan then." She shakes her head and smiles bitterly. "I just couldn't, though. I didn't know who to trust. The woman found me while I was in the other universe. She'd been trying to trace Lasinha through the Society too. I wonder what happened to her."

"He killed her, I'm sure. Did she tell you why she was looking for him?"

Ana shakes her head. "All she would say was that he was more dangerous than I could imagine. She didn't try to fight him at all when he came to confront us with—" She almost says you, but catches herself before she does. "I've never understood that."

"Did she tell you where she was from?"

"She said it was a ruined world. Everything was either

desert or swamp. She called it the 'fenworld at the end of time.' Said it like I would understand what it meant."

I turn in Ngurawan's direction, and he approaches, followed by Suon and the Black Robe. After telling him what Ana has told me, I ask if he can find Lasinha's world.

"There are several universes where the locals give that name to the earth, as you might imagine," the Seeker says. "It would help if I had her name. I could trace her through the Society records."

"She called herself Aghavni," Ana says. "I don't know if that was her real name."

"That may be enough. We shall see." The Seeker inclines his head and looks to the Black Robe, who moves toward the river, looking to Ana to follow him.

"I guess this is it," she says, looking at me.

"It is best that we don't linger here," Ngurawan says, and I nod.

Ana doesn't budge. "I imagine I won't be seeing you again."

"No," I say. "Better for you that we don't."

"Well, I hope I was some help. And I hope you get yourself out of this mess, Laila. Don't get yourself in too deep. It never ends."

I laugh. "I'm in plenty deep enough now. It's what I am. But you've helped more than you can know. So don't worry about me, Ana. Just go. Leave all this behind and live your life."

"I will."

Ana smiles, touching my arm, before following the Black Robe down to the river. I watch until she disappears into the willows and poplars. There is the faintest pull of another universe as a channel opens, and she is gone.

36

Stepping through the channel is like walking into a wall. The air is heavy with humidity, so thick it feels like I am breathing in exhaust fumes. Above, the sun glares through a break in a thick convoy of dark clouds making their way across the sky. It is not the sun I know. This one seems distorted and misshapen, a bent oval rather than a circle, while its color is a copper red.

"Don't look into it," Ngurawan says, though he has given us sunglasses to combat the effects of the rays. In addition to the glasses, I carry the unbinding sword, while Suon has a pulse rifle, as advanced as any I've seen. If the Seeker has a weapon, it is concealed on his person, but then he is a weapon on his own. All of us have a small transfer box, which Ngurawan also provided, which will return us back to the building in Jakarta should the situation demand it.

I flinch at his words and take in our surroundings. We are in the midst of several crumbling edifices, on what must once have been a large thoroughfare. Now it is overgrown with what appear to be mutated reeds and ferns. The ground is soft under my feet. Every step feels as though I am going to sink deep, the boggy mud pulling at my boots as I drag them free.

"So this is Calgary," Suon says, raising a skeptical eyebrow, and probing a frond of one of the plants with her boot. I move over to join her, and she glares at me. All I can muster in response is a pained expression.

Ngurawan ignores us both, scanning the area with his eyes, trying to locate any sign of the Unmakers or their equipment. It was through his efforts that we are here. He managed to track down Aghavni through Society records, tracing her to this universe. Now we just have to find them, which will be easier said than done.

"They were clever to come here," he says, shaking his head. "The sun interferes with my sensors and masks the signatures of the equipment."

We have transferred here roughly five hours before the Unmakers are crossing over, to give us time to locate their transfer point. Whether because of the effects of the sun, or the masking equipment the Unmakers used in setting up their transfers, the Seeker was unable to pinpoint exactly where they transferred to. The crossings were, in his words, blurred, the exact point at which this universe was connected to my own obscured. It is near to where we are now, no more than a few hours' walk, though we have no idea what direction.

We also have no clue if there is even anything here for the Seeker to trace. There were no transfers in the days, months, even year leading up to the crossing later today. If there had been, it might have given Ngurawan enough information to pinpoint where the transfers were going, despite the blurring. That there were no such earlier crossings suggests that all the transfers made from the warehouse are set to arrive here within the same narrow window of time, helping to further confuse any tracking we might do.

"We should be so lucky," Suon says. "How the hell do we find them if no one's coming for five hours?"

"I saw the crossing," I say, careful not to look directly

at her. "I would recognize the view, if we can somehow find those buildings."

Suon throws up her hands. "Sounds like we still have the same problem."

I resist the urge to snap at her. It is my fault she is she is as angry as she is. When we were in the transfer room in the Seeker's Jakarta headquarters, the channel just beginning to form, I was seized with terror that I could barely contain. I wanted to flee the room, to flee the universe itself. It was all too much. The Aurellanos. All those terrifying voices. They wouldn't stop. It is horrifying to feel the shape of someone's life—of thousands upon thousands of lives—within you, a part of you. In that moment, I could not bear it; the weight of it was too much.

I turned to Suon, regretting my words as soon as I spoke them. "You don't have to come. This isn't your fight."

"That's a hell of a thing to say to me."

I hung my head, my face flushing. "I'm sorry. I just don't want to see anyone else I know getting hurt."

She looked at me, her expression curdled with anger. "All the universes could be destroyed. I'll get more than hurt if I don't do anything to stop them."

I find myself flushing again as I recall the moment, and walk away from Ngurawan and Suon toward one of the ruins. The voices ebb and flow within me, and I ignore them as best I can. They are like extra appendages I cannot control. If I could cut them off, I would. Just like this body. If I could destroy it, I would without hesitation.

Like most of what is left here, the ruined building is no more than two stories tall, though it is obvious that once it stood much taller. It shows no sign of having collapsed. What is left appears solid if somewhat dilapidated. It is as if the rest of the building simply dissolved in the tropical rains.

I go inside to look for signs of life and find only a

cloud of insects to disturb the quiet within. Strangely, the building appears to have just one large room on the main floor, but no windows. It feels unfinished somehow, as though construction was abandoned partway through, with only the frame of the building in place.

Before I leave, I go to one of the walls and study it. There is a pattern of mold running across it, which glimmers slightly in the shadows. When I look closer, I see that the mold isn't growing on the wall—it is within its strange alloy, a spreading infection. This city was like Ngurawan's Jakarta once, I realize, the buildings alive and responsive. Now everything is dead or dying, except for the ever-encroaching foliage.

Is there anyone left? There must be if this is where Lasinha came from, but none of these structures are inhabited. So where are they? Without thinking, I put the question to the multitudes. There are as many answers as voices, a debate between them all, that seems to happen in an instant. I clutch at my head, the world spinning. The cacophony is deafening, and I have a vision of falling into a mass of humanity at the bottom of a pit, all of us scrabbling at the walls to climb up.

I return outside, squinting at the glare of the sun. Suon and Ngurawan are standing just beyond the building, staring at the opening as if they have been waiting some time. The anger on Suon's face has been replaced with concern, and she watches me closely.

The Seeker looks me over from head to toe. "It is unwise to enter the buildings until I ascertain their safety."

I ignore his statement, telling myself that I will have to try to keep the multitudes at bay. They are getting more demanding. It feels like it will only be a matter of time before they rise against me. "Where are the people? Is there anyone living here?"

Ngurawan looks around, head up, as though he is sniffing at the air. "There are. Not many. There is an encampment of some sort not far from here."

"I think we should talk to them."

"We should take care. They may be allies of Lasinha."

"Maybe," I say, crossing my arms. "But maybe they'll know where he grew up. Where his family is from. That's where this is going to go down. He'll want to be on familiar ground."

"It is possible."

Is Ngurawan's tone grudging? Perhaps. It will bear watching. The voices warn me to keep my guard, and I will.

"Lead the way."

Ngurawan gives what for him amounts to a shrug, then turns to lead us east, into the sun. I follow, and Suon goes last, still watchful.

The last inhabitants of this Calgary sit huddled on the only patch of dry land for kilometers, a rise that sits above the fetid swamp, where the vegetation has somehow yet to encroach. Looking around at the stagnant waters and the profusion of plant life, it seems an inevitability. But for now, it remains a human domain, with houses built from the surrounding jungle and lined with ferns. There are what look to be gardens around them, though their production appears meager, given the precipitation and heat available.

They watch us approach from the swamp below with a practiced wariness, along with a resignation, as if they have been expecting us all along and know that nothing we can do will matter. They may be right, I find myself thinking. All of this may be for naught.

We stand on the edge of their village, not wanting to intrude further, and wait for them to approach us. Ngurawan takes the lead as a straggling crew comes near, looking us over with a hostile indifference. Their clothes are not so different from those that we wear, though are ragged and bleached by days in the sun. They don't appear armed, though I don't either.

"We are looking for the Lasinhas. Do you know of them?" Ngurawan turns his eyes upon those who have gathered before us, and I can feel the awful pull, compelling them to speak.

It takes a long time for any of them to reply, so much so that I wonder if they are somehow immune to the Seeker's powers. Perhaps English is no longer spoken here, having transmuted over the centuries into something else. Lasinha had no problem with my English, but Lasinha was able to put on any mask he desired.

An old woman, with grey and curly hair she has tied up above her head into a sort of crown, pushes her way forward to glare at us. "What do you want with them?"

The accent is immediately familiar, a more pronounced version of Lasinha's. I look at the woman with undisguised fascination, which she responds to with a look of disgust, as though I have said something vile.

"We have business with them," Ngurawan says, his tone ominous.

"We just want to talk," I add quickly.

"Talk. Sure." The woman shakes her head. "What business could your kind have with anyone here?"

There are nods of agreement from the others gathered around us. More are coming from the huts and fields as they notice us. For now, it is hard to determine their response to our presence. The woman seems hostile, but the rest are difficult to gauge.

"We mean no one in this place any harm. If you could just point us in their direction, we would be much obliged." Ngurawan speaks slowly and portentously, so much so that I could almost believe he is deliberately attempting to antagonize them.

"Obliged how?" This from a man standing near the front of the group. It is difficult to determine his age. He looks young and aged at the same moment. They all do—the effect of the sun, no doubt.

"What can we do to help?" I say before the Seeker has

a chance to speak.

"We know what your help means." The woman looks around at her fellow villagers and receives many nods of confirmation.

"What does it mean?"

"Someone comes around asking for the Lasinhas and says they don't know what help means. You know what it means."

I smile and hold out my hands, though I don't know why I think the gesture will make any difference. "Believe me, I don't. We're just looking for the Lasinhas. That's all. We don't want to bother you more than that."

"Sure," the woman says, glaring at me again.

"It is the truth." Ngurawan's tone is infuriating. I want to tell him to keep his mouth shut.

The man shakes his head, looking at his compatriots as if the Seeker has confirmed their suspicions. "No Lasinhas in these parts. Hasn't been for years. They all left."

Something about the way he pronounces left, as though it were a curse, tells me what scares them about our being here now. "They left and you stayed, but they didn't want you to." There is no response from any of those gathered, though they all watch me intently. "We're not here to convince you to leave, or to take you anywhere. I swear it. We just want to find where the Lasinhas lived when they were here. Point us in that direction and we'll be on our way."

No one replies, though I can sense their changing mood by the subtle shifts in their stances. Some of them look relaxed, the air going from their chests. The old woman still gives me a furious look.

"We're not going anywhere. This is our home and this where we intend to live."

"I have no home anymore," I say. It is true after a fashion, with the Church gone and nothing to replace it. If given the same chance Ana has now, where would I go? "So you'll understand when I say that I would never take that from you."

A look is shared amongst all those gathered, and one man steps out from the crowd, leading us away from the village. He points at a collection of buildings, the decayed tops of which just peek above the foliage of the swamp. At this distance it is impossible to tell whether one of them is the building I saw through the channel.

"Before they left, that was where they lived," he says before walking away.

I nod my thanks, and the crowd disperses, all interest in our presence gone, everyone returning to their daily tasks before the heat gets overwhelming.

The Seeker fixes his eyes upon the buildings. "Is that where you wish to go?"

I am about to reply when Suon joins us. When the man took us aside, she remained standing where the crowd gathered. Even now she turns back to look at them at work in their gardens, looking troubled. "There aren't any children," she says.

I look at the village again, though I know she is right. There are no children. These are the final remnants of a dying people, who have chosen this place to live out the days that remain to them. It both heartens me and fills me with despair. After one final glance, I turn my back on them and set off to the buildings where Lasinha awaits, Suon and Ngurawan following.

37

There are five buildings in the cluster the native pointed out to us, each forming a small island in the middle of a lake of brackish water. As with the other ruins we have seen, they are only a couple of stories tall, the rest of their structures having decayed. All have ground floors that are submerged, while a profusion of vines and other crawling vegetation has begun to climb up the walls, as though preparing to pull the buildings into the swamp to complete its annihilation. There are gaping holes in the walls of three of the buildings, revealing nothing but shadows within.

"What do you want to do?" Ngurawan sounds unsure of himself, which frightens me.

I can understand the feeling, though. Being here now, I am far less confident of my ability to pick out the building where the transfers will take place. Standing here, there seems nothing to choose between them. Or any of the others we've passed on our way here.

Stalling for time, I say, "There's no one there? You're certain?"

"I am. Are you certain this is the right place?"

I swallow, ignoring the hard seed of doubt germinating inside me. The voices clamor within, but I ignore them too. "I am. How long until the crossings?"

"A little less than an hour." There is an air of challenge in his voice. Now is the time for you to demonstrate your capabilities, he seems to be saying.

Now indeed. I feel queasy, a nervous energy moving through me, demanding I do something. The moment, whatever it is that awaits me, feels very near.

"We could wait till after they transfer," Suon says quietly, looking out at the lake. "It wouldn't take long to get across to whichever building it is."

I fidget, picking at my shirt, which is soaked through with sweat. "We can't risk taking that long to get over there. And we'd be exposed crossing the water. Sitting ducks."

"The alternative is that we make an educated guess as to which building it is and hope we are correct." Ngurawan doesn't sound happy with his suggestion. "I agree we don't want to cross the water to the buildings once the Unmakers are here. The water is deep around them. We will have to swim to get to any of them, and it will be difficult to get up to the second floor from the water. And that is without anyone in them trying to stop us."

"How do we make an educated guess?" Suon puts the edge of her boot in the lake, sending ripples across the water.

"I saw the open channel as well," the Seeker says. "There were two buildings in view from the building where they were crossing. That would eliminate the far building. If you were looking out from there, you would see all five buildings."

"But you would have to include the near building here as well." Suon points at the building closest to us, which doesn't have any visible breaks in its wall. "We can't see the far wall, but if it does have a hole, you would be able to see these two buildings here."

The Seeker doesn't answer, which means he concedes

her point. Both of them look to me for answers. The wrong choice here will likely doom us, but we won't know whether I am right or wrong until it is too late. The multitudes beckon to me, and I allow myself to listen to a little of what they have to say. They have no answers, at least no definitive ones, and I decide I am better on my own. If the burden must fall on my shoulders, I should be the one to make the choice.

I stride into the lake, not uttering a word to either Suon or Ngurawan. They stand on the shore, looking at each other, before following. I choose the farthest of our three possibilities, reasoning that we will have no chance to get to it if I choose one of the others, but from it we can certainly reach at least one of the other choices in time. A two-out-of-three chance. It's the best I and all the universes can hope for.

It takes nearly thirty minutes to cross the stretch of water to the building I have chosen. Only once we are past the nearest structure, which does have an opening on its far side, as Suon feared, does the water come above my shoulders, forcing me to swim. The lakebed is tangled with plants, hidden under the surface, that we continually get caught up in. While on foot it is a simple thing, but swimming it is difficult, and the three of us have to pause often to help one of us who has been trapped by some mutated seaweed.

The water comes up about two meters short of the second level of the building, and the wall is slick with grime, offering no obvious handholds. The three of us tread water, looking up at the opening, just beyond our reach, feeling the seconds tick away. Ngurawan, the tallest of us, makes an attempt at reaching the second floor, but it is beyond his grasp.

"We have no other choice," he says.

Suon and I nod, knowing what he means. He takes a gulp of air and dives below. We stay above, treading water and avoiding looking at each other. He surfaces after an agonizing minute that has my lungs aching for him around the corner of the building.

He wipes a long and slimy strand of vegetation from his face. "There is an entrance below."

"Is there a way up to the second floor?"

"There is only one way to find out."

The Seeker dives below. With a sigh, Suon follows. I go last, moving slowly to let my eyes adjust to the darkness. Even so, I miss the entrance to the building. Suon grabs me by the arm as I swim past. The interior is overgrown with vegetation and utterly dark. I stay near Suon as we go forward, using her movement through the water to guide me, hoping she knows where the Seeker is and can see better than I.

My lungs begin to burn from the lack of oxygen, but I force myself not to panic, to keep at my steady pace. Thrashing about will only result in me getting tangled and wasting what remains of my air. The darkness grows deeper the farther in we go. I am reminded of the void the Acolytes put within me, of the vast emptiness beyond the hut when the Aurellano revealed itself to me. It makes me want to turn around and flee, back up to the surface.

Somehow, despite my absolute focus on her presence and movement, I lose Suon. I am unable to contain my panic then, reaching out for her. The last bit of air seems to go from my lungs, the burning extending out to my muscles, while my thoughts seem to go dim. Frantic, I plunge ahead, only to find long strands of some underwater flora wrapped around one of my legs. Though it is soft and pliable, it does not break when I try to pull free.

The Aurellanos are loud and quiet at the same time. I can see them here, all around me, reaching out to entangle me and pull me deeper and deeper into their abyss. There is no escaping them. There is no leaving this darkness. It continues to encroach upon me, my senses diminishing, until it doesn't even feel as though I am in the water any longer. There is only darkness all around.

I come to with a gasp, coughing up water, rasping desperately and fighting to try to get out of the water. Suon holds me down, pinning my arms, murmuring, "Easy, easy."

The Seeker is there too, peering down at me with his alien eyes. Looking within me. "They will survive."

Suon helps me up into a sitting position as the coughing subsides. There is the taste of bile and swamp water in my throat. I take in my surroundings, realizing that we are on the second floor of the building. The broken wall is before me, letting light stream in. I look out at the view of the lake and the other ruins. My heart sinks at what I see.

Following my gaze, Ngurawan shakes his head. "It is not the correct building. It may be the one we went past, though it is difficult to say with any degree of certainty."

I don't hear what he says, collapsing back to the floor, a flood of despair overwhelming me.

"It's okay," Suon says, squeezing my arm. "We'll just have to wait until they cross over and hope for the best."

Ngurawan looks away out on the lake. I know what he is thinking; I am thinking the same thing. We cannot hope to survive crossing the water to wherever the Unmakers will be.

"How long?" I croak.

"Fifteen minutes." He holds up a hand as I begin to get up, while Suon grasps me by the arms again. "We do not have enough time to get across, even if we could be certain which building it is. Suon is correct. We will have to wait for them to come."

"You're in no state to go anywhere," Suon adds.

I open my mouth to protest, sparking another coughing fit. When it subsides, I nod mutely, conceding that they are correct. There is nothing to do but wait.

Suon helps me up to a seated position, propped against the wall, and joins me there. We look across at the Seeker, who stands vigil by the broken wall, staring out at the lake as though it has secrets to reveal. Maybe he is wondering why, with all the wondrous technology at his disposal, he did not think to bring a boat with him. The thought has crossed my mind, though it is an unkind one.

There is no sense succumbing to bitterness now. It will not help. All we can do is wait and hope. The voices within me clamor for attention, but I ignore them. My mind wanders to Ana. I may fail her again, along with so many others. Whatever happens, I will never see her again. I feel no sadness at that thought, only a measure of satisfaction that she, at least, can be free of all this. If I can somehow manage to stop the Unmakers. I never can be, as the teeming voices within continue to remind me.

Suon is looking sidelong at me, though I can't tell what she might be thinking. She is concerned, most likely. Worried about my state of mind after this failure. After all the struggles of these last days. Having to see Ana and say goodbye. Being forced to confront the fact of this false body. It is always here, always a part of me. Yet, so often, I can ignore all these sensations, unfamiliar and wrong, that being in it engenders. It became easier to do the longer I was in it, but the dissonance never truly went away.

How could it? These aren't my lungs aching with water. These aren't my hands shaking from my ordeal. How am I supposed to face Unmakers in a body that isn't mine and with a mind that is filled with so many strangers?

"We need to talk," I find myself saying. About what?

"Yes," Suon says, not giving an inch, forcing me to speak my mind.

I make a helpless gesture with my hands, my eyes burning with tears. "I'm not...I'm not what you think I am. This..."

"It's gone, isn't it? Your body."

I nod, biting at my lip, not wanting to give in to the emotion. I have avoided this for so long. "Lasinha destroyed it. They thought maybe it would stop this—the Aurellano—from happening. Now this is what I am."

Suon leans over, resting her shoulder on mine and putting her hand light upon my knee. "I know what you are, Laila. This body, all of this, doesn't define you."

I snort in disgust, the tears coming now. "It's a body, Suon. It is me. Besides, you barely know me."

She flinches, but doesn't move away. "I know enough. You weren't nearly as good at hiding your true self as you thought when we were together. I always saw you for what you were. That's why I'm here."

"I'm not what you think I am, Suon. Especially now. I'm not that person."

"You keep saying that. You keep saying I don't know you that well. But I do, Laila. I can't imagine how difficult all this has been for you. It's unimaginable to me. But you're still you. That always shines through. Whatever may happen. You are you. You can't hide that."

I meet Suon's eyes and attempt a smile. "I don't deserve this kindness. I've treated you—I've treated so many people—so badly. You should have gotten as far away from me as possible the first chance you got."

"I love you. I may be a fool for doing that, but I can't pretend the feelings aren't there." Suon takes my hand, holding it tight.

I look at Suon. The words aren't there, only tears. I squeeze her hand.

"I'm here for you until the end. We both are." Suon looks over at Ngurawan, who is still casting his gaze out over the water. "And I love you, whether you think you deserve it or not."

I am still crying, but it feels good to. Transformative. The multitudes don't seem so filled with bedlam. They are voices again. Individuals I can hear. I find my own voice again, though it is choked with emotion. "I love you too,

Suon. I do. Despite myself. It's hard when you hate yourself. Hate everything that you are. It's… I'm sorry. I'm sorry."

Suon doesn't say anything, just holds my hand tight. We rest our heads together and look out at the ruined world.

"Five minutes." Ngurawan turns away from the lake and comes to stand over Suon and I. "You are recovered?"

"As recovered as I can be."

"Good. We need a plan for how to get across the water once they arrive."

"Swim. Unless you've got a boat stashed in your pockets." Suon attempts a mocking grin. The Seeker stares awkwardly, uncertain whether she is being serious.

I ask the question of the Aurellanos without hesitation. What do we do? They respond at once, thousands upon thousands of voices, seeming to multiply. Yet I can hear them all as if we were having an orderly conversation. It takes only an instant. One response in particular interests me. The others take it up and debate it. A consensus is quickly reached, one that I agree with.

"You don't think that the Unmakers' tech is the reason you can't pinpoint the transfer location?"

The Seeker shakes his head. "No. I would be able to separate out whatever interference they tried to use to obscure the channels. I don't know why I was unable to pinpoint the crossing. The sun does affect our technology, but that should only matter when I am in the universe itself."

"The blurring you talked about—the one that means you can't pinpoint the location of the crossing—could it be caused by another transfer?"

Ngurawan considers my question. "There is not a second transfer."

"What if it's because the universe they are transferring to hasn't been created yet?"

The Seeker goes still. "You are suggesting that they will transfer to the new universe created by their transferring here."

"To exactly the same spot. Yes." I get to my feet, unable to contain myself. "If they go through and create a new channel as the new universe is created, would you be able to see the crossing?"

"Perhaps not. It would depend on how much time needs to pass after the universe has been created for them to transfer into it."

"We can assume they're cutting it fine." I clap my hands together and go to stand at the edge of the building, looking across the swamp at the other ruins. "How much time?"

"Seventy-five seconds," he says. Ngurawan and Suon move to stand with me.

"Will you be able to pinpoint where they're going?"

"Yes. We are close enough that even with the sun, I should be able to follow the channel. Sixty seconds."

"What's our plan, then?" There is raw tension in Suon's voice. It all suddenly feels real. "Go across guns blazing?"

The voices are speaking in such a flurry that I almost don't hear her. It takes a moment for me to respond. If this happens when we are over there, it will mean trouble, but strangely, I feel no panic, only a rising certainty that I will actually know what to do and be able to act. "Something like that. We just need to get across in one piece. They'll have to open up a channel to put the unbinding weapon in. I have to make it into that channel."

"Understood. Thirty seconds."

I draw the sword from its scabbard behind my back, and Suon unharnesses her pulse weapon, clutching it tightly in her hands. "Do we need to keep the channel open?"

"Don't worry about that. Once I'm in, look after yourselves."

Suon makes a face like she wants to argue, but she

doesn't say a word. I smile at her. "It'll be okay once I'm through. Just watch yourselves. They'll be after you."

Suon nods, swallowing loudly. I feel a serene sort of calm that I know is false. I am in the eye of the storm, the worst still to come. We will be tested sorely, but I understand what I must do. That is a relief.

The multitudes rise within me, telling me to prepare the emergency transfer engine the Seeker gave me for the battle to come. My hands move in a blur, calling up screens I did not know existed within it. In a matter of seconds, I have managed to disable all the safeties, allowing me to enter the crossings. Ngurawan watches me, no sign of emotion on his face, but there never is. He turns to look out on the other buildings, scanning them in advance of the Unmakers' arrival.

"Fifteen seconds."

Suon and I follow his lead and look to the buildings, though we won't be able to see the channel opening. We should be able to feel it, though, the pull of my universe.

"Ten seconds…nine…eight…seven…six…" The Seeker intones his countdown with an exacting rhythm.

There is a sharp intake of breath. Mine or Suon's? She reaches out and takes my hand, squeezing it tight. It is damp with sweat, as is mine. I don't mind. It feels right.

"Five…four…three…two…one…"

38

For the barest of seconds, I am certain we are wrong, that Ngurawan or the natives have somehow led us astray and we are not in the correct universe, or far from the crossing point. The pull of the other universe, when it finally comes, is almost knee-buckling, a dozen or more channels opening simultaneously. The Seeker points at the building where they are coming across, but there is no need.

Fortunately, there are no openings in the building on the side facing us, so we don't have to worry about the Unmakers spotting us. "They can't detect us, can they?" I ask, wanting to confirm my assumption. They can't detect the Seeker, can they? is probably the more accurate question.

Ngurawan doesn't turn away from the building, intent on watching it for what happens next. "They can, if they choose to look. We can only hope they do not have the time to do so. I will also be able to tell if they are trying to find us. And perhaps counteract it."

I shift on my feet, still clutching Suon's hand, the gravity of what is happening suddenly landing upon me with full force. Everything depends on what happens next. If the Unmakers realize we are here, stranded in the wrong building, they can simply stay where they are and open the channel to unleash the pulse weapon instead of crossing to the newly formed universe. There is a chance the Seeker could open a channel that would allow me to intercept the weapon, but it is fraught with difficulties, according to the multitudes.

The channels close, and we wait. Thirty seconds and then a minute. I look at Ngurawan, and he shakes his head. "They are not scanning. Or opening a channel. Yet."

When the crossing is opened, the pull of the other universe is dim. I notice it immediately, though, every fiber of my being intent upon that familiar sensation. Suon and I look at Ngurawan, waiting for confirmation of what is happening. I am sick with dread, expecting to hear the worst.

"One channel," he says. "To the new universe, as you suspected. They are going through now."

I sigh with relief. "As soon as it closes, we go through."

"I am already preparing the channel. Where would you like to arrive?"

I ask his question of the multitudes and receive a response that makes me quiver, though I can see the sense of it. "Right in the middle of the main floor."

Suon releases my hand, looking at me with a shocked expression. "It'll be flooded too."

"Undoubtedly," the Seeker says.

"Yes. If we cross over to the second floor, they can pick us off as we come across," I say. "They can't do anything to the main floor without damaging their position on the second, and maybe the building's foundation. Too risky with the unbinding weapon. We'll be underwater, but Ngurawan can still determine what's happening above. And I can use this to get us up there." I wave the sword, feeling like I've gone somewhat mad.

"Are you certain?" Ngurawan says. "It will take some time to establish where it is best for us to go through."

"Do it," I say without hesitation.

Suon shakes her head. "I hope you're right."

I don't reply, looking to Ngurawan. "It is done," he says.

As he speaks, we can feel the channel opening before us. The other universe comes into view, an unmoving darkness that is so familiar and so terrifying that I have to brace myself to quell my fear. Suon is breathing heavily, almost hyperventilating. So am I. The thought of walking into those depths is unbearable.

"It is time," Ngurawan says. "Steady your breathing before you cross. Deep, long breaths. Once you step in the channel, you will need to hold your breath. Go together and let the water carry you. I will find you."

We nod, and I take Suon's hand in mine. Her touch steadies me, and I let my breathing go deep, calming myself. There is still fear, but it is manageable. I look at Suon, and she squeezes my hand. We walk into the channel, Ngurawan a step behind, moving steadily toward that inky blackness.

The many-faced Aurellano emerges in the crossing. One moment I am stepping across from the ruin in the engulfed city to the brackish depths of the other universe where the Unmakers await us, and the next I am back in the nipa hut adrift in space. The darkness reaches everywhere, but I can see their shifting faces clearly. I recognize some of them now, matching faces to the voices I have heard within me.

"You have done well," they say. "Finding this world."

"You led me to the other. I couldn't have done any of this without you. But the hardest work is what's left."

"We will be ready," they say. "It will take all of us."

I look at them, overcome by emotion. "I know."

"It will be like your battle with Harith. When the time comes, turn to us. The more you do, the easier it will be. The more we will be as one."

"I don't think we will ever be just one."

"No," they say, turning to look out at the distant sparks of light that surround us. "That is our strength."

I follow their gaze, my eyes drawn less to the stars and more to the vast expanses of darkness between them. The thought of that great emptiness makes me shudder. Or is it the fact that all these other people exist within me, are somehow an inextricable part of me? It is still an awful thing, one I don't know that I can become used to. I glance at the Aurellano, and they smile at me, a reassuring smile. An understanding one.

The sensation I expected was of descending into the water, the liquid gradually enveloping me as I moved out of the channel and into the new universe. Instead, the transition is abrupt and brutal, from air to water in an instant. It is like a punch to my chest, and I almost open my mouth to gasp before remembering that I will need every last breath of air in my lungs.

Suon's hand is still in mine, and the sword is in the other, so I tell myself to remain calm despite the rising pressure in my chest and the increasing panic I feel. I look in her direction, but I can't make out her form. She moves close, pressing her cheek against my own, letting me know she is okay. This relaxes me, and I go still, letting the water take us where it will.

There is no current, the water still, and as a result, we slip below, descending from the roof to the bottom of the lake. The vegetation is thick there, tendrils draping around us. It is our descent that is causing it, not the plants themselves moving to ensnare us, as it feels like. I close my eyes, but that just makes me recall the last time I was at the bottom of this lake in another universe, trapped and running out of air.

My chest is burning, the air all used up. From the tightening grasp of Suon's hand, I know she is feeling the same: dread and desperation, along with a growing certainty that Ngurawan is not going to find us. He can, I tell myself—he is a Seeker, after all. Whatever the effects of the sun on this world, he will still be able to locate Suon if she is in the same building as he is.

What if he is not?

Ana told me not to trust him. I have no proof that he is my ally and not an Unmaker. Every chance he got, he sent me back to the Church, where Lasinha was able to keep watch on me. Now I have let him send me to the depths of this lake, with only his word to trust that it is in the universe the Unmakers have crossed to. Only his word that he will follow and drag us from these depths. He was behind us, and though I think he entered the channel, I can't say for sure he actually crossed over. My faith is dwindling along with what remains of the oxygen in this body.

The Seeker materializes before us in the brackish water, seaweed trailing his long hair. Suon is visible beside me as well, her face strained with agony, as mine must be. I struggle to understand where the light is coming from, wondering if this is a hallucination of my dying brain. Ngurawan reaches out and takes Suon and my clasped hands in his own, and begins to swim above. After a few seconds, where my mind refuses to believe what is happening, my body responds, kicking through the water to aid him in his efforts.

When we reach the ceiling, the light emanating from the Seeker allows us to see that the water doesn't reach the top, and there is a thin pocket of air, no more than a few centimeters. Ngurawan releases us, and we both arch our heads back so that just our faces are out of the water. Hungrily we suck at the air, which is warm and stinks of mildew and rot, yet no breath of mine has ever been sweeter.

Once our lungs are filled, we descend beneath the water, where Ngurawan awaits us. He leads us to a corner of the building and points above for me to use the sword. I clench its pommel tightly, letting its warmth grow. When it is burning in my hand, I thrust it up into the ceiling. As before, the ceiling disappears, revealing stacks of equipment against the wall. It is impossible to determine what they are or if any are in use, with the water putting everything out of focus.

There is no one standing nearby that I can see, so I let go of Suon's hand and reach up through the passage the sword has created. Ngurawan reaches up as well, using his incredible strength to pull himself through the opening with one arm, while keeping his other hand in contact with me. When he is safely through, he reaches down to take hold of Suon and pulls us both up and out of the water.

For a moment, nothing happens. We crouch on the floor, dripping wet, the detritus of the swamp falling off us. The Unmakers appear as though they were frantically moving about in the vast, warehouse-like space of the building, readying for something, but all of them are now frozen still, staring at the three of us in disbelief. I see Lasinha and Harith standing near a stack of transfer engines, their lights blinking, the pattern not in synch, though it is getting closer. Tingco, the man from my Aurellano dreams, is with them, looking over everyone.

There are maybe twenty others spread out across the building, mixed in amongst various pieces of equipment. It seems such a small number to have created such havoc in so many universes. Of course, there were many working with them, like Molijc and the Acolytes, who had no idea of their true aims. And this may not be all their loyal soldiers. The number of transfer engines suggest more may be on their way.

There are more than I can count, their lights all blinking—how many channels do they plan on opening? Meredith and Gloria stand in the opposite corner to us, on either side of Morris. He cradles something in his hands. An explosive. That is the answer to how they plan to explode the universes and not get caught in the channels. They will have Morris go in with the bomb. What they will do in the meantime is unclear.

We all hold still for what seems like minutes, though it must only be a few seconds, if that. The three of us stand up, and the Unmakers begin to move. There is a sound, like everyone is exhaling. After that, everything happens at once, in a blur where I am just reacting without any thought at all.

"Finish your work," Tingco shouts, breaking the strained reverie. "Whatever you do, don't let them stop the work. That is all that matters now."

Before he has finished speaking, Suon begins shooting, spraying pulses around, sending people diving out of the way. Two collapse to the ground. The Seeker turns to the transfer engines nearest us and pulls out an unbinding dagger, plunging the blade into the guts of the machines. They go dark. Two Unmakers rush to him, but he shrugs them aside and continues his path of destruction.

"Morris," I hiss under my breath at Suon, as she continues to lay down a spread of pulses across the room. She turns and fires at him, but Gloria is ready. Another unbinding sword in her hand, she steps in front of him, the pulses bouncing off her without effect.

I unleash my own sword at her, but she flicks away the blade as if swatting a fly. She grins insolently, striding forward, exuding fury with every motion. "Now we finish what we started, Aurellano."

I let her approach, keeping an eye on both her and Morris. He is my ultimate goal. If I can get the bomb from him, the unmaking ends before it begins. Meredith has stepped in front of him to act as a shield. The voices cry out within me, and I let Josefina assume command. I send my sword at Meredith, but Gloria parries that blow as well.

"Don't get distracted, Aurellano. This is between me and you."

She launches herself at me as she is speaking, leaping into the air and sending her blade toward me. I manage to fend off the blow from her sword, but cannot get out of the way of Gloria. She kicks me in the chest as she lands, sending me sprawling and knocking the air from my chest. I am left gasping for air and trying to get to my feet as she approaches, a look of grim satisfaction on her face.

Another voice assumes command. There is an ease to it, just as the Aurellano told me in the crossing. We are many beings acting as one, with a speed and unity I can barely comprehend. Will it be enough?

I clench my blade, letting it grow warm as Gloria comes near, allowing her to come as close as possible. She approaches warily, expecting something. I wait until she is almost beside me before touching the blade to the floor, creating a path through the particles for her to fall. She is too quick, though, darting out of the way and swinging her sword at me. My blade responds automatically to counter the blow, returning the floor to normal.

I scramble to my feet, trying to put some distance between myself and her, but Gloria presses her advantage, launching blow after furious blow against me. Even with the blade's protective qualities and the knowledge of my Aurellano counterparts, I am hard-pressed to fend all of them off. She backs me into the corner where we came through the floor until I am pressed up against the wall with nowhere to run.

Suon is gone. I don't see where, though I notice that the firing of the pulse weapon has ceased. Over Gloria's left shoulder, I can see the Seeker in a desperate struggle with Harith and Tingco, facing two unbinding swords with his dagger. The other Unmakers, including Lasinha, go about their business as if there is not a battle for the fate of the universes going on around them, making sure the engines that Ngurawan was unable to destroy keep cycling.

"I'm glad you're here, Aurellano," Gloria spits at me. "You can see the end of your precious illusions yourself. That's why I'm not going to kill you. I want to make sure you see the end. Maybe you'll even catch a glimpse of what you've spent so long denying us."

She thrusts her sword at my midsection. I twist away in response, deflecting her blow, just as she intended. Her sword plunges into the wall, which evaporates behind me. I am suddenly perched on a precipice above the swamp, teetering on its edge. Gloria shoves at me with her free hand, and I am forced to drop my sword so that I can cling precariously to the wall.

Gloria laughs, kicking my now-retracted blade into the swamp. "You're nothing, Aurellano. Just a collection of fools we already killed. What makes you think you'd be any different?"

"I have friends," I say.

Gloria blinks and narrows her eyes, realizing my meaning too late. Suon, who took cover behind the remnants of the transfer engines the Seeker destroyed, crashes into her from behind, pitching her off balance and over the edge into the water. Gloria grabs hold of my shirt as she goes by, intending to take me with her to the depths. But Suon has a hold of my arm and is pulling me back from the brink.

It is a desperate struggle, Suon and I on one side fighting against Gloria and the steady pull of gravity. I kick and punch at Gloria, trying to shake her loose, but only succeeding in putting myself more off balance, threatening to take Suon with me over the edge. Gloria laughs uproariously as though she cannot imagine a more suitable ending for me.

"Let go," the voices have me tell Suon. To my surprise, she does, sending Gloria and I tumbling into the water. She loses her grip on me as we hit the water, both of us thrashing around frantically. I am trying to get away, and Gloria is trying to get hold of me, our struggles sending us bobbing up and down, water spraying everywhere.

From the corner of my eye, I catch a glimpse of Suon trying to aim a pulse rifle at Gloria, and I immediately dive below the surface, going as deep as I can. Gloria is frozen by indecision, unsure whether to follow me below or flee to avoid the shot. She is still for only a second, but Suon does not hesitate. I can feel the pulse from her shot reverberating through the water, numbing my hands and feet. Hovering above me I can see the shadow of Gloria's form, though it is impossible to tell whether she is still moving. To be certain, I wait a few more seconds to see if Suon lets off another shot before resurfacing.

"Jesus. I thought I got you too," Suon says when I emerge. There are shouts from behind her, along with the sound of repeated blows from unbinding blades clashing together. She glances over her shoulder, ready to shoot, but holds her fire. "Get over here."

I swim over to the edge of the building. After checking over her shoulder again, Suon kneels at the edge of the building, extending the butt end of the rifle down to where I can grasp it. She pulls me up, showing a strength I didn't know she possessed, until I can gain purchase on the floor and pull myself up.

Seeing me safely inside, Suon whirls around, ready to fire. She does not, for the Seeker is in front of us, mounting a desperate defense against Harith and Tingco, who are attempting to drive us all into the lake. The rest of the Unmakers continue their work, ignoring the struggle happening right beside them. Even Harith and Tingco aren't hoping to defeat us; they merely want to delay until the channels are open and they can enact their plan.

"Shoot them." I point at the Unmakers busy at work on the engines. "Ngurawan can handle himself. I need to get to Morris."

Suon nods, sending the nearest Unmakers scattering with a few blasts. Under the cover of her fire, I sprint out of the corner across the building to where Morris and Meredith were. Only when I duck behind a stack of equipment do I realize they have moved during all the confusion. Scanning the room, I see Lasinha and Meredith at the far end of the building, heads together in conference.

"Do you see Morris?" I say as Suon scrambles to join me.

She shakes her head. "I didn't see what happened to him."

"Have they opened any channels yet?" I didn't feel any opening during my struggle with Gloria, but I was so focused on saving my life that it is possible one did without my noticing.

"I don't think so," Suon says, trying to catch her breath.

"Good," I say, as much to myself as to her. "We still have time."

As I say the words, I feel the sudden pull of a dozen or more different channels opening all around us.

39

There are multiple crossings opening along each of the walls surrounding us. Between us and Lasinha I can see glimpses of several other universes forming, the farthest ones distorted by the nearer like an image receding in a funhouse mirror. I can see the heart of a volcano in one, a black hole in another. Even the floor has channels opening into it. Making our way across the room is impossible. Every step could potentially lead us to another universe from which there will be no possibility of return.

"It's a fucking minefield," Suon says in horror, looking around.

I nod, almost afraid to move. There is a universe behind us and one to our left, cutting us off from Ngurawan. He is still locked in combat with Tingco, saved from Harith, who is stranded on the other side of a channel. Both Travelers have lost their unbinding weapons and are resorting to hand-to-hand combat, their limbs moving with a blurring speed.

Lasinha moves toward us, stepping around the open channels with a practiced ease. He barely glances at where he is going, knowing exactly where the channels are, his eyes intent upon mine.

"This is the end, Laila." He doesn't bother to disguise his accent now. "You can't shoot or talk or bluff your way out of this."

"That was your way."

Lasinha laughs. "Yes, yes. You could never admit that we were the same. We did anything, sacrificed anyone. All for the cause. The only difference was you believed in De Gofroy's bullshit. I had a higher calling."

"If you consider mass murder a higher calling." I don't watch Lasinha, scanning the room for signs of Morris. The voices tell me to be ready when he enters the channel. All this talk doesn't matter; Lasinha is just doing what he always does. Distract and obfuscate, while setting his plans in motion.

"This isn't living."

"It is for me. It is for everyone else in the universes. But I guess that isn't good enough for the likes of you." There is no sign of Morris that I can see, though Meredith is lingering by a stack of transfer engines, some distance behind Lasinha in a way that arouses my suspicions.

"Oh yes, what a fine existence I was given. Have you seen this world? Do you know what it is like to live with the perpetual knowledge that your future is doomed? That your children will see the death of the earth? What kind of life is that?"

Lasinha is shouting now, the rage and hate he kept carefully hidden all these years bursting out. "But you wouldn't know anything about that, would you, Laila? You were given a good life in a decent universe, but that wasn't enough for you. You made sure to destroy it. You ruined your relationship with your family because you needed more. It wasn't enough to be a Regent; you had to be De Gofroy's chosen vessel. You and Molijc were so easy to lead around. Even when you had something good, it didn't satisfy you. You threw Meredith away at a word from Dejian, and for what?"

I swallow, my face hot with shame. He is right. In so

many ways, he is right. I meet Meredith's eyes, and she is triumphant in her anger.

Lasinha cannot stop. He needs me to hear this, I realize. It isn't just about keeping me occupied and distracted. It isn't enough to destroy the universes—he needs someone to understand why.

"I refuse the terms of these universes. Why should I, and everyone in this universe, be condemned to a short and brutal life, while others have the power to go to whatever universe they want? Do whatever they desire, without ever once asking what the people who live in these universes want? Where's the fairness, the justice in that? There isn't, and you know it."

"I won't pretend there's justice in any of this." My voice is shaking with emotion that surprises me. "The Society, both sides of it—there has to be a better way. But that better way doesn't involve destroying everything. Killing everyone."

From the corner of my eye, I see that Tingco has Ngurawan on the ground, pressing his knee into his throat to choke the life from him. The Seeker's face is still a mask, but his mouth is tight with strain, betraying the agony he is undergoing. With the channels between us, there is nothing I can do for him. I have to try something, though.

I ask the multitudes what can be done, and I receive an answer that seems impossible. Some of the voices within me agree, saying that doing what is proposed will only result in us being lost in the channels between the universes forever, unable to do anything to stop the Unmakers. For some reason, I can't get the image of the hut floating in space from my mind. All those points of light. What are they?

Lasinha doesn't appear to notice my distraction. "You were always afraid, Laila. Afraid to stand up to Molijc and me. Afraid to do what you needed to do to save Ana. Now you're afraid to do what's necessary. You must see that it's necessary."

I give Lasinha a cold smile, an echo of all the ones he gave me over the years. "I know what's necessary, more than you ever will. The universes don't owe us anything. They exist so we can exist; that is all. What we owe, we owe to each other."

I take the pulse rifle from Suon and set it to overload, putting it atop the nearest stack of transfer engines. Suon looks at me wide-eyed, and I squeeze her arm in reassurance. Lasinha is suddenly quiet and watchful. I cast my eyes about the room one last time, trying to find Morris, but he is nowhere to be seen. Meredith is still standing awkwardly near the equipment Lasinha and Harith were working on when we arrived. She has not moved from the precise spot she was standing, I am quite certain.

I note the spot, as well as the space where Tingco is squeezing the life from Ngurawan, before taking Suon by the hand and leading her into the nearest channel. A vast and empty blue expanse awaits us in a universe we will never reach.

There are shouts behind us as we enter the crossing and leave the universe behind—Lasinha giving frantic orders to the other Unmakers. Does he know what I am going to attempt? He must suspect it. Suon clenches my hand, clearly terrified of what is about to happen. She has some idea of what is going on, though she has only heard the Seeker talk of what befell those who tried it.

With the reprogrammed transfer engine, I am able to override the crossing the Unmakers created, closing it off at either end, leaving us stranded in the channel. As I do, the universe we are crossing to vanishes, the blue twisting to black with an abruptness that leaves Suon gasping. She twists around in time to see the building in Lasinha's drowned universe fade, as if it were only a trick of the light and nothing of substance at all. When it is gone, there is only darkness.

"Is this…?"

"Welcome to the channels." I smile at her, hoping I am reassuring. I am not.

"There's nothing here. How can we see each other? How are we here?" Suon is panicked, sounding as though she is near vomiting. She clenches my hand tighter and tighter, her breathing unsteady, as if she expects to float away at any moment.

"All the universes are here." I wave my hand around. Our eyes have adjusted to the darkness that replaced the light from the two universes enough to reveal the billions of points of light all around. The same lights I saw in the last crossing when the Aurellano revealed itself.

This only frightens her more. "Jesus. Jesus. How are we even breathing? There's no air here. There's nothing."

I take her by both shoulders, compelling her to look into my eyes. "Listen to me. We're fine. There's not nothing here. These are the channels. The same ones you've crossed through who knows how many times. And you're breathing now, so there must be air. Right?"

That is not entirely true, I am informed by the multitudes, but I do not want to further confuse matters by elaborating on various theories about the nature of the crossings. How they exist and how they allow us to cross between the universes. The channels' existence is fundamental to the existence of all the universes, fundamental to their propagation. They are the things that connect us all, a causal chain of events, building one upon the other. If the Unmakers succeed in breaking them apart, we would all be destroyed.

Suon has regained her composure somewhat, though she still sounds on the verge of screaming. "So the people who Ngurawan was talking about who went here without a destination, they could survive here."

I know what she is imagining now. Us stranded here until we slowly starve to death, or worse, are lost here for eternity, never dying but not living either. So I attempt to explain it as best I can. "For a short time. The channels only exist because the universes exist and are being created. They connect them, which is why we are able to use them to go between. They're a little like the pocket universes the Society created, if you're familiar with them."

By her expression, I can tell she is. The thought of them and not this vast, endless space we are seemingly adrift in is enough to calm her somewhat.

"We can exist in them, but...they aren't stable. These..." I wave my hand around, searching for the words. "These have a temporal element. Which causes them to break down and re-form. Reconnect. Because the universes are always changing, always propagating, the channels have to do the same. In theory, we could stay here forever, if we could jump from channel to channel. It is its own universe, a half-universe, I guess, that doesn't follow the rules of our own."

"But you can get us out, right? We're not stuck here."

"That is the plan." I hold up the transfer engine. "I'm going to open a channel to the corner of the room where Ngurawan was, so you can help him."

Suon gulps, her whole body trembling. "What about you?"

"I'm going to where Lasinha and Meredith were. They've got Morris hidden somewhere there, I'm sure of it. Just waiting for their chance."

"What if they've already sent him into the channels while we're gone?"

"They haven't. I would know." I realize that is true. While I am here in the crossings, I can somehow feel every channel in every universe, as impossible as that seems. "Besides, we're outside of that temporal chain now that we're in the channels. I can always return to before they send him. They'll want to stop me from entering the channels. That's the only way to be certain I can't stop them."

"Then why not just stay here? Wait them out."

"There's no waiting them out here, Suon. There's no time at all." That isn't entirely true, but near enough.

Suon takes a deep breath, closing her eyes. "What do you need me to do?"

"Help Ngurawan. And then see what you can do to help me. I'll be coming. Hopefully the pulse rifle exploding has created a little chaos. If nothing else, they'd have to close some of the channels to get to it and stop it."

She looks around. "You're coming back here, aren't you?"

"If all goes well, yes. This is where it will end. If it doesn't, there will be nothing to go to. Are you ready?"

Suon nods, and I squeeze her hand, entering the coordinates into the transfer engine. It connects us to a nearby channel, the building where the battle is occurring blooming into color before our eyes. We can just see the Seeker and Tingco locked together in their bitter struggle.

"Walk towards it. I'll see you there soon."

I let go of Suon's hand, and she steps gingerly toward the light, glancing over her shoulder once, seeming to lose her balance as she does so. She recovers, laughing a little to herself, and goes, lifting a hand in goodbye. I close the channel as she steps through, not wanting to risk anything coming in after she is gone, and am left alone in this void.

Before opening another channel, I test my newfound awareness, using the transfer engine and my intuition to move from channel to channel with terrifying ease. I can feel crossings opening up, millions of them every second, as the Society, the Acolytes, the Church, and all sorts of other variants of ourselves move about. Sojourners all.

But we are the true sojourner, I realize. As disorienting as Suon clearly found it, this is our natural habitat. Everyone within me is connected by this strange place that is not a place at all. It is everything and all of the universes at once. The action of the Aurellano feels easier here, more like my actual thoughts than it is in the universes.

We are ready, the voices within me say. We are.

I open the channel and step across.

I arrive to chaos. The pulse weapon exploded and the wave has just passed through the building, shattering multiple transfer engines, and closing and distorting several channels. Unmakers are still ducking for cover, those that managed to escape the wave. The ones who did not lie on the floor, limp and unmoving.

Suon arrives as I do and crashes into Tingco, sending him sprawling to the floor. Ngurawan gasps for air, massaging his throat. As Tingco struggles to his feet, still dazed by Suon's blow, she shoves him into the channel that stands between them and Harith. There is something dark and swirling awaiting him on the other side. Tingco, realizing too late what is happening, lets out a roar of disbelief and fury, before disappearing from view.

"Quick. Close it. Close it," Harith shouts over the din.

The other Unmakers scramble to respond, but it is too late. I can feel it. He has crossed over. Harith lets out a cry of despair, coming to the same realization. The room goes still for a moment, in the midst of all that chaos, as if the Acolyte's sorrow is too much for any of us to bear.

The channel closes in the midst of that stillness, signaling that the chaos can resume. Harith charges at Suon and Ngurawan, his face twisted and flushed with wrath. He has an unbinding sword in his hand, which he has claimed from somewhere. Suon scrambles away from the blade, petrified, while Ngurawan stands his ground, armed with nothing.

This all happens in a handful seconds as I try to regain my bearings following my passage and confront Lasinha. The rest I do not see, for Lasinha isn't where I expected him to be. Meredith is, though, standing exactly where she was before. She has a pained expression on her face, her lips curled into a bitter yet triumphant smile.

I look at her, expecting her to say something. Instead, a

channel opens up before me and Lasinha emerges from it, leaping to kick me in the chest. I spin out of the way, diving to the ground, just avoiding him and another channel, leading to a raging fire, whose flames are so hot that I can almost feel the heat through the crossing.

"You're not the only one who can play games, Laila." He sneers at me, aiming a pulse pistol at my head.

"I'm not playing games." I step into the open channel as he fires, ignoring the searing heat. With the transfer box and the speed of the multitudes within me, I am able to close both ends of the channel before the pulse wave can reach me and before the crossing carries me into the fire.

When I return, it is beside Lasinha as he fires his gun at empty air. He starts to dive out of the way, and I knock him to the ground, clutching for the gun. It falls from his hand, clattering across the floor. I scramble up to get it, Lasinha making no move to stop me.

"You're too late, Aurellano," he says, looking up at me from the floor. The smile on his face is terrible to see.

I can feel two new channels opening nearby. One is where Meredith stands, and she disappears into it, is consumed by it. The other lies beyond Lasinha. Morris emerges from it, still clutching the unbinding weapon in his hands. I straighten up, grasping the pulse pistol, and shoot him. He crumples, the explosive clattering across the floor toward Lasinha.

"You're too late," he says again.

"Get out of here," I scream, hoping Suon and Ngurawan can hear me.

The channel Meredith disappeared into has closed. Traces of its passage still remain, the distinct pull of its particular gravity enough for me to find it again when I am in the channels. But I have to get there first, before the unbinding weapon destroys everything here.

I don't know how much time I have before the explosive begins to take effect, but there are half a dozen open channels a few steps from where I am. Lasinha lies between me and two of them, including the one Morris just came through. The others are behind me and to my right, some on the floor, some in the air, all intended to form a protective barrier around Meredith. It also leaves Lasinha as the only person able to stop me, but he will need to get himself into the crossings as well if he wants to escape the effects of the weapon.

"Close the channels. Close them all," Lasinha calls out, stunning me.

"Get out now," I shout to Suon and Ngurawan, before racing to the nearest crossing.

Lasinha scrambles to his feet, clearly intending to stop me from escaping. I fire the pulse pistol in his direction, forcing him to dive out of the way. As I come to the first of the channels, it closes, a terrifying and awe-inspiring view of the earth from the upper atmosphere dimming to nothing. I let out a cry, somewhere between frustration and desperation, as all around the rest of the channels wink out of existence.

I whirl around, trying to find some passage that is still open. If I don't enter the crossings soon, I won't be able to find the channel Meredith is in without a monumental effort and more Seeker tech than I have at hand. But that is the least of my immediate problems, for I can feel the unbinding weapon beginning to spread, disintegrating the room molecule by molecule in an ever-widening circle. Soon the whole building will collapse on itself.

I tell myself not to panic. Lasinha and the rest of the Unmakers must have a way out if they planned to explode an unbinding weapon here. I can feel that escape route forming even as I wonder what it could be, dozens of channels taking shape within each of the Unmakers. Harith disengages from Ngurawan as the channel consumes him. All of them back away, ensuring that none of us can escape into the crossings.

"You've failed, Laila," Lasinha says, his triumphant voice distorted by the channel that is already pulling him from this universe. "You're too late."

He is gone, as are the rest of them, before I can so much as move. I am paralyzed at the thought of my failure and our impending doom, only able to watch the widening circle of destruction left by the unbinding weapon. It has consumed Morris and much of the floor around where he lay, and is now spreading toward the transfer equipment. The building groans as its structure is gnawed away by the unbinding pathogen, which is feeding on all that it destroys and growing more powerful. Soon it will have enough energy to generate an explosion that will unmake everything in its path.

I have to get into the channels and I have to ensure that Ngurawan and Suon can escape the explosion. The altered transfer box is still with me, but do I have enough time to open a channel for all of us? There will have to be.

I go to pull it out, but one of the multitudes stops me. Let the Seeker deal with the channel, she says. An unbinding sword can generate an unbinding explosion. And two unbinding reactions can cancel each other out.

For a moment I am in a daze as she explains it to me, wondering what she is driving at. Utilized precisely, an unbinding reaction can cut off the chain reaction of another unbinding weapon, starving the explosion, so that it simply fizzles to nothing, with each unbinding reaction unmaking the other, neither able to feed and grow to its explosive potential. It is a precise maneuver, one that could just as easily result in the reactions being combined and the force of the weapons being doubled. She shows me how to do it, insisting that I must find a sword.

Ngurawan pulls me from these thoughts. It feels like I have been absent for minutes, but in reality, it was only a handful of seconds. "Come, Laila. There is little time."

I don't answer, looking around the room until I spot what the voice tells me to find. Ngurawan's unbinding dagger, which he lost in his battle with Harith and Tingco. It is lying on the floor, in the midst of some equipment, right on the edge of the unbinding wave. I sprint over to grab it, hearing Suon scream as she sees what I am doing.

A strange numbness overtakes my fingers as I reach out for the dagger, no doubt an effect of the approaching reaction, making it hard to grip the knife. I grab and hurriedly pass it to my other hand, which can manage a firmer grip. The numbness doesn't retreat from my fingers, though it does stop advancing up my arm as I move away from the unbinding wave.

With the weapon in hand, I retreat to where Ngurawan and Suon are standing in the far corner of the building, not wanting to take my eyes off the growing unbinding reaction. How long do we have left? Seconds, I am told. Ngurawan is already opening a channel, while Suon stands behind him, ashen-faced, unable to look away from the approaching wave. I don't know if we have enough time, but it is too late now to escape the blast radius.

The channel forms outside the broken wall of the building, hovering over the water. Ngurawan looks at me to go first.

"No. Both of you go through. I'll need to alter the channel, and I can't do that with you in it."

He nods, looking as though he wants to ask me the question that is looming in my own mind. Will I be able to find Meredith in time? Will I be able to find her at all?

Suon reaches out to squeeze my hand. "Go," I say. "Go. I'll find them." I stuff the dagger into my belt and pull out the transfer engine, so that I am ready to close the channel as soon as I enter it.

Ngurawan takes Suon by the arm and leaps into the channel, pulling her with him. I can see the room in Jakarta that we left only a few short hours ago on the other side. Numbness spreading in my back tells me the unbinding wave is getting near. It must be near critical mass for the explosion to be unleashed. There is not a moment to lose.

I jump. There is a sudden gust of air pulling me back as

I do, the reaction hungry for more molecules, pulling air from outside in. I have the sensation of dangling in midair like some cartoon character waiting for gravity and doom to take hold. But I am close enough to the channel that its pull restores my momentum, and I tumble in. Behind me, there is a roar as the explosion begins.

40

I don't recall closing the channel, though I must have, for I find myself stranded in the crossings. There is no sign of Jakarta or the explosion I left in Lasinha's universe. I am here in this space that is not a space, that is in between, where time is slower, dilated, as if we are being slowly drawn into a black hole.

That is the only reason I still have a chance to stop Meredith. Because the channels are causally created by actions in the universes, anything Meredith does in the channel will have to take place sometime after she left Lasinha's universe. And because only a few seconds will have passed for her since entering the crossings, while I remained in the universe for several minutes, she has likely not even initiated the unbinding weapon.

Unless the Unmakers knew enough to teach her how to move among the channels as I can. If that is the case, then she can move out of causality, as I will have to if I am to find her. But if she could do that, then I would surely already feel the channels disintegrating as the unbinding contagion spreads through them. That I don't gives me hope. All that remains is to find her.

I look at the transfer box, one of the multitudes taking

command to call up readouts on it, scanning to find the channel she entered. There are several leaving Lasinha's universe, though they all blur together in a way that is disorienting and hard to parse, even with the Seeker tech. It must be the Unmakers. That the channels overlap so closely suggests they have same destination, and that destination is Meredith.

Why are they going to her, when she will be ground zero for the destruction of the universes?

If nothing else, it has served to make it difficult for me to find the channel Meredith entered with the others providing interference. Fortunately, I can still recall the feel of that channel, the particularities of its gravity, and I can parse it out from the rest. At least, I believe I can.

Once I have located the channel I believe she occupies, I have to determine where to enter it. The closer I can get to the moment Meredith entered the channel, the better. Only a handful of seconds will have elapsed for her, but that may be enough to initiate the unbinding reaction. I shift the dagger to the scabbard on my shoulder, where it will be hidden, before checking the readouts one last time to confirm where I will enter.

There is no delaying any further. I look around at all the universes, those lights in the darkness, feeling the crossings connecting them all. There is a sense that this might be for the last time, though I am quick to push that thought from my mind. I locate the channel Meredith is in and step across.

It takes a moment for me to notice Meredith in the channel, my eyes slow to adjust. She is standing simultaneously close and far away from where I entered.

"You're too late. I've set it off." She sounds both exultant and terrified.

"Why, Meredith?" I study the readout on the transfer box and see that she isn't lying. The reaction has already begun, though only just. There is still time. But where is the weapon? She isn't carrying anything, and there is nothing obvious stashed on her person.

"He said you would you come. I almost didn't believe him. It was too good to be true. But you're here." She speaks in a dreamy voice, as if to someone far away.

I glance between her and the screen in my hand, moving toward her. The depth of the channel is very deceptive, and she is much farther away than I thought possible, given the time that has passed for her.

The unbinding reaction is progressing quickly, yet I cannot see the location of the weapon. Has Meredith hidden it somewhere? We are in the crossings; there is nowhere to hide it. So it has to be on her somewhere.

"I know what Lasinha wants, but what about you? You can't believe in any of this." Keep her talking, I tell myself, moving closer, though it doesn't appear that way. I need to be close enough to use the dagger if it comes to that. Assuming I can locate the weapon in time.

"I believed in you, Laila. I believed in you, and you sent me away like I was just a piece of trash you could throw out."

I shake my head, refusing to be drawn in. "We've already talked about this, Meredith, I don't know how many times. What more is there to say?"

With the transfer box, I try to seal the channel from the rest of the crossings, though I suspect it will prove futile. Each channel is contingent on the universes. They cannot exist apart.

Meredith's eyes come into focus on mine, sharp with emotion. "Just this. What are you going to save: me or the universes?"

The silence seems to last forever as we stare at each other. Meredith's eyes are red. I shift uncomfortably. The transfer engine vibrates in my hand, letting me know that the channel remains connected to the crossings. It isn't a surprise, but I am unable to keep the frustration from my face.

"I told you. You're too late. You're going to have to choose."

"What the hell are you talking about, Meredith?" I ask, though I am terrified of the answer.

"I am the unbinding weapon. They integrated it in me."

I shudder, despite myself. Looking at the readouts, I see that she is telling the truth. The unbinding reaction is spreading out from her into the channel. How is she still alive, then? Because the contagion is targeting the crossing, I am told, based on its programming. At a certain point, the reaction will gain enough energy that it will consume her, as well as me. But for the moment, she is protected.

"Then it doesn't matter what I do. You're dying. Why would you agree to this?" Whatever else she might be, Meredith is first and foremost a survivor.

"I made a choice. And now you have to make a choice too, Laila. Will you sacrifice the universes so that we can survive?"

"They've played you for a fool, Meredith. Don't you see?" I wave my hand impatiently, moving closer to her. The unbinding dagger seems to burn into my shoulder, its presence in the holster palpable. I will have to use it on her if I'm going to stop the reaction.

"No. They haven't. Look at your device. Look at what it really says."

I stare at it, one of the multitudes shifting the display, new readings appearing. One of them I recognize immediately. A new channel is forming within Meredith. I look up at her, and she smiles, proud to have outsmarted me one last time.

"I am the channel to the real universe. Whatever is out there. I will go through, and when I do, the channels, everything, will collapse."

"What about the others?"

"They have implants. Seeker tech or Acolyte tech. I guess they're the same, aren't they? It anchors them to me.

When I go through the channel, they'll be pulled through too. All of our people in every universe."

That is why all the Unmakers' channels were focused upon Meredith. She is drawing them to her and will lead them through to whatever lies beyond the universes. If that is possible. I ask the multitudes, but they have no answer.

"It won't work," I say. She is very close now. I can read her expression, see the tension in her jaw, almost feel the anger pulsating off her.

"Yes, it will. Lasinha's people have had lifetimes to think this through. This place only exists because of all the other universes. Any channel that opens can only connect to a universe or to here. Unless there is no here and no universes. Then it will have to go somewhere else."

I swallow, my hand edging up, ready to reach behind and seize the dagger. "What if there's nothing out there? What is this is all there is?"

"If this is a simulation, then there is something out there."

"It doesn't change the fact that you all are part of the simulation. How can you know you'll be able to survive outside it?"

Meredith smiles. "You think we haven't heard all these arguments before, Laila? You don't know. Nobody does. That's the thrill of it all. Maybe this is what the simulation is designed to do. Allow those us who are willing to do what's necessary to escape its confines."

I open my mouth to argue with her further, before stopping myself. This is what she wants. This is what she has always wanted. Another battle with me. It doesn't even matter who wins in the end, just that she forced me to her ground. Once it would have excited me, but now it just leaves me empty.

"You can come with me, Laila." There is a need in Meredith's voice that surprises me. "We can see what's on the other side."

The multitudes are screaming at me that the unbinding reaction is nearing the point of no return. I hardly hear them. Their voices are dim and far away. "You really think I'd be willing to sacrifice trillions of lives just for the chance to be with you?"

She flinches at the scorn in my voice. "You really think you can kill me, Laila? I think we both know whether you'd rather spend the rest of whatever time we have with me, or live out your days in simulated universe with no meaning to anything you do. I know, because I made the same choice too. Come with me."

"You don't know a thing about me anymore." I pull the unbinding dagger from the holster, its narrow blade flashing into existence, casting an eerie glow in the darkness.

"You don't really love her, do you? Come on, Laila. Do you really want to spend the rest of existence with someone like that?"

When you could be with me is the unfinished part of the sentence she doesn't need to utter. The multitudes are rising within me, demanding my attention and trying to compel me to act. I ignore them, thinking of Suon and Meredith. How unalike they are. One of them is a poisoned chalice from which I will always long to drink. The other loves me unconditionally, something I don't deserve. It terrifies me, that emotion.

Meredith smiles, certain that she has swayed me, or that it is too late for me to stop what has begun. "Take my hand. Now, before it's too late."

I reach out and take her offered hand. My fingers, already numb from my earlier brush with the unbinding weapon, go cold, all feeling disappearing from them.

"I love you, Laila. I've always loved you." There are tears forming in her eyes, from emotion or perhaps from the strain the unbinding reaction is putting her under. With Meredith, I will never truly know.

I can feel the reaction all around me, a coldness that

threatens to swallow me. It doesn't, so long as I am touching Meredith. The voices in me are screaming, like the deranged chorus of some Greek tragedy. Now, they say. NOW.

The dagger is ready, its warmth spreading through my left hand. Meredith's eyes widen, and she tries to pull away, seeing something in my face. I don't let her go, holding on to her hand tight. She twists and turns, but she cannot escape. I plunge the dagger into her chest. It cuts through her as though there is nothing there at all.

"Goodbye, Meredith," I say, my voice strangled, sounding monstrous to my ears.

There is a delay before the pain from the blade penetrates her consciousness. When it does, she lets out a terrible scream, which pierces my soul. The unbinding reactions interact, feeding on each other, neither able to gain momentum or end. It will forever be contained within her.

I release the dagger and Meredith's hand at the same time, my whole body feeling numb and limp. The competing reactions pull at me, trying to keep me in their orbit, but I am able to fight my way free of them, stumbling back. I fall, but there is no ground, only more of the endless void that the crossings exist in, and I am overcome by vertigo.

When I recover myself, I look at Meredith and quickly turn away. She has not moved—she cannot—and her face is contorted in an agonizing grimace in which it will remain forever. So long as the crossings exist, she will be trapped in this channel, the unbinding reactions fighting for a supremacy they can never achieve. The Unmakers will stay in their channels, traveling to Meredith, drawn by the crossing opening within her, which will never be able to open fully, as the unbinding reaction will never reach its necessary point to trigger the transfer engine implanted within her.

Will the Unmakers realize they have failed? Any

equipment they have with them will tell them they are being pulled to Meredith and this channel. It will appear just as if the reaction were approaching its endpoint, not that it is caught in an endless cycle from which there is no escape. Time passes very differently here. It may be a very long while before they realize something is amiss.

The Aurellano will always be able to find them again, though it will not be me. I will be long dead by then, I imagine, my time in this construction at an end. But I will have saved the universes as intended. The multitudes within are ecstatic, though I feel nothing. Just cold and numb. A broken thing. Useless now that my part is done.

It's over, I tell myself. But I look at Meredith, trapped in an eternal agony, and I wonder if it ever can be.

EPILOGUE

The seasons are changing, summer passing into autumn, and the morning is brisk. I can see the outlines of my breath on the air. Earlier there was a cascade of flurries, though the sky is clear now, the sun bright. The leaves on the trees have already turned yellow and begun to fall, littering the pathway we walk upon. I have insisted on arriving this way, though there is no reason for it, not that I can explain.

Suon is at my side. Sometimes she takes my hand in hers and we walk together. It still doesn't feel quite right. This body. Her hand in mine. All of it feels a little wrong, and perhaps it always will. It is something I will carry with me forever, and someday I may be used to that burden.

There are others. The voices remain, but it is different now. I find I can ignore them when I need to. Other times, I long for their company. I have gone to places in my mind I never imagined possible. All those memories. It is easy to get lost in them. They are always there should I need them, and there are times that I do.

The tower is only visible as we come up a small rise, crossing by the old Protectors building. It is empty, abandoned still, as are all the others. The Church owns them, but it no longer exists. The ones who held its accounts, who knew all its secrets, are now either dead or forever on their way to Meredith. All but me.

We stop, some distance from the tower, and look up at its windows gleaming in the sunlight. "You can go anywhere in the goddamn universes—literally—and this is where you choose." Suon shakes her head, but she is smiling.

"There's still work to be done," I say. There is.

Ngurawan and some Black Robes are waiting for us inside, on the top floor, where all Molijc's treasures still reside. "They were very thorough," he says without preamble when we arrive in the audience chamber. "Nothing left here. Very little left in the building north of here. It will be difficult to trace them."

"But we will. Every last one."

Ngurawan inclines his head in agreement. How many are left? I think of the grotesque faithful Molijc had in those last days. The half-things who had once been High Regents, Protectors, Hierarchy members, Regents, and friends. I owe it to every last one to try to find them, to restore them.

"What about all this stuff?" Suon is studying one of the massive codices Molijc stole from some universe.

"Return it to where it belongs. You can do that, can't you?"

The Seeker nods. "Of course. And the buildings? In all the universes. The Church still has substantial assets."

"Donate them. Sell them. Whatever makes sense. The money we get, we can use to help integrate all the Regents and Initiates back into society. Help them somehow."

"It's a lot of work," Suon says, coming over. She loops her arm around my hip. For the moment, it feels familiar. Right.

"We'll find others to help."

"Speaking of which…" Suon looks at Ngurawan with a raised eyebrow.

"The Society, both aspects of it, are still uncertain of you. They believe you, of course. The evidence is incontrovertible. But they fear you because of that and because of what you might do."

"Good. They should be worried."

Ngurawan smiles. I am actually beginning to recognize his expressions. "Yes. They should be."

We go through everything on the top floor, all of the Grand Regent's files that are left. There isn't much—Lasinha was always thorough—but there are old membership lists for all the various universes. It isn't much, but it is a start.

I leave the others to the work and go to my old chambers, ending up on the bed with the dead man's switch Ana gave me cradled in my lap. Here is where I feel most at odds with myself, where this body I am left with feels so false. I wonder how I can go through to the next hour or the next day. It all feels so unbearable.

There is a thought I allow myself in those moments, a forbidden one. Meredith is still there in the crossings, and she will be long after I am dead. I could go to her now and pull out the dagger, hold her tight and let the unbinding reaction take us to whatever place lies beyond this one. It is unlikely either one of us would survive, but we would be together, at least for an instant. She would know I hadn't betrayed her again.

It's a foolish idea, and I know it. I would never actually do it. But it's alluring because of that. To ponder what would happen. Some days, that oblivion seems so much better than this.

Suon steps into the room, trying to mask a concerned look with a smile. "There you are."

"Just thinking," I say.

"I know."

She holds out her hand, and I take it.."

ABOUT THE AUTHOR

Clint Westgard is the author of The Shadow Men Trilogy and the science fiction epic The Sojourners Cycle. In addition, he has published a work of historical fantasy set in colonial Peru, The Maleficio Chronicles, and a retelling of the Minotaur legend, The Trials of the Minotaur. Clint Westgard lives in Calgary, Alberta.

ALSO BY CLINT WESTGARD

Realm of Shadows
Volume One of The Shadow Men
An Alkemya Novel

Craitol and Renuih, two empires a world apart, divided by
the desert that lies between them. A desert ruled by the
Shadow Men.

An uneasy peace holds sway in both realms, hiding
longstanding feuds and bitter rivalries. Until a Shadow
Men raid on Renuih shatters the calm and sets in motion
events no one can control.

Masiph id Ezern, unfavored son of the Imperial Vazeir,
finds himself a hero following the raid. His father remains
unmoved by his exploits and, in his bitterness, Masiph will
find himself a reluctant participant in a plot against the
empire.

As he finds himself drawn deeper and deeper into the
conspiracy, he soon realizes there will be no escaping the
realm of shadows, where intrigue and betrayal abound.
And though the Shadow Men have gone quiet, they will
not stay silent forever…

ALSO BY CLINT WESTGARD

Council of Shadows
Volume Two of The Shadow Men
An Alkemya Novel

Discontent continues to fester within the realms of Craitol and Renuih, fed by intrigues carried out in the shadows. As rivals and apostates struggle for supremacy, a long incubated plan begins to unfold.

Vyissan, a mysterious alkemycal practitioner arrives in Renuih, the latest strike in a long war over who shall control the secrets of alkemya and Craitol itself. He carries with him a secret that, once revealed, will reverberate across all realms. Before he can reveal it though, the conspirators against the emperor will strike their own blow.

But now, a new and more powerful menace looms on the horizon. The Shadow Men have gained the secrets of the Council Adept's alkemya and no one can be certain what they will do with it...

ALSO BY CLINT WESTGARD

Dance of Shadows
Volume Three of The Shadow Men
An Alkemya Novel

War with the Shadow Men looms in both realms as the consequences of the Gvers' Council in Craitol begin to make themselves known. A war that could end in glorious triumph or bitter disaster.

Doubt shadows everyone's steps, for they know there are no certainties in the desert. Especially now the Shadow Men have made the art of alkemya their own.

No one has more questions than Vyissan, for he is working in service to a cause he is no longer sure he believes in. And now he must undertake a journey with those who both loathe and fear him. Before the first sword is drawn, his life will be under threat.

But his will not be the only one, for somewhere in the desert the Shadow Men lie in wait…

ALSO BY CLINT WESTGARD

Unspeakable Rites
An Alkemya Novella

A dead man of no family or account is what Gahryll, Chief
Magister of Tson, sees when the corpse of an Enir youth is
brought to the Magisterium. But Magister Mihuibel sees
something else: a conspiracy involving false adepts
practicing an outlawed form of alkemya.

Against his better instincts Gahryll authorizes an
investigation that draws both Magisters into the seamy
underbelly of Tson where the rich and powerful prey upon
the desperate. When the inquiry implicates one of the most
important families in the Realm of Craitol in forbidden
practices and false alkemya, their positions and ranks will
be threatened.

But that is only the beginning. For the killer will stop at
nothing to ensure his secrets remain hidden and Gahryll is
brought face to face with the unspeakable power of
alkemya that has been unleashed. It forces him to make a
choice. Will he risk everything to fight for justice in a
realm ruled where rank and wealth are all that matter?

Set in the same universe as The Shadow Men Trilogy,
Unspeakable Rites, further explores the nature of alkemya,
its terrible power, and the heavy price paid for its use.

ALSO BY CLINT WESTGARD

The Maleficio Chronicles

Luisa is always more than she appears. Rumor and mystery surround her. And strange events seem to follow wherever she goes.

Born in Lima, City of Kings, to a noble family, her father so fears her true nature that he banishes her to a convent. There she falls under the suspicion of the Inquisition and decides to flee.

Disguised as a man, she embarks upon a series of wild adventures, dueling, carousing, and gambling her way across colonial Peru. But everything changes when someone recognizes her for what she truly is, and soon she finds herself fighting for her very survival.

In a world where she will always stand apart, Luisa undergoes a strange journey, marked by betrayal and murder, terrible powers and mysterious strangers. *The Maleficio Chronicles* is her incredible confession and a story like no other.

ALSO BY CLINT WESTGARD

The Trials of the Minotaur

In the fifth year of the rule of Auten the One Eyed a
minotaur is born to one of Colosi's most important
families.

Taken from his mother as a newborn, exiled and cast from
his family, the minotaur vows to return to the imperial city
and take his rightful place as a patrician in the empire. But
the patriarch of the family, his grandfather, will stop at
nothing to see this blemish to his honor destroyed.

And so begins an epic journey, through lands beyond
imagining, marked by despair and exile, triumph and
betrayal. At its heart lies a quest to be free.